NICO LEE

A Good Lie Ain't Easy

A life-affirming story about not staying true to yourself.

First published in Great Britain 2016 by Mega Dodo Publishing

ISBN 978-0-9544528-9-6

For P.

MEGA
DODO

Contents

A GOOD LIE AIN'T EASY

1. Ad Astra

All across Old Glory's western seaboard, from tattered edge to shining reverie, out spread the Golden State's sour serendipity, as cherry black and star spangled as the onset of a New Year's night can be, pregnant with misplaced metaphor and fumbled chances, bloated on root beer, Twinkie bars, jumbo bags of corn chips and the expectant promise that we were about to witness the greatest spectacle of human endeavor since Marco Polo landed on the Great Wall of China and shot fireworks at the moon.

"You know, for *this*, I thought he'd keep his pants on."
"It's the only way he knows how to salute the flag..."
"...kinda reminds me of Evel Knievel..."
"God Bless America and the right to bare ass?"
"More the sideburns..."
"...didn't he die?"
"Just the once."
Only time will tell if our own hirsute hero will be as lucky.
You'd think so.
After all, over 150,000 people do die every day.
Just probably not like this...

Upon leaving the makeshift ramp, the wheels do their best to mimic the atonal whine of jet take-off. Still laboring under the full weight of a 120 lb Seven Eleven cashier, the office-chair takes wing directly over the badly creased stars and bars banner that was hung way up here just to yell there's nothing more American than a convenience store, the plastic casters ceasing to spin with the ferocious inevitability of a boulder barrelling through the guts of a booby-trapped Mayan temple, and now, with the help of good old-fashioned wind resistance, delivering tonight's first and only fanfare for the common maniac.

Who would have thought they could produce a sound that shrill?

A single wailing resonance, with all the comforting warmth of an Aztec death whistle. Still, if this is truly how it has to end? Then I can't think of a more suitably tuneless epitaph than that solitary keening note, certainly not for one as deaf to the sweet music of good sense as our would-be king of the wild blue rodeo.

Except 'Who Let the Dogs Out' by the Baha Men.

But that goes without saying. I mean, let's face it, it's got to be the go-to choice when throwing oneself off the roof of a building. Surely? Perhaps you could even argue that this three-minute musical marvel has already taken its place in the pantheon of disposable pop as the de rigueur soundtrack to *any* act of life-threatening stupidity. I know I've rarely heard its plaintive strains without the accompaniment of someone yelling, "Holy fucking shit, my leg, it's got my leg!" or the perennial favorite, "Is this supposed to be on fire?"

Previously you'd have to guess when you were in the presence of impending doom, but, as we all know, its clarion call has come to preclude speculation.

Sadly, none of us owned a copy.

So, instead, bereft of that musical succor, we were filled with such regret as tinges the ages with the tears of the damned...

To be honest?

It wasn't as if we needed its neo-calypso caress to signpost the way.

Even Boyd, grasping the sweaty headband of the battered chapeau he time-shared with his brother, is suddenly and most finally realizing that, in not letting go of his mobile throne before the edge of the roof, he has probably committed his last and most spectacular act of daredevil joie de vivre.

Still, at least he wasn't wearing dirty underwear.

I mean, he wasn't wearing any, but it's the thought that counts, right?

Especially when one is facing down mortality.

That this day's short journey into night will be far worse than the whiplash from the time they strapped nitrous to their neighbor's lawnmower, and far less predictable than the 'misunderstanding' with the snakes, is, after all, by now a given.

Ever since they saw Indiana Jones and the Temple of Doom as kids, Boyd and his brother William had sworn that when the hat, both literal and metaphorical, was thrown into the ring, then one of them would have to rise to the other's challenge. The shallow parabola Boyd was currently carving through the early evening ether was surely inscribing the final arc of that covenant.

Time to pray?

During childhood, Boyd and William felt that religion was a disease to be kept at bay through frequent involuntary exposure. That and training to be Jedi- an option their sister, Alice, never considered, despite bearing more than a passing resemblance to the young George Lucas. It wasn't as if they didn't help by pointing that out to her. Several times. Mostly on Sundays. In fact, it was sacrosanct to do so. Righteous even. Just like Don Henley's 'Boys of Summer', the pig iron they peppered with BB pellets in the backyard or the hobo's gumshoe fedora that they had bartered their dad's beer for.

Pop's faith, in contrast, was more parochial, that old blood and thunder holy rolling, rolling, rolling, day in, day out. Heck, the side of a milk carton had looked a much cozier place for them to hang a high school graduation snap than any of the ingle-nooks the family household had to offer, and certainly Sis had bailed, first chance she got, struck out for some galaxy far, far, away, somewhere under the rainbow, and, except for that one postcard years later, never once looking back...

She left that for saps like Lot's wife, Indy's old nemesis the hapless Dr. Rene Belloq, or perhaps even for Boyd- who now momentarily did cast his gaze homeward, back east, across the skies, across time itself it seemed, as he hung in the air, feigning stillness... almost, with significantly more than that damn fedora's edge flapping in the twilight breeze, a whip-thin statue of buck-naked flesh and bone, this bruised token of all our capacity for great acts of heroic stupidity, held there, it appeared, for the briefest, longest, loneliest of moments, rapidly rediscovering an intimate knowledge of every devout invocation known to Midwestern man.

Dear God, won't anyone think of the children?

Or at least those, like Boyd, who surely must have a similar IQ.

Would this déjà-voodoo prove enough?

Here in sun-kissed Sausalito?

Hardly.

Gravity loves office furniture more than God loves prayer.

"Shit biscuit finger dick!"

A curious last plea for divine intervention, but then again Boyd was never what you would call entirely orthodox.

Possessed maybe.

No longer lifting our gaze, hoping he would clear the horizon, we ran instead to the low wall that edged the flat roof. Three pairs of sneakers in a thuddle of slapping rush.

Peered over.

I remember musing that there but for the grace of brains go I. What did we expect to find?

Boyd's?

Could we envisage such a sidewalk stain?

Less a gestalt map of Los Santos' sprawl, more likely the floor plan of a very small, very pink Barbie house.

Still, as Malcolm X never quite said, '...whatever doesn't kill you makes you blacker...'

Except perhaps vitiligo.

Incidentally, Knievel survived trying to jump the Snake River Canyon.

Even with his pants on.

It was life that got him in the end.

Certainly that's easier to spell than idiopathic pulmonary fibrosis.

Then again, what isn't?

Vitiligo again?

Still, I'd rather try to spell I.P.F. than have it.

Unfortunately, Evel didn't have a choice.

I bet he still misses the crowds... just like we miss the sideburns.

They linger, those furry tokens of alpha-masculinity, basking in the afterglow of childhood recollection, independent sometimes of the face, bathed in the same dying light as the memory of your first pet or perhaps that toy, lost to the long grass, never at the time the most favored, but which now grows in swollen significance with each passing year till one can't help but mourn the shadow of the X-Wing lain in the field outside the window pane...

One more talisman of fading youth.

I expect such memories comforted Boyd as he sailed towards the clouds with the grace of an anvil. Weighted with heavy anticipation, that fecund pause as fat as a fart in a coke bottle. The last sound he heard before he and the chair hit the dumpster below... Lynyrd Skynyrd.

I'd almost forgotten what was actually playing.

All our memories have holes- some almost as many as that lump of treasured pig iron they kept out back as kids, so I can't confirm that the track was Free Bird, though if it was, come to think of it, doesn't that count as a fanfare too?

Then Boyd went deaf for five months.

Actually deaf.

For five whole months.

Back then, before box-sets?

That was nearly half a year.

Not quite long enough come summer to warrant sharing the inside of a way-too-compact Chevrolet Aveo with three other pilgrims, but hey, whatever doesn't kill you... well, you know the rest.

Sarah, our token Brit, curiously jingoistic for once, had argued vociferously for a Vauxhall, but we couldn't find an ad for an Astra this side of the pond, so if... can you just, yeah, move your leg a bit, bit more, yeah... thanks.

No that's fine- plenty of room...

We've got loads of time to grow fond of cramp.

We're still miles from Burning Man, wondering why flies spend so much time washing their legs, when the greasy hat is thrown down once more. Boyd, one hand on the wheel, thankfully fully clothed, but even now still with wool in what Sarah, so quaintly, calls his 'lugs', Brother William tamping a pipe with surgical cotton dipped in something which, whilst not strictly illegal, surely could not have been intended to be smoked...

Still we'd had a good lunch to soak it up.

Nothing like a scotch and soda sandwich.

"A scotch and soda sandwich?"

"Yeah, just hold the bread..."

Thanks for that William.

Never let the prospect of laughing stand in the way of a 'good' joke.

Who drinks scotch and soda, now?

James Bond?

He's as anachronistically old fashioned as a drunken maiden aunt indulging in the semi-scientific labelling of ornithological taxidermy, 'The Fleming is a curious bird that smells like a casino at 3 AM and is prone to throwing the odd afternoon off a cliff...'

So, anyway, for spies like us, it's on with a barrage of vodka martinnitus, time for the postprandial debate, the monologue masquerading as discourse, what we do best, shouting over each other's divine right to the floor.

"...Inch High Private Eye had a Napoleon complex? What about Illya Kuryakin?"

Like I said, not exactly a dialogue, just William's torturous attempts to corral reference for the sake of a series of ever decreasing punch lines, the kind that only a man with fond memories of sock suspenders would appreciate- and I do... at first. It's not exactly real vodka either, just a close medicinal cousin, like McCallum's Russian accent in The Man from U.N.C.L.E. William starts to hum the theme tune, then shifts tack to blather on about forgotten cop shows of the 70's.

We're somewhere near Barstow and I can barely hear him over the air-con and a tape cassette of Richard Pryor that sounds as if baby bats had chewed it, though I gotta say Mr. Pryor's delivery was still smoother than William's- certainly when we finally kicked into the question and answer section.

"... and that's why Kojak really got cancelled. Hey, you think you could jump from a moving car..?"

I hold the door handle tighter, sea-sick and dusty, praying for my own dose of heavenly intercession, or at least another shot. Religion is, after all, the poor man's opium, something we only grasp for when the ethanol runs out, or that girl leaves town...

On the back seat, Sarah Appleyard squirms in my lap. She stares up at me from under spider-lashes, heavy and hot, a lumpy twenty-four going on forty, homely as all hell and the only one I'll ever really love, at least till the next. She has *her* smile- for an English poppet that's a real distinct lack of European teeth. The last facsimile of what I lost was more accurate around the eyes but the incisors weren't even close. To say this is fucked up would be an understatement.

I never chose to be a doppelgangbanger, so I take the traditional route, accept the mystery pipe, and, forgoing my immediate chances of standing for President, inhale, hoping it'll get me somewhere that Jung never could. We all have ways of self-medicating; hazy analgesia, or a shot of adrenaline to the heart...

Boyd slows the jalopy, then William, one hand still in his pants, rolls down the window and tests the wind with a wet digit in an attempt to answer his own dare. When blacktop and countenance embrace it will be the kiss to end all love stories, at least William's, surely?

Chicks dig scars, but only when they're attached to something like a face.

He tenses, the whip slows still further and then he's gone, brakes squeal, Boyd yelling, "Yowsa!" as Bill bounces out...

It's true, mortality really has a way of bestowing eminence upon the asinine.

Would posterity record this as the moment we lost one of our great holy fools?

When we get to a gas station William presses wadded towel to his knee, the only thing he'd fucked up as he bowled himself down the fast lane. Sarah told me once that Anne Boleyn had a royal brother called Crown Green. You really can't trust the Brits.

I feigned ignorance- which is easy, especially when you are in fact ignorant.

She then told me that the English prefer to bowl in the open air, free-range as opposed to our battery of lanes.

Right now I'm in a restroom holding my tripe-white pin, the last chicken in the store, pissing sitting down because the pipe's made me ill, the stall closing in like a cage, William standing in the door ruing the one time he let Boyd drive.

"I oughta keep some record of what's comin' outta me..."

He'd been complaining about his guts for days. Blaming some 'foreign-sounding' almond cake shaped like the fluted scallop of a pilgrim's sea-shell. The deleterious effects of one small sponge fancy?

I have my doubts.

"I wanna write a diary of my shits..."

A remembrance of things passed.

I fart.

I fart big and consider whether William should really be chowing on a corn-dog.

Jesus dude, don't eat in here, I'm pinching a turtle's neck.

Touché, mon ami.

"Yup, that's the last time I let Boyd drive."

Like *that* was the poor decision, and not deciding to exit the vehicle whilst it was in motion.

Some people are born with foresight; perhaps one day in the future William will wish he possessed it.

Boyd though will always just dive into whatever's in front of him.

When he was very small he used to really like cat food.

Always managing to find his way into a tin.

That's some trick when you're only four and your dad doesn't own a can opener... or a cat.

He was persistent though.

Like I said, he really liked it.

But cat food didn't like him.

Maximum velocity at both ends.

I imagine if you're on a diet that has its advantages.

As a toddler though I guess he didn't watch his weight and now, to be honest, well, I've already mentioned, he's as thin as Dr. Jones' most favored weapon... so when faced with the prospect of the mildest exercise or an emetic?

He'd rather go bowling.

And he's not a big bowler.

Though if you want to change your shoes?

Bowling is the less messy of the two options.

I've only been once.

Never again.

It wasn't Crown Green and I didn't like the natives.

Like in here, in the john, you're separated from them in lanes- well, that's what I'd been promised- but there weren't any walls to disrupt your line of sight, and, as always, sound carries, has no respect for arbitrary lines in the sand...

That voice, redolent of Marlboro Lights and despair, resigned to it being another shitty day, it sticks in my head like tire tracks on roadkill.

"I only like big, bald men..."

The poor woman was only in the Ten-Pin-A-Rama to get her parking validated. The guy being rebuffed just wanted to shoot his mouth off, was five foot two and as follicularly frolicsome as a Shetland pony or a Greco-Roman Michael Bolton- 'kefalos' being the Greek for 'mullet', Sarah now *reliably* informs me, the Latin being 'mullum'? What my fellow Americans usually refer to as a party in back.

Look, what I'm trying to say is, a full head of hair and a lack of height wasn't this lady's thing, or maybe she was just lying- just wanted an end to this caveman courtship, guessed correctly things were gonna get outta hand, who really knows?

"I only like big, bald men…"

"You'll love these then, baby…"

He dropped his pants.

Two coconuts and a cocktail weenie.

A high girlish scream.

His.

I guess even if you're one of those men who are big-balled it still hurts.

Maybe more so?

She'd kicked like a mule, stall or no stall.

And incidentally, did anyone tell you that you can't help but stare?

Well I can't.

Not if they're hung like Jagger is…

Allegedly.

Not even when I'm in a public restroom.

And I've been here before.

Lots of times.

Bowling- like I said, only that once.

Oh, and the moral of that story?

Never look a gift horse between the thighs?

Or always kick one in the balls?

Or, perhaps never listen to my bullshit?

Even the true life stuff tends to meander if I'm taking a crap…

You see, when I'm on the toilet I often like to imagine I'm in a mid-price Swedish hotel. Whilst that takes the edge off the usual quality of the surroundings, it does mean I find it even harder to concentrate on anything but the job in hand, and when I don't? Like I said, I just… wander off.

I wake from my reverie, look down at a stack of toilet rolls still in their plastic wrapping. On the side it says, 'Classic Toilet Paper- Scrunch or Fold' with a diagram showing both methods of how to prepare the tissue to wipe your ass.

I give this species of ours twenty years tops.

So, if I'm going to be leader of the free world, I guess I'd better get a move on.

During the seventies, as well as truly great stuntmen, there was a President called Jimmy Carter who was nicknamed the Peanut Farmer and criticized for his comparatively non-aggressive foreign policy.

By which I mean he never invaded Poland.

Nowadays though I think they want you to put more of an effort in.

That protestant work ethic is even more American than a flag made in China.

Or the Korean convenience store from which it flutters.

Me?

I can be a little indolent.

Just lolling around, dropping a kid off at the pool.

Laying pipe.

Feeling the breeze between my knees.

Not Velcro on my shoes lazy, but still…

Outside, Sarah's re-plaiting her laces. I kiss her eyebrows, between, over the bridge still red from this morning's plucking, maybe wanting to go further but somehow… maybe when Boyd and William aren't around?

Who am I kidding?

When are they not around?

They even took me bowling once… that was fun.

We oughta go again, sometime.

I loved it, such interesting people.

Possibly it's the only thing I love more than shouting.

Boyd is calling from the car.

Then his voice turns to static.

The sun half blinding me, scorching back memory into dust, all I've wanted, just to lose the way…

Haloed, Sarah's shadow outline becoming solid, real.

I wake from daydreamin'…

"Hi Mrs. Sarah, what's that?"

"That, my friend, is twelve inches of high octane motor-oil-infused pork rind in a prophylactic sheath of extruded corn huskings, wanna bite?"

"No thank you my dear, it looks like a mortuary Muppet's wing-wang."

"To be honest it tastes like a mortuary Muppet's wing-wang…"

"Yeah?"

"...that's been dipped in mustard and sugar-dusted."

"Ok, I'll take a bite, but just for old time's sake."

"For the regiment..."

Together.

"For the regiment..."

I have no idea of the origin of this Limey ritual.

Boyd spits.

We all look at the spit.

The spit looks back at us.

He really is quite ill.

William is exploring his nose, so we all focus on him for now as it's far less disgusting than staring at what's just come out of Boyd, Sarah half kneeling in the heat and dust. Sahara, Sarah, playing with syllables... aren't we all out of Africa? Eden?

I've gone through so many fads looking for a home that isn't home, and at such a rate of Gordian knots: Buddhism, Hinduism, Dude-ism, Sufism, Kantian Transcendentalism, even Christianity for old time's Chrissakes. Now I try to keep my distance from the immortal, just another subset of celebrity. Maybe I should just take up picking my nose instead? What mysteries may reside within?

Soon we are as far out as can be, here, where nothing grows except the crowds, this disparate family thronging toward the totemic statue of metal and flame rising in the distance. I put my ski goggles back on and draw my cowl tighter as we approach her flaming bush. This year's Burning 'Man' resembles woman, a belly full of iron junk, thighs of tempered steel. Stuck in earth yet it seems she wants to run, to head out East...

At a far from sweet sixteen, in a ninja flurry of Marie-Celestial finality, my Sis left behind the moisture farm and hitch-hiked her way, no doubt, we thought, to her eternal damnation, and... there she is again on my mind, like the one that got away, Moby Dick, Andy Dick, Dick Cheney, a list of old lovers or male strippers? Playing with names, seeing just the one face, not so much blazing a comet's trail for her brothers to follow as simply winking out from the familial firmament, not even the enamel glint of her sincerity-lite smile could be glimpsed as it disappeared into the night... and surely that's something to admire? Nothing impresses like oblivion.

Not even a bitchin' tattoo.

Drums.

Rockets shoot off into the purple dusk, I flinch and the earth spins on. I fart. Sarah farts. William farts. Boyd is not so lucky. We head back to the Chevy to try and find him some spare pants.

We end up sleeping in a pile, the Howard Marx brothers, my face in what you would hope was Sarah's highly European armpit, getting a boner, high on desert funk. In the morning we'll try and head on, away from the stars of Vegas, but the car won't start, it takes hours, but what can you do?

Let it drift...

We were drawn together by fate, William, Boyd and I.

I lost my sister to the road when I was young.

They did too.

My sister's name was Alice.

Theirs was too.

These coincidences can seem miraculous.

Would have been too if all of us hadn't shared the same last name.

Let it drift...

Isn't that what brothers do?

Sisters?

We hadn't known her long enough to know...

What could we do at the time?

Nothing would replace her... would it, could it?

Let it drift...

Or not.

Sarah and I near sleeping, perversely her eyes grown so big, the lashes clogged and heavy, Amish chin beards strung around comedy breasts, mouth like a broken pomegranate, such duplicitous teeth, those two strands of bleached hair, wheat dipped in Robinson's Golden Shred, just stuck there to the lips, magnetized, Seville gold ambercising, the palest copper melting darker, conjuring its own verdigris from the depths of her liquid gaze...

I'm more in love with the words than the truth.

I open my eyes, hours later?

Staring at what was once porcelain.

Another gas-station rest-room.

Another fly, this one more concerned with hovering haphazardly than surfing a windscreen, emulating that lazy approximation of flight with a real cartoon relish.

I think I'm gonna be sick, my belly swollen.

I can afford to, I've taken a hippocritical oath.

I prod myself in the bread basket, disgusted by my corpulence, then suck my gut in to reveal my spine.

I shake again.

Did I shake?

Leaving the stall, which stall?

I see a pair of sandals in the next dunny.

God is watching me?

Does Jesus ever take a shit in the Bible? It's been a while since I read it. A while since I spoke grace. Pops had always shared that chore between us boys- well, after Alice left.

There- I said her name again, but please not three times next to a mirror.

We're heading south-west, away from her bearing...

Parting the red sea of sand, on into the promise damned, the graceless land, to the sound of Paul Simon on the radio and two steps from any county line we collapse into Los Angeles, population less than zero, at least what you'd call sentient life. Nowhere was twinned with there once, but then it got wise and voted for Dusseldorf instead. Sarah's got an ice-cream, all I got is popcorn, some smokes, oh, and this lousy t-shirt, but at least we're finally here.

Once again I've sat still and the universe has turned around me. Does this constitute a journey?

An odyssey?

As a family we tend to like those. Certainly I've read one set in Dublin and one in the Greek Islands, and then William capped the trilogy by completing the final level with the alien called Abe on the original Xbox.

Which is the greatest achievement?

Oh, Boyd also almost understands where Homer Simpson got his name from- which must count for something too, right?

Sometimes though?

With that kind of adventure it feels as if there's too much sweat from the participants, too little effort on the part of God. Let's send them off in that direction, I'm sure they'll learn something...

I'm on the edge of an empty pool, folded space. The couple of sun-loungers look like Venus fly-traps- even for the wary. I take another mini-donut, shake off the sugar, then wet my finger, pat some up, lick it. I can almost see William's as it tests the air, surfing it from a car window, was that yesterday..?

We oughta get moving?

Time is money.

Least till you try and pawn a watch.

This day's already drained to the concrete dregs.

A crow walking round the coping.

Lost?

How do you tell when a bird's off course?

Do they use the night sky?

What happens during the day?

A girl, about fourteen, big belly, big arms, big legs, but a tiny head, she waddles past in a one-piece bathing suit, smiles.

She's carrying a duck.

A real live duck.

A plane goes over.

The gap may be closing on what makes species unique.

Other species use tools.

Other species enjoy recreational sex.

So far as we know other species do not use tools for recreational sex.

Which I guess makes the Rampant Rabbit mankind's greatest achievement?

I'm waiting for a cotton-tail to walk past with the watch he's trying to pawn.

I stare out into the dark, brush and concrete.

The scent of dog-shit baking white, sun-block and pool cleaner.

The next morning I'm spreading some spray-can fake cheese on a cracker and Sarah's trying to open one of those non-dairy creamer mini-tubs.

"Is this California or what?"

It's kinda convincing, but I guess that *is* the pure essence of the place.

A mutt goes by, low and slow slunk, something in its mouth, a tiny red ball or a tumor. I can hear a tuba, oompah from across the way. A sudden recollection of cassette covers, red-headed family bands in leather shorts who share one set of false teeth on a roster. Yes folks, live from Bavaria, it's Boyd and his dangerous musical irony. I'm still in my clothes from the night before but even though we were vacuum packed beneath the sweaty sheets they still don't seem to smell, least not to me.

Speaking of vacuum packed, a guy in speedos and a Stetson follows the mutt, Hank Walliams the swimming cowboy is what Sarah chooses to call him years later when she recalls this, even then I was always too hung-over to care about the explanation, even now the reference bobbing away on the tide, knowing as she speaks that all of this is irrelevant, all these moments will be lost, like beers in the brain...

For now I watch the sun catch the gold hairs on his legs.

A few heartbeats later, and somehow it's the end of the line and the condom bursts, the IUD fails, the cap collapses, the pills dissolve and Sarah's going to be a mother? Is that all it takes? If only we got to choose our origin, our relatives, our offspring, A to Z. We all want more life, father- you'd have thought Roy Batty would have gone for a progenitor with more foresight or at least better glasses?

If Sarah is anything to go by the baby will have the family smile, just to light the way... but we're not there yet are we?

By a few heartbeats?

Well, it seems I didn't just mean a morning's worth- after all, it's still movie land and don't they just love a flashback?

Sorry, flash-forward?

The dog walks back again, my bow-legged unicorn, a magical moment of stillness, stock footage, what's the symbolism?

The TV is propped on the door-sill.

A bird's eye view of a compact car hurtling down the road...

I flip off The Shining or the studio sanctioned end of Blade Runner.

Shopping channel selling cheap baubles.

"Is this California or what?"

It's like hanging in air, time just...

Before we got here, too many days just hanging outside Boyd's work.

I never could figure the place. What kind of Korean hires a feckless drop-out like Boyd to do the night shift? Mr. Tham was an enigma, a peanut-faced patriarch whose sons were far too smart to be continuing to work the counter after 8th grade, but who, himself, was also far too busy painting oil colors to be bothered with the actual day-to-day running of the store. He was the least ambitious Asian I had ever met and one of the most foul-mouthed. You couldn't help but love him.

"You think I fuckin' know fuckin' kung fu, you fuck-nugget?"

Fair enough, Boyd's question had been ignorant.

Isn't it Taekwondo in Korea?

I remember William took just the one karate class nearby at Kristie Kenpo's. He'd have been better off looking for tips on self-defense at Suzie's Nails next door. The talk was tougher, but then again the coffee, somehow, even worse.

What did Bill know about a tasty beverage?

More than Boyd is a given.

His knowledge of coffee is commensurate with his knowledge of… well, anything to be honest.

It once took me a full ten minutes to explain why the erotic works of Anne Honeymouse were something Boyd would never actually find, despite my previous exhortations for him to search our local library. Sometimes I wonder if he still thought Tom Braider was an eminent archaeologist. Or that Louis Armstrong was the first black man to play trumpet on the moon? What's the point in a joke you have to explain, a reference you don't know?

I'm thinking too much, so maybe I should drink more caffeine? To make good coffee you need a healthy sense of the absurd. It's a drink made from beans for Chrissakes. A methodical approach is also preferred, and everyone knows Einstein can sleep safe in his grave knowing Boyd's pickled grey-matter was still at least second choice when it came to filling the cavity atop the neck of a re-animated super-smart robo-gorilla. Yeah, Albert, you're probably coming back as an ape zombie, just as soon as we've ironed out those bugs…

I really need more caffeine, just like that gorilla needs a hole in his head… for Einstein's brain. Whatever happened to Albert anyway? Everyone's into Hawking these days. Come to think of it, whatever happened to Boyd? To William? To all of us? To good coffee and all those things you didn't have to clarify?

Back then I walk over to the edge of the pool, crane style.

It looks like it was once filled with butter.

It's the only way to explain the stains.

It ain't no hot-tub time machine, so I guess we'll have to live with the regret.

Inside the regret though? Is that really necessary?

Wonder if I look like a crow.

The one who sold both his wings to the devil for the promise of snow.

Now I can't place that reference either, then fate pulls the lever, lines up three birds in a row, and the duck scoots by, minus the girl.

Then the dog, again.

Circles?

Then finally the kid.

Where's the anonymous swimming cowboy?

Any second now I really am expecting that rabbit with a fob-watch.

Or a tree to fall whilst I'm not listening.

The cowboy will do.

Seems though I can't keep staring, apparently I have the attention span of a corvid.

Am I a crow?

Or am I a man?

Or am I a crow and a man at the same time?

Is that what happened to me?

Boyd tried to put me in a black fright wig once as part of some prank.

I remember the taste of pumpkin.

That's when I decide I'll have cheese and crackers and not cake for breakfast tomorrow. That's when I suggest we forgo the two weeks in Tijuana and drive to Chicago instead. Brother Bill sides with me, and after much friendly debate, we come to the amicable conclusion that as it's William who organized the fucking car and it's mostly William's fucking drugs... then it's my way or the highway that is my way. Which of course is his way. Regrets? We'll have a few, no doubt. Boyd sulks, even after the hat is rather perfunctorily thrown down at the last minute and the ancient rite of challenge is once more invoked. Two cut thumbs later Sarah still sits on the fence, then performs magic.

With a flourish full of theatrics, an easy camp charm, she produces from her WWF rucksack sacrosanct relics, the illustrated scriptures that will provide sacred knowledge of the celestial pathway we shall follow for the next seven-eleven days. Three 1959 Route 66 travel place-mats. Sold to Mom and Pop restaurants up and down the mythical highway- before McDonalds closed it, or whatever happened, and printed on vellum, or some other high quality wizardy shit from

17

the days of yore. These blessed maps, still stained with the gravy of the ancients, list the whereabouts of several holy grills. Or, if you prefer, the actual, real-life locations of the only tourist attractions that still truly matter. The ones no longer there and therefore infinitely cooler than any of the crap you'd find nowadays.

And so, lo, it was then that the supplemental oath was sworn.

That, without Google or other electrickery, we would hunt these great bastions of…

Even we weren't that stupid.

Even we knew that most of these places were so long gone we might as well be hoping to find Indy's lost ark.

Instead, Sarah brought forth the mystical…

I can't keep this up.

The plan, in plain American, was this.

We'd drive whatever was left of this once-great nation's most holy asphalt from L.A. to Chicago, maybe fly on to New York, and, along the way, we'd compare what we found today with the guileless promise these simple road-stop guides of yesteryear once offered. Re-discover these now kitsch delights even if they weren't actually there anymore.

Perhaps our trip would leave a bitter taste too, perhaps we'd yearn with true aching nomstalgia for the forgotten delights of the Liberty Restaurant's finest charbroiled steaks and chicken, or wonder why we now have a Cadillac Ranch where once buffalo roamed… back in the 50's? Perhaps we'd also do a little more historical research as we journeyed.

Whatever.

We can't back out now. The hat's been thrown big-style, the plot's been plotted, the dream dreamed, the quest… sequestered?

I need to sleep.

For God sake it's morning, what kind of time is that?

Do I need to sign off on this?

Besides, why not take William's stance that commitment is about leaping into the moment? He won't even look at these ancient atlases. Like any form of map, last will and testament, first novel, any plan too complex to be conveyed without further resort to paper and pen, they are to him something to be burnt before reading.

In short, they are not to be trusted, being neither a reliable tool for navigating life, nor the final true version of events, lacking both artistic truth and the three-dimensional topography that really constitutes the prison bars of our existence. He will trust to the road, that which will lead the way.

Pseud.

Life is not a problem to be solved, but a reality to be experienced?

Kierkegaard may have written that, but Peng Jiamu lived it, and even he could have done with a map in the end.

Something to lead him home.

Sarah puts her big old hand on my skinny little knee, smiles lopsided, asks for her pen back, and... again? Really?

I feel smaller, smaller, and then the wind whips up and the light changes, clouds stutter, sputter, slip to a halt around the sun and then the memory of my sister is gone.

The map grows dark, and I can hear William on the phone trying to sort out a pick-up for the Chevy in Chicago with the rental company and then Sarah's hand takes mine, swallows mine, she leads me back inside. In the doorway she kisses me and I can almost taste cream cheese through a recent memory of peppermint gum. She tickles, grabs, pushes me over easy onto the motel mattress and the rest is pin-sharp but single flashbulb shots like the start of the Texas Chainsaw Massacre.

A freckled breast and dirty nails, her jeans shorts half off, my pelvis against the bottom of her back, my face buried in her neck, her hair, deep brunette spattered with indecisive bleach, the choppy thick bob spilling up onto the pillow in an orange and brown fan as she lays on her side.

Upon the bullish neck an anenomole with three dark fronds, sea-caught within the rich dark black and brown of thick hanks of wet hair that hang across her face now in tangled clumps, in coiling serpents, those still oily strands of thick brown and black.

Afterwards the clock says 1 PM and I wonder about where that came from in this month of Sundays, and also about Knott's Berry Farm- our first destination, America's first theme park. Not of how much it will differ from the 'authentic recreation of the Gold Rush Days of 1849' as promised by one of the place-mats, or how that was already a nostalgia for a past that never was, but just that nebulous, sinking feeling of my own history with roller coasters and log flumes, that fear of rides you just don't want to ride, and then those pin-sharp flashes

again, pink flesh, wide-eyed pupils, and, butting in, right now, in an appallingly inaccurate slow southern drawl, "Lawks a mercy, Mister, you've left me wetter than the fat kid in the front row at SeaWorld."
Sarah is sniffing her fingers.
The English are a disgusting, filthy-mouthed bunch of fuckers, and I will be too if this charming love affair continues.
She laughs, sashays to the bathroom on chubby calves.
"I'm gonna take a shower now honey, y'all wanna join me?"
I follow, too tired to argue.
We rub each other towards clean, but nothing much else happens.
Instead she tells me about a trip she made to the British Museum and finally shaves her legs.
She went to attend a talk on, '…the History of Burlesque…' which she claimed ably illustrated just how far a national institution can go in rejecting the pursuit of providing an erudite scholarly education for the masses, especially when the higher prize of fickle middle-class public interest is at stake. Lord knows it pulled her in, so who is she to be withering?
In a hot, very hot room, which appropriately enough displayed the architecture of a Turkish bath-house taken to the most ridiculous and opulently delicious excess, they sat, or mainly stood, the whole panoply of leather-jacketed suburban couples, gay blades, girls dressed like Velma from Scooby-Doo, (the popular repressed lesbian from the popular seventies children's cartoon), and other assorted geeks, freaks, and bearded tweaks, including her, *obviously*, totally normal self, just to hear a panel of 'experts' fail to put questions to themselves about a topic which is as elusively diaphanous as a stripper's filmy underwear, or the putative ethnicity of a Damascene diplodocus.
Then, after some amateur-level tableaux vivants of Great British historical moments, a man dressed as Steed entered, (the popular saucy spy from the popular saucy sixties television show the Avengers), and the crowd murmured amongst themselves.
Sarah then realized she could have simply described a city gent-bowler, suit, umbrella, except this Steed's outfit was bright red and tapered to a pair of woman's stiletto shoes. Though I point out, to assume I didn't know who Steed was could be construed as a tad patronizing too. She continued, describing acoustics. How the

murmuring then fell to a lower buzz, whilst the ersatz Macnee performed an energetic striptease to that show's uber-dramatic theme.

Beneath his Steed outfit he wore a corset, pasties, and upon whipping off his trousers revealed tiny briefs with twirling tassels hanging from his big bouncing balls.

No-one kicked him in the nuts.

I guess it wasn't a very balanced bill.

Like a girl with a duck under only one arm.

When we get out of the shower Sarah puts on the glasses that make her look like a tougher Johnny Depp but still... nothing much, nothing much.

Again though those flash-bulb shots.

Her mouth harridly devouring my flesh.

Harridly is a compound word- hurried and harridan, like she is in her late fifties, older...

A tear for lost youth yet unspent?

Should I weep over the edge like an old man's cock, spilling over the side, the gush long gone? Propped upon a pile of once-was-cotton, cascading, as musty as a pauper's winding sheet...

The sun is on my arm, she's smoking on the balcony. We kiss, her body still damp from the shower.

Libido apparently at an all-time low, I go for smokes, slip on a terry robe and a pair of Bulgarian combat boots and head out into the midday sun. Strangely, even in this mufti, I'm the straight man by default.

Halfway to the store there's a Spock-eared black guy on crutches holding a twelve inch Pee Wee Herman doll. He's dancing it against the window of a broke-down Krispy Kreme wannabe, whispering beat-box noises under his breath, his one be-gloved hand the puppet-master. Two skater kids are trying to get the doll back off of him. In the window of Crunkin' Donuts Michael Madsen's double is pointing at a bald dude across the booth behind triple thick glass.

"I could make a million with this." The kids don't believe the black guy about the doll, any more than I do.

In the window the bald dude mimes cocking a pistol at him.

"I was in Kuwait fucker, that shit don't scare me..." Inside the booth of course they can't hear Tuvok Shakur, they're just watching a mime.

Spock takes off his one glove.

It's filled with Vaseline and what's left of his hand.

Napalm nightmares rear up, a smell of disinfectant and ass.

He starts telling the kids how he got through Iraq ok, but then how he lost the skin off his fingers afterwards in a drug bust when his brother tried to throw lighter fuel over a cop.

Then the bald dude in the window, continuing to stare straight at Mr. Madsen, puts a bullet on the sill and the black guy leaps four feet backwards. Even on crutches it's still pretty balletic. I walk on, consider whistling... reconsider. The skaters ignore the bald dude and Madsen, they still want their doll back- they're only kids. They might not think they're immortal, but they feel it, believe it, so hard, so keen, in their soft little bones. It's gonna be one of those nights. Just as soon as we've got through this afternoon...

2. It Sure Ain't Hollywood

Scrub, scrub, scrub away, scrub till your fingers are red raw...
Ostensible morning.

At 3 AM in the real concrete deep dark blue dark hell of true morning I thought I had heard my dead father calling to me from the back of a Wagnerian cavern. Just Sarah's breathing echoing through the mattress.

I'm trying to stand on one leg wrapped in a towel, which according to Sarah is just about a passable crane style- though I don't think the towel is entirely necessary. You ever see Jackie Chan in a towel? I bet he can dry himself just by concentrating his Chi. Cleaning the crud from my fingers I can hear Boyd and William impersonating competent human beings starting to pack for a trip, but it's about as accurate as Sarah's southern belle from the day before. In a little while, she and I sit eating crackers by the empty pool. The dog comes closer, closer. I throw his red ball and then he just sits there looking up at me, waiting for me to go get it.

By the time we're on the road L.A. isn't so much a freeway as a parallel parking lot. Sure it has some pretensions towards movement but no actual success.

Richard Pryor has given way to Frampton as the in-car 'entertainment'.

It could be worse.

Just.

It could be Boyd's oompah.

At least, thank God, we're heading towards the O.C.

A sentence very few people have thought down the years, but the traffic is supposed to be lighter in that direction at this time of day. Lighter, it turns out, is a relative concept, like Microsoft Help.

When hell freezes over and Boyd's declared Pope we finally arrive in another luxuriously appointed piece of paved paradise. We must be collecting car-parks. Still, this one knows its place. Its place is too far from Judge Roy Bean's hitchin' post for comfort, given the state we're all in, and yet, somehow, Sarah and I make it to the Knott's Berry ghost town. Eager to see what's left of the original amusement park and more importantly find a place to lay down outta the mid-day sun, we opt to stay, fairly, put. I had been hoping for something like the railway station she showed me in Sapphire and Steel, what we get is somewhat less spooky. In the end I'm glad, as the light shifts and suddenly I'm remembering my morning's dream in more detail, the Otranto mask falling from a fried egg sky, perspective slipping and I'm left staring at lips grown the size of baked goods, van tires, the visor cracking like fresh bread and my own face revealed beneath the giant's helmet. I sit. Sit very still. Waiting to be entertained by what the real world has to offer.

Boyd and William go in search of more vertical thrills on the boardwalk. Rides that are just like the Pope, too near to God and with all the thrills and spills of hoarding Nazi gold. See you later, Pontiff William and High Cardinal Boyd. Why are they called roller-coasters when the one thing they hardly ever do is coast? Technically yes, but my stomach disagrees.

When the first gun-shot goes off, even with five minutes preamble from the 'actor-guide-edutainmenter' I still shudder. Visions of black Vulcan flesh spattering the face of a tiny plastic Paul Ruben in a gory bukaki splurge threaten to re-acquaint me with this morning's crackers. The morning's other images that then pop into my mind pin-sharp from nowhere are somehow worse? Why is sex such a mess in memory? Just mine? I concentrate on the moment, settle in to watching some highly trained middle-aged stuntmen fight a slow-moving gunfight in the shadow of an enormous wooden ride.

I look at the program.

Saloon girl can-can.

Panning for Gold.

Dr. Ezekiel Bordello's Medicine Show.

Native American, blah, blah, blah…

Then it all culminates with Abbey Road, a tribute to the Beatles, and finally the Snoopy spectacular.

I look again.

Try and remember what Boyd's contribution to the pipe smelled like this morning.

I'm fairly certain embalming fluid wasn't one of the high notes.

I look again.

Four photocopier salesmen's smiles stare up at me from beneath mop-top wigs, and, let's be honest, whichever way you turn the picture you can't mistake a seven-foot Snoopy dancing with Day-Glo-clad cowgirls.

I'm fairly certain the last two attractions weren't in the original vision of an 'authentic recreation of the Gold Rush Days of 1849'.

With the sounds of shotgun blasts echoing across the prairie I decide to explore further afield despite my fatigue.

There has gotta be a food court, right?

Sarah is particularly keen to move on.

Ever since her pops scared the piss out of her with the Yellow Submarine when she was six, she has always associated the Beatles with damp bedding and a peculiarly English sense of whimsy she finds both claustrophobic and somewhat sinister.

We drove from Hollywood, so we pass on by their branch of Pink's, and Mrs. Knott's Chicken diner too- even though it's been there since 1934 and historically that's gotta count. Though you'd hope they'd changed the oil in the fryers. It don't matter. That's not what Miss Sarah wants. Miss Sarah wants home on a bun, a particular kind of mouthfeel.

The kind of thing that will take her straight back home to Blighty.

TGI Friday's is dark, as welcoming as a womb can be.

At the table next to us a guy in a red suit, with eraser hair so ginger it's pinker than his face. He's ordering a cheeseburger, hold the cheese. The lack of logic seems Herculean, till that attempt is crushed by the waitress who informs the human pencil that they don't do special orders. He switches to pasta with a side order of the rest of the menu, Sarah skips the semantic conundrums and, aching for that taste of England's dreaming, goes for the California club sandwich which she had grown to love in Norwich.

Sodium arrives in chunks and blocks; this is the arterial end, the lust highway, licking lips, losing track of hips and feet swelling with defeat, prostate like a bladder, bladder hard like a golf ball, teeth like forget-me-nots, forget the nuts, I'm drowning in the white stuff, drinking the ketchup, can't hold the salty tale even with the hints, need a flagon of coke, a piss ball, mouth cotton-ball, dream of tin tear drops and too much heat, too much heat. Loosen the waistband, the map spilling over the sides, mountains of flesh. Unlike the svelte Boyd, I'm nearly up to 130 lbs, at least! Surely? Which way now, Captain, with your hearty heart of beef?

I burp.

Sarah burps.

The burp ain't so lucky, it's got nowhere to go, nothing' to do but bubble up and go, go, go, again... if only a burp could burp.

We wander back towards greater heat, trying to roll out the door.

Eraser head lynches his fork with a spaghetti noose, dive-bombs a basket of fries with his free mitt. It's the American dream made manifest. Supremacy over all other cuisine is paramount, everything must be bludgeoned into a double-carb stupor.

Man vs Food.

It's like we're in a piece of speculative fiction where Mussolini didn't win. Yeah, there'd be more people I loved, including myself, but can you get real Italian? Of course a few years after the axis victory we were told cannelloni had always had frankfurters in it anyway. Then all opera except Wagner was banned, and oompah became a world-wide craze.

So, the world could be worse, either way.

Don't forget her name is Sarah.

Thank Jehovah.

That's the comfort of victory, the moral superiority it affords you.

Remember that next time you can't get your parking validated, or someone flames your blog.

Thank god for the fourth Reich, all heil the Republic, at least it's not Teutonic.

You know what?

I tell Sarah she should get a tattoo of Il Duce- maybe she'd get more respect from William, seeing he's the Pope an' all.

She's standing in Independence Hall, bathed in the glow of light refracted from cool marble-ette. Actually it's probably the real deal, shipped all the way from Italy, but Sarah says you can't take anything for granted. I consider how taking that stance leads to nothing but heartache, and speaking of misery, just then I catch the flash of Boyd streaking past the Liberty Bell, singing, "...starry, starry night..." and clutching the legendary fedora- unfortunately to the top of his head rather than where God intended.

The guards here are fast, somehow Boyd's faster and he's back out the door. Should we give chase too? I look at Sarah.

"So anyway, you wanna go look at the volcano?"

The whole of California is a volcano, a crack in the ground, a tremor waiting to happen. Ok, so the volcano part is not so active nowadays.

We Californians hold earthquake very low on our list of possible ways to die too, just over cougar attack and way below jogging or the heart-stop of drive-by wounds, and therefore... walk? Actually walk to see a hole in the ground? Even if it gushes steam, somehow that'd be an insult to the golden state we're so umbilically tied to by dress, modes of speech, other, nothing less than ephemeral, loyalties. Nothing more than ephemeral either. No-one is born here, we all drift in on the tide like jettisoned cartons of 'tax-free' cigarettes. That should make Sarah, who washed up first, more Californian than me. For Chrissakes she's a Jew, what's more Hollywood than that? However she's also British and that's a special case, like Billy Idol or 'that bloke from the Sex Pistols'. I remember once, her telling me she sees the whole of America as essentially a struggle between Tarantino and Spike Lee for them to decide who is the most racist. An explosive opinion and possibly one that could only be held by someone who's never seen a volcano. Yeah, I'm not sure how that works, either.

Apparently they don't have them in England anyways. The rain put 'em all out, or somethin'. So we go to stand around a hole in the ground fully expecting Boyd to pop right out of the lava holding his frazzled wiener, which, I'm guessing here to be honest, would still need more than dipping in mustard to make it palatable, even if it's been sulphur-smoked and sugar-dusted. Not even for the regiment...

"You think we'll ever get to the center of the earth?"

"God, I hope not."

When we get there the boiler's been turned off, due to maintenance.

It's not a real volcano of course.

That'd be ridiculous.

Knott had it installed, then upgraded in the 50's or 60's. A sign reads, "This is the apparatus that controls the volcano. It was made by Henry Legano, and is operated by the gentleman turning the crank. (Sound effect by Bob Halliard)".

The last bit kinda gives it away, that it's all sham.

Up until then I would have fully believed that man had tamed the power of lava. Then again William can't even tame his bowels.

"You wanna get a cheese stick?"

'Strictly On A Stick' is calling, its singular approach to feeding the befuddled masses seems irresistible, but still we decide to resist.

William's cell is dead, so is Boyd's.

Maybe security aren't that slow.

We're talking again about how the shape of the noose would go across her shoulder. Still how many people would recognize him, strung up there like a fat Parma ham? Photo-realism is not her thing either, though shouldn't a tattoo be personal, indecipherable?

Sarah still has signal, and is surfing, looking through 'not right in the head'; there's a guy with an ink that says, 'Never Reget Anything', another a full back piece of a steaming turd, Robocop in pastels riding a My Little Pony Unicorn. Suddenly a famous Italian fascist dictator seems like reasonable subject matter. Silvio Berlusconi blowing a shirtless Putin? It's all up for grabs. Now she's studying a link about how one hour's TV a night is worse for you than smoking.

I almost call my dad's old number.

That's becoming a habit.

The sun has rotted off.

A busted bruise.

I turn up my collar, Sarah hugs herself.

If TV *is* worse, do most people having read that article a) watch less TV, b) smoke more?

Sarah's trying to roll a cigarette but her hands are shaking with the sudden chill.

I don't smoke, but I am missing the pipe.

Three dwarves walk by.

Rather than looking for a punch line they're discussing how a job in movies used to be a shoo-in but, now there is CGI, that's all- as Sarah often says- 'gone to tits'. One of them says he works at Disneyland in the CCTV security control room, watching 'fucking giraffes'- i.e. someone over 4' 10"- dressed as Snow White's companions, stealing jobs, and he's riffing on how, if he had his way, there'd be camps for them. Then I realize they are watching me listening to them, one by one they turn full on towards me, like a really cute version of Left 4 Dead, and I can feel their eyes burning into mine, staring up with a tight-lipped intent.

"Whaddya want, Andre?"

"Andre?"

Sarah points at what is actually a Wrestle-Mania rucksack on her back, and I realize he's referring to Andre the giant.

New Jersey accent, not so cute.

"You fuckin' heard me, you great Brobdignagian piece o' shit."

By now there are kids of all ages watching as the gang of goat-height goons does that thing all mobs do when faced with underwhelming odds, leaning forwards, rocking on the balls of their feet, poking their collective intent right at you, like West Side Story recast with bobble-head dolls.

Then the blonde one with the Enola Gay t-shirt starts cracking up, I start to realize that this has been what Sarah calls a 'wind-up', and William, who is at least, thank god, fully clothed, de-cloaks from behind another piece of plastic that Walter Knott, the park's progenitor, would have been hard pushed to recognize if he jumped up outta the ground.

William is telling Sarah how Enola Gay's wife was always coming in Boyd's Seven Eleven bitching about what a practical joker her husband was. She waves from the back, long-suffering, jeans skirt, loud lipstick. She does work at Disney, it turns out, as an animator. She's English too, her dream job, ever since she saw Dumbo as a kid in Brighton, to work for Uncle Walt.

I'm thinking if I had intimate ties with the magic kingdom, I wouldn't go to a theme park on my day off. Too much like work? I guess there's no connection. She sits drawing on a Mac in an air-conditioned office and this… this is forty degrees of hell. Don't they have height restrictions on the rides? Turns out she likes watching people on the water chute. Her husband just likes jerking people around. Where better than here?

He starts bitching about how his kids can't see any of his movies.

An actor in California, who would have thunk?

They all tend to be horrors apparently- the kind with torture as a metaphor for foreplay.

In the last one a mother is forced to pleasure herself with the femur of her dead child. He expresses his disgust. I concur. Then he tells me that he helped write the thing. The guy just can't stop yanking my crank.

A marriage made in heaven?

His wife is telling Sarah an ancient joke about an MGM child-star, whom she calls 'Ruby Garland'- in air quotes- just to make this shaggy dog story seem libelous and therefore more believable. A Hollywood Party, or orgy as it's sometimes known, Ruby orally servicing the entire male contingent of little people who had followed her down a certain jaundice-bricked road, all at the behest of an English Director with low morals and an excruciatingly grating Dick Van Dyke accent.

After munching kith and theatrical kin 'Ruby' can't stop, of course, and then moves on to the waiters, Hoagy Carmichael's lawyer brother, various vaudeville legends… the tale ends with one of the most appalling Michael Caine impersonations I have ever heard, and I watch the Late Show religiously.

"Oi Ruby, you're only supposed to blow the bloody dwarves off!" Sarah's in stitches. I get the reference but perhaps there's another a layer I'm missing- is this another damn Limey thing? Just like thinking Americans still call the English Limeys. An incoming call curtails the hilarity.

Boyd's cell's started working, given the guards the slip, turns out he's made it to the parking lot somehow, and is locked in the trunk waiting for the hand of justice. So we should go, get him out? It's only dogs that die in hot cars, isn't it?

William's had enough. Already puked twice. That's where 'Enola' found him, in the cubicle filling the bowl with cookies. So we head for the car anyway, Sarah telling me we oughta call him 'Willie Wanker' now, but is that really politically correct? Then from Charlie and the Chocolate factory we get on to *bad* films with Gene Wilder and she, off-piste as ever, brings up the worst moobie she's ever seen.

Moobie is a compound pet word comprised of slang for man breasts and movie, a signifier for any film bad enough that Matthew McConaughey would agree to take his shirt off in it, or in other words pretty much any film that is bad enough to have Matthew McConaughey in it, period- and, as most bad films did at one point have Matthew McConaughey in them, it then takes a while to narrow it down. I hadn't seen Tropic Thunder, and I've since heard that's alright. But I don't think he's in it that much and I've also heard he doesn't take his shirt off, which must count as some kind of coup, a cinematic miracle even. Apparently he's made a run of decent projects since then, too- but if he ever wins an Oscar I'll lose 100 lbs, grow a moustache and move to Texas. Sarah is primarily referring to 'Fool's Gold', a film where Donald Sutherland has an 'English' accent and Ray Winstone an 'American' one. It's set in the Caribbean. She's telling me that, as a film, it looks like it was a damn good holiday.

I'm singing, "Doobie, doobie, do…" Strangers in the Night to a reggae back beat, when we reach the car, and, as this is *our* vacation, we're having trouble with the lock on the trunk. It's like we're baked, and then I remember we probably are. When we finally get in, Boyd is curled like a hairy fetus reading a paperback by the light of his own eyes. 'Hitler's Niece.' It's Sarah's. Twenty-five English pence from a charity shop in Peckham. The British are fascinated by the Nazis, even more than we are. They hate xenophobes.

Especially if they're German.

It's not a noble trait, just one fostered by nobility.

And, yes, I know the current Royals are Deutchlanders, real blue-bloods, descended way back, from the Hessian with the biggest club and the toughest swing. You gotta respect that, haven't you? It's like the mob. No, what I'm getting at is the English love of hierarchy, one that is positively incestuous. Can you imagine our leaders handing down power, one generation to the next, Sr to Jr? Ridiculous, a simian fantasy that makes a mockery of evolution.

Of course you could choose the third way and just stagnate instead. It worked for the British Empire. There's a confidence in the superiority of knowing nothing matters anymore, that you're better than world politics, above it- one that has, as its public justification, a misguided belief that you possess an innate tolerance that the rest of the world surely does not. A Royal patronage of the ex-colonies and beyond. 'We must be better than foreigners, we think everyone in the world is equal- as long as they understand that and remember to *stay* in the rest of the world, and as long as we preserve the status quo, eat steak and kidney pudding, requisition jumpers for goal-posts, keep calm and carry on, indulge in the deathless recitative repetition of old glories...'

Sarah clued me in to that... and so, of course that doesn't stop me accusing her of it.

Our policy is more like the Borg.

I'm telling her how we Americans aspire to the principle of tolerance too, but we are all actually foreigners, and besides we don't have the advantage of a hereditary class system to really point out how ridiculous that smugness is, so we want to make everyone in our image, an image we all made up out of off-cuts, bits of movie fiction, old songs that all promised us that they were the future, our shared dream of progress...

Boyd chips in, something about who invented concentration camps, and so, given any reference to the Nazis in an argument instantly disqualifies you from the privilege of participation in discourse, we instantly ignore him. Besides, now he's too busy segueing from the Nazi zombie classic 'Dead Snow' to his idea for a movie called 'Night of the Liturgical Dead'.

Ooh, we've got a screen-writer in the family.

Remind me to inform the Academy.

I always knew the Boydster, El Boyderino, the Boydinator would come in handy one day for vast cash sums. How could he fail to rise when living in spitting distance of a town that prized the uncommon common touch over all? I even remember getting out of a cab once and promising him that, yes, if his remaining leg was on fire, I would indeed piss on it... honest, and wouldn't one do the same for Jerry Bruckheimer? It's like they're twins. Thinking about it, shouldn't we at least be grateful that our little genius wasn't the kind of half-wit who just sat in a chair and wet himself on his own time?

Good for him.

Good for us all.

Good for our sense of humanity.

He was overcoming adversity from the inside.

While we're making character references... he wasn't *that* much for throwing up either, and, unlike William, only opened up his nose on religious holidays- Ramadan mainly, which seemed kinda random for a guy brought up handling snakes. Oh, and he'd stopped peering in girl's windows too, even though he was happy to pass on tips. So, what can you say? A virtual saint, and now surely a born scrivener.

Meanwhile, William is, I think, supporting my point, the one which I've now already forgotten. He extrapolates, tells us that he likes to think Americans are too spread out to constantly use our sense of patriotism for evil. That's what state-hood is for. Every time we bomb some shitty sand-hole he thinks that maybe California'd be better off invading Alaska and stealing their oil.

"You think we would have lost Mexico if it was worth keeping?"

Some pauses, some heated debate. I pick it up with Miss Appleyard again, "...if you ring fence your borders, you'll have an even smaller gene pool..." Just to prove a point, Boyd, that ultimate small town boy, is still riffing on his movie pitch, "...the irreligious can't get infected, they just get eaten, but the faithful can pass the virus on to other believers who then become holy zombies too..." He's painting a picture of sanctimonious corpses tub-thumping in a clinical-nymphomania of eternally frustrated fervor, hordes of the clerical undead who switch between their unquenchable, ravening hunger for conversion and their equally ravening carnivorous hunger for dismemberment.

Fellini it ain't.

To be fair, even Woody Allen had trouble pulling off that trick.

Not just being Fellini, I mean.

William then develops that look which questions Boyd and his genetic connection. It's one thing to jump off a building, it's another to be as dumb as a Michael Bay movie. That takes something that so closely resembles talent you'd almost be forgiven for thinking there was some form of intent. Like following a map, speaking of which...

3. Frying Pans And Other Fires

When you rely on the road to provide your destination and not the other way around, strange choices are made.

Welcome to the Marine Corps Logistic Base in Barstow. Actually they don't welcome you.

I thought it'd be like NCIS.

I thought we'd be greeted with open arms, invited into their high security facility for a jolly hour of procedural drama and 'jokes' about extra strong coffee, all by a nice old man in a bow tie and glasses and a goth girl in a Jessie J. Halloween mask who's built like that guy you expected would end up a star quarterback in high school, but then, despite his height and strong jaw, never quite filled out...

Not so.

Apparently they don't investigate murder here, instead they rebuild and repair ground combat support equipment. Which is a shame. A TV detective would probably be able to figure just where we turned off the straight and narrow. To tell you the truth, when I said I thought it'd be like America's number one crime show, actually, I didn't think it'd be like anything, as actually I didn't expect to be here at all. Thank you brother, no really, thank you, and your 'internal compass', it is as ever a marvel of misplaced iron filings...

Somehow we've ended up six kilometers east of Barstow.

The Naval Base's electro-magnetic pull leaving Boyd guilty as charged.

The day could only get worse if we managed to pick up a kid in a Mickey Mouse t-shirt and ply him with the contents of William's pipe. As it is, my own personal fear and loathing resides in everyone wearing a uniform and the median age seeming to be that exact point where sense is yet to kick in but the capability for violence has already reached an all-time high. Testosterone and Walmart body spray. I don't think I've ever been called Sir so many times by boys who didn't mean it. Marines, you gotta love 'em. The terror threat is currently brown- 'in...' as Letterman always put it, '...my pants.'

Don't get me wrong, I'm glad someone's willing to die for corrupt corporations... I mean, the American way of life, but face to face? Sarah starts chatting and we're getting nowhere, just no help. It's all, 'Like, yeah, I could fillet a man, rip out his scrotum through his left ear, no problem, but commit to giving tangible advice about directions to a stranger?' It's the first time in my life I wish I had a blonde, pneumatic, play-bunny girlfriend, some way maybe to melt the ice? Aren't the military supposed to reach out to the public nowadays? Goddamit, the Navy made friends with Cher for that video, and she was an old hippy. You'd think they'd want to get rid of us as quickly as possible, at least. They do just keep pointing away from the base, back down the road we came, and giving the vaguest speculation as to what our movements should be after that, probably go forth and multiply...

Finally, someone everyone starts calling Ma'am strolls over, honey-blonde ponytail, camo cap, actually built like the guy from your high school who *did* become the star quarterback. Full beams Sarah with perfect naval orthodontistry, starts giving directions with nothing but genuine politeness, even asks if she's ever thought about serving her country- I think she must assume Sarah's from Boston rather than the dark satanic mills of the West Riding- is that where Norwich is?

Ow!

And again she punches me...that's becoming a habit.

Once we're back on the right trail, it's an hour before we stop teasing her. I'm the worst- William and Boyd's fervent interest in lesbians is something I've never really shared, but any chance to make fun of your girlfriend cannot be ignored.

I believe we started with girls climbing an assault course sniper tower to indulge in some 'K.I.S.S.I.N.G', followed by a variation of the old 'two nuns in a bath' joke- replacing the nuns with female navy seals. Proceeding through the esoteric and somewhat weak ramblings of Boyd's script, to the backing of an egregious country mix-tape, we then get to...

"How many lesbians does it take to change a light-bulb?"

A pregnant pause whilst Hank Williams gets real lonesome on the only acceptable track.

"One. They're just as capable at fixing problems round the house as any man. But I'd prefer it if there'd been two of them, just so I could watch…"

This was usually one of what we called Boyd's 'specialist subjects'- things about which he knew nothing and therefore felt an unquenchable desire to tell the world. I can't remember where it ended. Probably in tears. Probably mine. The navy really could use a punch like Sarah's. Or at least hands that big.

I start to wonder what she'd look like as a recruit. I try to imagine a crew-cut, but personally it's doing nothing for me, or indeed her. What's wrong with loose, unkempt bangs? Is Johnny Depp any less the man for having them, or the young David McCallum? Please don't answer that, I simply will not have them impugned. It's that kind of rampant, misplaced homophobia that wastes time otherwise better spent on jokes about dykes…"

Another punch.

At what point had I started talking aloud again?

Don't judge.

For if we as three grown boys cannot tease a 24-year-old girl, what is left sacred? What do men have? Better pay, more power, greater status? Mere trifles, surely?

Sarah has a look on her face that's reminiscent of what Boyd, growing up, used to call a bit-pull terrier.

What was I saying, and so unfortunately out loud, oh yeah, dykes…

"Some of them call themselves that…"

This is no excuse for using that word, especially if you're not one yourself, and Sarah is wise to that.

"…I don't hear you using the N-bomb to describe anyone black…"

Fo' shizzle, she has a point, William used to use it as a term of affection for Boyd, but that was a passing fad long before we'd met Miss Appleyard.

So I pull the oldest bull-trick in the book.

"One of my closest friends is a lesbian."

"You don't have any close friends."

"Yes, but if I did, one of them would be… Surely..?"

Whimsy is not cutting it.

"You don't have any friends…"

"Steve."

"Steve's a lesbian?"

Boyd chips in, "Not through lack of trying."

No-one is quite sure what he means by that, but he still receives a hard stare from Sarah. I counter.

"Yeah, Steve's gay."

"Steve's gay?"

"He cried at the Phantom Menace."

This time I really deserve the punch.

"Everyone cried *at* the Phantom Menace."

"I threw up."

Was that why we cried? Some memories are too bad to… well, be remembered? Let's get back on track.

"What about Jessie?" I offer.

"Jessie's your close friend?"

"I hang with her all the time."

This isn't strictly true, especially since she upped sticks to the mysterious black hole known as 'Europe' last fall.

"She owes you money."

Actually I owe her, but the guilt made me spend far too much time with a woman who thinks that… when did this go back to being in my head?

It was then Sarah kissed me on the nose and I felt even more of a shit-heel for using the word 'dyke', even as shorthand in a joke. What the world needs now is mutual respect. Surely something that simple is achievable. An old blues comes on as they've switched the mix-tape, and so William chooses that moment to say how much he loves that, "…pussy-licking nigger bitch, Ma Rainey…" as the car takes flight with a whirlwind passion, two of the passengers at first attempting to restrain the other from landing a solid crack on the driver and then deciding, after a moment's reflection, to help. All this drama to the strains of the Black Eye Blues.

For a moment the sky seems to dip to a deeper blue. The desert folds round and I keep expecting to see two suns descending in the east. West? Hey George, which way to Mos Eisley? No one could doubt the Baker Boys and their fabulous sense of direction.

How hard can this be? It's one highway, it's rumored to be the best. We won't get lost again, surely? It'd be a black day…

It seems more than oddly appropriate that the next stop on our griddle greasin' map is the El Rancho hotel built by R.E Griffith, the brother of legendary Hollywood racist D.W. This was where Errol Flynn worked all day and drank all night, whilst John Wayne was rumored to do whatever John Waynes do in the Monument Valley- so the only gossip to float back to Gallup would have been in the Navajo dialect, smoke signals dissipated by a lack of skilled translators…

Never trust a legend.

Do people still say Indian giver?

Not around Rich Hall.

She turned me on to him too.

Still, Sarah does have a key-ring with a Robinson's Marmalade Golly in a feather head-dress hanging from it.

I once kissed a Native American.

It didn't go well.

We were in the dark womb of a cinema showing the 'Green Berets'.

I'd pulled my date to a kitsch revival.

One marked by audience partici… pation to rival the Rocky Horror Show. Every time the Duke saluted we downed another shot from a shared Dixie cup.

Boyd is always trying to tell me that most women have terrible taste in movies, and yet they also tend to have no time for John Wayne.

The El Rancho is still there, if you can afford to stay. For us, tonight was going to be one of the ones we had to spend under the stars that William had stuck to the roof of the jalopy. It was the only way to make this economically viable. Hotels depend on the blindness of strangers, the eyes closing in defeat, the 'Bus Stop', must stop, of hicks pulling over to sample the local talent. Monroe never stayed here. Never made many horse operas and no, her last movie don't count. Ironically this was one of the few attractions along Route 66 that was killed by the road's success, not its eventual decay. As the road became more travelled, its seclusion dipped, mirroring the public's interest in the western and deterring Hollywood from staying. No longer did John Wayne walk into the desert looking for God, pussy, whatever it was... a cure for cancer?

It was sometime in the middle of the night that we discovered Boyd had wandered off in search of mine shafts. Curious, he never did like John Wayne. I tried to get him to understand the parallels between westerns and all that space-opera crap he still loved but Boyd always distrusted metaphor, I think he felt it came between a boy and actual experience. Though how much you could argue he'd actually touched the stars? You'd have to ask the pipe. We only knew he'd be safe once we'd discovered he hadn't taken the fedora. Surely his innate homing instinct would bring him back to us... If only I could have persuaded William to Fed-Ex it to Chicago we'd never get lost.

In the dawn's early light we thought we'd found the devil-may-care scamp extricating his penis from a cactus barb, actually it was just his thigh, upper arms, neck and torso. He'd sleep-walked right into a passionate clinch with what he believed was a plump Mexican girl with very green teeth. Luckily for Boyd his morning glory had found the one spot where the plant was a tender, pulpy orifice rather than an exacting torment. This was a delicate operation, at one point he instructed William to, "...get out of my cock space you regency water closet...", an epithet so atypical that William took the opportunity to tease him that spiders often built their nests in cacti and that right now the babies were probably lining up to burst from his balls in a tribute to James Cameron. I always thought if you had to pay tribute to James Cameron, Aliens was a good place to start... and end. Speaking of blue balls, I've always thought that if you had to find women attractive then Sigourney Weaver was a good place to begin. For a start her teeth weren't green. Strong jaw too. Just like Snake Plissken.

Both William and Boyd violently disagreed, citing Monica Bellucci and Rosie Perez respectively.

Sarah chipped in with Anne Heche.

We wished.

Could have kept that teasin' going till the Grand Canyon.

It was impossible to gauge her taste in men, let alone any theoretical 'curious tendencies' she might have.

Rafael Nadal. Steve Buscemi. Lloyd Bridges. Thane Krios. Steve Jobs. Jeff Goldblum. Chow Yun Fat. Michael Madsen. Pee Wee Herman. Nick Nolte. Newt Gingrich. Ok, the last one was a lie but you wouldn't be that surprised to see the Dali Lama or Kim Jong Il in there. She didn't even bother mentioning Johnny Depp, too obvious. That was just a given for her generation. Her taste was so much wilder and wider than anything I could offer on my side.

"Alien."

"Alien?"

"You know, Ridley Scott's…"

"I thought you said you didn't like girls."

"Only the queen's a girl, I like the drones, the original design, like in the first movie."

So that's normal then, they're guy Aliens.

"If I was a man I'd like to look like Sigourney Weaver."

Thank you Boyd for that profoundly disturbing thought.

What did I look for in a partner? What did Sarah's taste say about me? I had time to think. After all, she *was* choking on an insect.

"Could be worse…"

"…worse..?"

"I'd rather be you than the fly."

Saw one walking on a mirror once and thought: well, there's another way of looking at it…

The Aveo was having a problem. Wanted to stall. We'd have to take it slow. By the time we'd get to The Calico Ghost Town it would almost be midday. I know what you're thinking, another ghost town?

Boyd and William wanted to press on past.

This was going to be different.

Firstly it had actually been around since the Great Silver Strike of 1881. Second there were actually over 500 mines there. And thirdly it was bought by… wait a minute, it was bought by Walter Knott too?

Who 'restored' it during the 50's.

Fudge.

Where to start? Maggie's Mine? The Mystery Shack? Or the Calico-Odessa Railway?

At least there wasn't a petting zoo.

I'm wondering, did celebrities always keep wild animals? Did the Duke have a fondness for monkeys?

I once dated a freshman whose mother had remarried a stuntman.

I remember sitting on plastic furniture whilst Bucky, or whatever his name was, recounted another Hollywood party story, another oral tradition, this one where he claimed the center-piece was a buxom prostitute being paid lip, tongue and teeth service by big-leggy himself. It's best to take such tales with a pinch of bromide. Dreamland is a breeding ground for misinformation. The only real truths are the ones strong enough to climb all the way to the San Fernando Valley and become solid fable. The ones that both the legitimate and illegitimate industries cling to. Porno's number one rule is the same as Hollywood, never work with children or animals. The myths about those that did are as grave as concrete, and never end well.

I will play with a cat, but I will never befriend a lama.

Boyd on the other hand is trying to feed a prairie dog, and with his other hand. Look, see Boyd throw nuts at the vermin. See the vermin run. See the vermin run at Boyd. See Boyd run. See the vermin throw nuts at the Boyd. Let's get down a mine *before* he hurts himself?

Boyd wants to beat us to the punch line by heading for the hills…

'Warning: Mines in the Calico Region are EXTREMELY hazardous and must not be approached for any reason…'

We conclude a burro ride would be safer.

How wrong could we be?

Let Boyd prove us wrong.

Still I daresay if puberty proved it could happen once I don't see why a testicle can't descend a second time.

What's the difference between a fedora and a sportsman's protective jock strap?

Everything.

Of course the real tragedy is now William will be doing all the driving.

We forgo camping- primarily as we don't have a tent- and press on towards our next port of call, Amboy- gateway to the stars.

Apparently Tom Selleck would pockmark his career with stays here.

But as Harrison Ford grabbed every role he was ever up for... well, the bare flat Mojave welcomes both this alternate reality's Han Solo and the real one who could actually afford a Millennium Lear Jet. In fact the latter gets his own landing strip. Harrison was your big brother in Star Wars, your cool uncle in Raiders, your embittered older self in Blade Runner and now your earring-wearing, much younger girlfriend humping mid-life crisis-a-go-go chump, in a slew of average thrillers and ill-considered revivals of earlier glories. Harrison got stardom. Selleck got a fan-page dedicated to his moustache, but not really to him, oh and the keys to Hawaii- though how that compares to a hangar at Amboy I'm not sure.

Boyd staggers into Roy's Café.

Points at a picture of a cheeseburger behind the counter.

"I'd like that, but without the cheese..."

"...only what's on the menu."

Oh those Americans, so sarcastic.

Still it couldn't have been more obvious if they'd named the place Burger-King. I can't imagine that woulda fit with the retro-futurism of the humongous sign outside. Red. Yellow. Black. Blue. White. BOLD. Atomic architecture, an apoco-lapse in taste I happen to like. Inside Anthony Hopkins and Harrison grin down at us from the walls, their respective signatures a battle between fine penmanship and loose swagger. Sarah orders fries. I order fries. William orders fries which he looks black daggers at. Boyd's just fried.

Once we grow tired of burping we wander into the street, try to figure out precisely where it ends and the desert begins, but it's all so flat, eerily beautiful. Some of us are thinking about breaking into the school next door, or rather you can see the trouble-twins eyeing up the possibilities for a challenge. They keep the wistful home fires of mayhem burning in their retinas as we drive east, till eventually that pull is extinguished by the hypnotic power of a palo verde tree bearing the track-meet strange fruit of a thousand sneakers.

God's own stinking bush.

It's bigger and yet less impressive than I imagined.

Then something…

A twist in the light, a feathered brush stroke of wonder.

My attitude changes and up high above us, or rather high above the tree it seems, a patch of rainbow. Not a cut off part of the usual curve, for there are no clouds, but a smudge in the grease-lensed sky we are looking through- two, three, more… floating there. Hard to describe them, like a flotilla of improbable light, in a flash I have seen a colony of weightless sprinters running through the air, standing upright, at top a scared trinity, John Carlos, in the center, 'hung' by his feet from the tree. No-one has much of an interpretation for this personal epiphany, as yet. They're too busy cooing over the rain-not-bows. However, in celebration of this holy vision, William does do a massive roaring donut to echo the rings of the twisted silver arboreal and the loss of the sky's curve. Clearly there is only up and down now, the earth is flat, we are doomed to run its bitter salt flats for eternity, ironically a circular hell of repeated… or William needs to crack a window when he's smoking.

Even with the 'clouds' we're still drawn inexorably to the glorious ugliness of mankind's sports footwear hanging there like a gnarly beard. The branches all seem too weak, even compared to the eyries offered by the dented roof of our aluminum chariot. Boyd descends, the steel hollows popping up to greet the vaselined sky. He plummets softly to earth, now that the rubber is clearing from our burn-out even he conceding that this most sacred of shrines must remain untouched by our tainted honky hands. Now he's categorizing my moment of fervent psychosis. Deciding its meaning. Slavery is a serious business and what will one day become the holy trifecta of John Carlos, Sebastien Foucan, and Edwin de la Rosa must always be respected, even before it exists. For now, as this is Carlos' tree, we just stare at this searing indictment of our forefathers.

Sarah burps.

William burps.

Boyd this time is lucky.

Though how you would shart your throat?

Vomit?

Bile?

Like I said, he's lucky.

We are not.

An olfactory 'delight'.

"What the fuck was that?"

"Cornflakes, squeeze cheese, and jalapenos..."

"What?"

"...the breakfast of Mexican champions..."

"Cornflakes?"

"They're sweeter than nachos..."

"Sweeter?"

"More breakfasty..."

"What kind of an egregious, philistine..."

"What kind of an egregious..."- he hadn't copied my voice in a while, a habitual Boyd-ism he hadn't yet dropped from childhood, just like burping.

I thought he'd stopped, but now we get his rendition of 'My Country Tis of Thee'.

Thankfully he gives up before the third verse.

"What's a rill?"

"I don't know, but if it smells of squeezy cheese and jalapenos they can keep it."

"A rill is what makes America great..."

"You have no idea..."

Sarah interjects.

"It's a small cut in the landscape, the erosion of topsoil, the start of a river..."

"The Rio Grande..."

"The Mississippi..."

"The Mighty Hudson..."

"John Wayne..."

"Mark Twain..."

"Kate..."

"Kate?"

"Kate Hudson."

"It's what made this country..."

"The home of the breakfast of Mexican Champions..."

We spend a quarter of an hour deciding whether that's racist. Being in the shadow of St Carlos' Tree of Life is perhaps making us feel this burden more keenly.

There is only one solution.

Chloride.

Like Moses I will lead my people to their rebirth.

The only thing we planned on this trip, apart from the route, was a visit to the chloride beds in the shadow of the Amboy crater. As the shadows are growing we must hurry. No-one likes skinny dipping in the pitch dark, it's un-American. Besides who could deny the local fauna its chance to not only bite Boyd in the nuts but to be captured on camera-phone doing so?

My flash is useless, his flashing hysterical.

We needn't have worried.

The light may fade but man is ever ingenious…

After a short drive and a lunch of tinned nori and soda bread a long nap in the lee of the car is in order. Never let it be said that a feeling of urgency has ever impinged on my brothers' sense of life's pitch, its roll and pace. We awake to the nuclear glow of arc lights and phosphorescent swearing. Like the holy fools we have become we head in that direction, stumbling on speedball grit, one moment a slow glide, the next a flurried flail. Three shapes form into well-fatted tablecloths, the only logical explanation for the existence of that much checked cloth. Two of them carry long-barrel rifles, the third is crouched over hammering at something you'd guess would be better served with a more complex engineering tool.

Still it seems to do the trick.

The motor roars into life and I'm handed a beer as I'm offered a seat on a lawn chair.

"He wanna go swimming then?"

"Fuckin' nuts?"

"My brother…"

I'm not sure how this explains things but it seems to also do the trick.

I get a wave of feeling I've been accepted.

I'm not sure it's the kind of thing you'd want to get used to.

They train one of their vehicle's lights on a distended rill of glowing blue.

"Knock yourself out…"

Boyd is already down to his under-crackers, William is slower, Sarah is a hundred yards away being shown how to cock the skeet-gun. Seems she brings out the nurturing side in anyone with access to firearms.

You never fired a gun, you must be from that England?

The first thunk.

A swift moving disc of Day-Glo yellow is rocketed skywards. William and Boyd scream out in wonder.

What?

That's better than a rainbow cloud?

Next an almighty boom like one of Boyd's stentorious eruptions rips the night sky and I kinda collapse/lean into the guy who handed me the beer. In truth I wanted to jump onto his lap.

I don't have to.

He puts his big paw on my leg.

This guy was clearly a corkscrew, the kind only brought out for social collapses, he was... without him no drama, no offence, no party, and then back he goes, into the drawer with the knife with the weird prongs on the end and those red rubber bands, one solitary cocktail umbrella, face down into... you've almost forgotten him as much as he forgets himself, but then he's a good story, so you open up the drawer again. Of course, one day he'll fall down the back, and you'll say, whatever happened to...

"That your girlfriend?"

"Yes..."

He's looking straight at me now, eyes wetter than the water that just shot up Willie and Boyd's collective asses as they dive-bombed into clear blue.

"Does she know?"

Does she know..?

"My wife doesn't..."

His hand is a little higher now.

4. From Needles To The Falls

The radio is on.

I can't quite believe it.

Let me explain.

As a people, you'd probably be surprised to know, we Americans under-exploit the opportunities for heinous behavior without retribution that this great country of ours offers. Sure, we all love an overseas aberrant adventure but on our home soil we're usually quite restrained. We're also not fond of curse words, except those of us who are, of course, very, very motherfucking fond.

What I'm trying to say is if our token European knew she had this much land to disappear into and a strong enough radio transmitter, she would fill the airwaves with potty-mouthed epithets and leave the religious proselytizing to the glory of the landscape and its unspoken word. Hence my surprise to hear these airwaves gently caressed by...

'...this is a story about pussy. Don't snigger. I don't mean Tom, or Sylvester or Felix, or indeed the comic cuts of your domestic kitten when you tease it with a ball of string. I'm talking about the serious business of what lies between beauty's legs. A thick furl of jungle curl, a neat little triangle, a smooth egg of quivering pink, the dusky, the pallid, even the pornographically vapid... au naturel, Brazilian. I'm talking pussy, pussy, pussy...'

He ain't jivin'.

"Who is this cat?"

"That's the pussy-cat, el Duderino..."

"What's a Brazilian?"

Middle America, the mild open prairie, you can take the boy out of the corn fields... of course, he knows what a Brazilian is...

Surely?

We ignore Boyd anyway.

"He's been on about an hour."

"On about an hour last night too, but you were sleeping..."

"Why didn't you..."

It was obvious.

You couldn't tell anyone about the Pussycat, you had to find him yourself. Of course that wasn't his only topic, just the one that William had right then decided gave him his name. Seems the Pussycat's mission was to dial up your conscious, slap it about for a half hour or so, on any number of subjects, and then disappear into the ether...

"His range must be..."

We tried to imagine the broadcast tower, a giant phallus rearing its ugly head above the wasteland- its shadow a Lebowski scribble cast long upon the ground. Cock a doodle do, this wasn't the breakfast show though.

"...I'm more of a night-owl, oh shit, is that the time? Goodnight."

The abrupt sign-off kinda threw me.

We pull up in the near-dark outside the Needles skate park, say a quick prayer for Tony Hawk and someone mentions Sam Kinison. Sarah votes for Dan Louden's murals in the morning, I just want a proper bed, right now.

We try to find Lynn's Broiler and Cocktail lounge as food and drink is an adequate substitute for sleep, right?

I paraphrase William.

The Broiler is long gone.

Instead the squeeze cheese yellow and muscovado brown of Wagon Wheels Restaurant. Big rigs, cop cars, mini-vans, a couple of fifth wheelers. Could this be the deep-fried nirvana of Boyd's dietary fever dreams?

Inside western-welcome-horns above the door, a quarter-gobbling kiddie horse ride, tiled floor, wood paneling, a spoke-wheel-ended bench.

"...like the trench, you say the trench and everyone knows..."

They're off topic, discussing how Star Wars was the last 'cultural' event big enough that everyone knows the references without that sacred bond of shared experience being broken by the internet- a tool which gives all men all knowledge and renders specific shared experience meaningless. Who the fuck are the Knutsons? Just look it up. Helios Creed? You don't have to hunt down the records now to know what he sounds like.

Boyd is wearing a Route 66 t-shirt he bought from the gift shop, to replace the one he dribbled squeeze cheese down earlier, a t-shirt which up until five seconds ago wasn't smeared with Swiss mushroom omelet. Now he's using it as a napkin despite there being plenty of paper ones on offer.

"…if I say the trench now, though, I bet you just see clear blue…"

He's directing that at William. They're back off the road now, under the starlit sky, floating on their backs in the clear blue chloride, held aloft by physics and a little magic, already nostalgic for yesterday, was it?

"You shoulda come in…"

No thank-you.

I never swim.

Besides I'm saving up stories for your grandkids, for when you die of chloride-related cancer '…yeah and whilst your pappies experienced the marriage of salts and water, tested the resilience of a local buoyancy phenomenon, I experienced a local salty boy's testing of the phenomenon of his marriage, the hand gripped tight upon the thigh…'

"…it was…"

"Cajun hot link, fried eggs over easy, home-style potatoes, diced bell peppers and onions and a side order of biscuits and gravy, thank-you…"

We look over to the next booth, expecting Godzilla.

A tiny Mexican with pink-eye is already starting to tuck in to his other breakfast of champions, just as soon as it arrives he'll begin the physical manifestation of tackling the mountain he's already climbed six times over in his head whilst driving here.

The waitress with the star tattoo on her wrist is bent over, holding her back, straightening herself, her wagon wheel t-shirt riding up on her saddles. I think William may be falling in love.

"Solid."

Boyd and I laugh.

He calls me Homer like he used to when we were teenagers.

I used to play the Battle of Olympus on the NES all the time when we were still just about growing up.

"Solid."

We know what he, and only he, means by that, and you can't look it up on the internet.

You can probably play Battle of Olympus on your phone now.

Sarah lifts hers to show us 'Solid-Babes.com'

We change the topic.

Boyd takes offence for no reason, "You're not wrong William, you're just an asshole... and you..?"

He uses his fork to point a flobble of egg at me.

Sarah stays out of it, staring at the mosaic of orange, white, yellow and green glass that tops the wall of our booth.

I think of English cathedrals, Harry Potter.

"My Auntie had something like this in her downstairs loo."

I get up for a piss.

On the way back get pulled into the notice board, a habit, little lives other than my own.

Most of them are adverts for truck repair, RV campsites or discount photocopying. However, next to a friendly faced middle aged lady with glasses advertising who knows what, I can't remember now, is a small green card with a radio tower, a frequency and the epithet, "The Ball Headed Broom- sweeping the unholy dust from your ears..."

Shouldn't that be bald headed?

What's ball-headed?

"What's ball headed?" Too tired I call it over to the table.

My order is immediately filled by Boyd dropping his pants.

"This is a family restaurant..."

The voice is so school ma'am-ish Boyd pulls 'em up real quick.

Thank god it's just Sarah's disapproval and not one of the staff. I'm waiting on toast and a coffee and I'd like it in here not in the parking lot.

"...legs over easy..."

What?

It's just this one guy joking.

A Mormon looking douche in a gold joke-shop cowboy hat, the only person to have noticed Boyd's mini-striptease, he wags his finger, but I don't think he'll tell. Nothing's getting past those teeth, they are the fortress of surfactant.

Then we get some real interaction with the locals.

"…I am the reggae ambassador, hey, hey, hey…"

He's leaning over, trying to pimp this 'cool' place called the naked pirate beach cove or something, he's friends with the dj. 'My bro' as he puts it to Sarah. Thankfully he's going now, on his way out…

We stay almost to closing at 10 PM

Spill into the lot smelling of chicken fried steak and lighter fuel.

I get my photo taken by the cinder block wall with a Louden locomotive and the 66 logo sweeping cross them. Up above on the porch roof a little wooden wagon beckons the attention of Boyd, but you can tell he's only yearning for the old glories, for the squeak of an un-oiled caster, the warm embrace of an un-jetted dumpster, that ever-green night flight to pain. Nostalgia for anything other than Han drawing first will not be tolerated. The gas station next door is still open. Perhaps chewing gum will take the taste of lost time away. A hard call I know…

"…Billy Bass, what's it called over here..?"

Sarah talking about the animated singing plastic fish they had on the wall next door. If this is the last generation's Rubik's cube, surely we're devolving?

I look at Boyd and William, am made certain of my conviction.

Then it all goes kinda black and swirly…

Are we there yet?

Have we been here already?

We make Oatman double quick.

I remember Oatman.

From when?

Are we even there yet?

Didn't we stop at the hotel for ice-cream?

There were dollar bills plastered all over the bar walls and ceiling and a sign saying Carole Lombard stayed here with Clark Gable for their honeymoon, though he spent a lot of that time whooping it up with the boys, playing cards with grizzled miners.

The Hotel's pink adobe, as garish as a Liberace-approved chorus line. I feel like the Road is mocking me. Like the reason I don't need metaphor is that history is just repeating itself without need for allusion.

Speaking of predictable.

How long did we think it would be before Boyd tried to ride one of the tame burros ambling down the streets?

They're descendants of the ones the miners used.

They've been here since the early 19th century, seen it all.

Maybe not felt the warm press of naked Boyd butt on their back before, but…

Then I consider how lonely a miner's life can be waiting for Clark Gable to show up. Boyd hugs the shaggy neck, whispers sweet nothings, a tender moment in a back alley.

I blink and his clothes are back on.

What was the point?

"You ain't done nothing till you've done it naked."

Passed the bar exam? I try to imagine Boyd as a lawyer. How self-evident would truths have to be before he could hold them?

Echoes.

Mountains.

The English language fails me.

I try to recall the opening lines of a great book.

As it was not a 'dark and stormy night', I was kinda stuck.

In the beginning God created the heavens and the earth?

How about, "The scenery round here sure is nice…" Volcanic, bizarre, hard to do it justice. It's like the earth has opened its sulphurous back door, offered up its plump haunches to… when I came across the Glory Hole I knew the town really was mocking me.

It's a curiosity shop and museum.

Three hundred inches tall, uncut. A two tiered artful wreck that creaks like an old ship flying at half-mast, the musky scent of prairie dust and Edwardian assignations. You know how some people just love antiquing.

I love my girlfriend.

Yes I do, mister.

Even if sometimes she can't get on with my brother, all that chafing against William's wit.

Sarah has a carved burro in her hand.

Boyd is at the door.

"This is Sarah…"

Not that Sarah with the donkey…

There's a girl standing next to him, red-blonde hair and sallow skin, trail-burnt to a jaundiced hue, (Australian?) a leather cowboy hat tipped back on her head and a backpack much bigger than her. Her t-shirt is faded grey, she's not wearing a bra and I feel, feel something stir in me, like a primal thing, I guess?

Mockery.

Yup, primal bitchiness.

One boob's almost twice the size of the other.

A circus love.

"This is another Sarah."

So now we're collecting Sarahs.

"Sarah-Jane?"

It's not like she's sure, it's like she just wants to help. Like that isn't really her name, or not one she uses, but hey, if it'll stop any confusion…

"Can we just call you Jane?"

William takes her hand and Boyd looks worried.

I don't like trouble.

I think back to the oil-stain on Deadman's curve where the shop-keep told me two Harleys collided back in '97.

I don't like having less space in the car either.

Or in my chest, can't really breathe…

I do like breasts? That seemed kinda surprising. Especially when they're not exactly a pair. Had I forgotten? It sure came outta nowhere. I still can't breathe. Maybe I'm just tired of the Sarah that isn't Jane. Maybe? Maybe if I had some real sleep?

Jane's laughing. Even her eyes are yellow.

Jane's still laughing.

The rest of the day's a little…

When I wake up, it's night.

My temperature had reached over one hundred, my vision blurred to gold. No-one is sick save me, that's why we're sleeping in the desert- all for one, my ass. Jane's gone. Boyd's got a black eye. Then I understand it's not the stars above me but flashes in my vision. I hear the words 'cool springs' and 'King's man' echoing in my head and someone says we're in Antares?

Isn't that an X-Wing pilot? And... I'm back in the trench. First the darkness, then the smell. Like the bottom of the laundry basket was your pillow. Who leads a dying man here? The room is growing thick with smoke, Jane's armpit is in my face.

Sorry, Sarah's.

It doesn't stop the morning glory, it calls it forth, goddammit!

My brothers are nowhere to be seen, so we climb back into how things used to be and it's good. Comfortable. I'm happy fucking for the first time in... I'm fucking, really? Is any of this real?

Sarah's breath on my neck, soft sleepy voice, "Where are we?"

"You don't know?"

"I wasn't expecting you to, it was just rhetorical."

The steel door comes aside with a scrape.

Well, what do you know?

"Hello Boyd's wang."

It returns the greeting with a display of virtuoso genital origami that owes very little to puppetry of the penis and a whole lot to Jim Henson's Creature Workshop.

"Welcome to Master Bates' Motel." Thanks for that one Sarah, it's not even yours, goddammit.

Boyd comes towards us waggling it. It's not that time of the morning, is it? He hasn't given us time for the three-way rock, paper, scissors which decides which one of us stooges takes him for a walk, and where is William when you need him anyhow?

"Please don't, I haven't eaten yet."

Sarah throws a shoe at him instead.

I could have died of altitude sickness, no-one seems concerned, but hey, just like the egg said, at least I got laid.

Didn't I?

Eventually we stagger into the southern fried sun to be greeted by a fourteen foot tall green Easter Island head- more road-side tomfoolery, anything to trap the tourist back in the day.

Apparently, even this mighty totem was not enough to deter us from breaking and entering.

I must be getting better, as my next sentence is, "We need to get food."

William is holding a bolt cutter and I'm wondering where he got it and what poor defenseless fowl will get bludgeoned for breakfast, let's hope Boyd's cock isn't on the menu.

Damn, I could eat a stadium.

When we find the Hackberry General Store our hopes are not high, but then they're raised and dashed.

The place is the most ramshackle I've ever seen. There's a red corvette and an old Buick out front of these tumbledown shacks crammed full of auto parts, rusty signs and then... nirvana- 'chicken sandwiches for 35 cents'.

"Last chicken died years ago..."

I resist the temptation to ask why he still has the sign up.

We stock up on candy and sodas, praying we'll find proper sustenance before the inevitable comedown hits. Along the road are dotted Burma Shave signs. A series of semi-rhyming couplets designed to play out mini-motor mysteries to which the final answer is Burma Shave.

1. Big Mistake
2. Many Make
3. Rely on Horn
4. Instead of
5. Brake
6. Burma Shave Logo

We invent our own. Boyd's haiku is a riff on the original and an ode to the old-fashioned trouser fastener.

1. Zip not button
2. Encloses mutton
3. I rely on horn
4. But already torn
5. Ouch!
6. Burma Shave Logo

William's a tender love poem.

1. Bitches Come
2. Bitches Go
3. Never Come Between
4. Me and my bros
5. Down with hos
6. Burma Shave Logo

This blatant attempt to curry favor with Boyd and I is met with silence and a punch from Sarah whose own attempt is strangely surreal.

1. Cherry wine and Hadacol
2. King of Kings and lowly vole
3. Rented tuxedo, borrowed sleep
4. Butcher gambols, priests weep
5. That's the way the hickory goes
6. Burma Shave Logo

I finish the task in style.

1. There was an Old Man from Kilkenny
2. Whose illnesses were very many
3. He greased up his ass
4. And expelled all the gas
5. And now it smells just like peony
6. Burma Shave Logo

I wake up in a Motel 6.

At least that's how I remember it now, this part of the trip so jumbled.

There's a postcard under my pillow, an old picture of nowhere, a hometown we'd all left behind, the writing is loopy and reckless, drunk? The return address reads like orders, a cold efficiency in sharp contrast to how it makes me feel to read the name at the bottom... I roll over, it falls into shadow.

The $10 TV is bolted to the furniture but it's showing HBO so why I'm complaining... must be hallucinating though, I mean HBO? C'mon...

I'm sweating badly, and all I can hear in my head is Boyd singing, 'Will It Float' from the Letterman show. He must have been serenading in the shower earlier. The 'funky' round shower looks like a Star Trek accessory I had as a kid. You'd press a button on top and the Spock doll would spin round and then blur, finally disappearing when the identical empty chamber replaced the one containing him. It was a great old-fashioned trick but being a single chamber the toy didn't in any way resemble the Enterprise's transporter room. Also Spock was kinda crammed into the space, with as much room as you'd get in... Oh, I don't know, a Motel 6 shower stall, I guess?

Still, the water's cold.

The room's empty.

Taupe walls and bedspreads with a vomit of pastel countryside- bucolic grain buildings and strip-farmed fields.

The towels were fluffy though.

I slip on some clothes and walk out into midday heat.

Sarah's got her feet in the pool.

William has got his feet in the pool.

Boyd has got his head in the pool crooning underwater, giving William and Sarah a polite hillbilly Jacuzzi with his rendition of 'Old Glory'.

He says it's staying in training.

Most karaoke bars have really big reverb on the vocals, muddy sound.

When he comes up for air we all know it's time to hit the road.

The first mural of the morning is a gang of Peanuts celebrities- Snoopy's brother Spike is Needles' most famous son. The background is an eye-searing red meat that reminds Sarah of childhood blancmanges at her granny's house. We also seek out Roadrunner and a milkman that coulda stepped out of a Max Cannon strip.

Boyd does his cow walk, we laugh, time passes...

We need to get going, the Grand Canyon beckons.

I wonder how slick an office chair Knievel would need to be able to make that jump.

When we pass through Peach Springs I'm dozing again, my sleep patterns screwed. We're heading for the Havasupai Lodge.

What do we think of when we stare at the majestic sight of nature's wonder? The tall stacks of rocks, the thrusting trees?

I've only started to use 'presidential' as an adjective to describe my penis since Obama got in. I'm walking down a broken trail, remembering joshing with the night-clerk, last evening? This morning. Slipped away from the room just after 3 AM, my usual semi-insomnia. It's kinda racist what I said and he's kinda black but it's an aside nearly no-one minds. You can see his face wrinkle, smirk 'he's talking about his penis', then, maybe he thinks, it's sorta out of line, but, at least it's pro-forma affirmative, and finally the kicker. The next thing everyone thinks is, no matter how much he fucked us, I bet George W. had a small cock, especially for a Texan. They would wonder what they were getting worked up about a minute before, as they're now too busy imagining the beady eyed fuck in his boxers with a semi. Don't matter which side of the house you're on. I mean I've never tried this trick knowingly on a Republican, to be honest- you can never guess who is. This Great Nation of ours can be tricksy. But we are all united, one nation under God, indivisible in our opinion of Bush Jr's winkie.

Europeans won't believe we voted him in.

They like to portray us as stupid, but won't accept that we're *that* dumb.

You know, if you asked Sarah, you could probably wear a t-shirt with a print of 'gay-niggaz-4-life' in and around Compton, regardless of the political demographics, and, if you'd kept shouting, '...the President's got a small weenie...' then, probably, just probably, before Obama got in, you probably, maybe, hopefully wouldn't have died in a hail of sprayed tech 9 bullets. Just saying. Probably. She's not that familiar with the Watts neighborhood, or what we colonials really think of our forty-third President... or his cock.

Soon we'll be run by my generation, the ones who think that it's ok to kiss your sister, as long as it's for luck, and then what next?

There are a lot of poor Republicans. Even more poor patriots. Still, I guess, she was just shooting the breeze. I can say what I like as well, well almost, especially to the night-clerk. We share a hobby. I'm sure there is a joke here about not, really, liking Bush... although, you gotta be careful, I've even met black Republicans and Sarah'd never believe that- shows what she knows about the history of the Democrats...

The mud's thick, slippery, not what I'd expected.

The trail forks, but I think I know where I'm going.

I've never been to Compton.

I've never been to Texas.

I did read a profile piece on Dick Cheney once. He came across like Tony Soprano's whistling left nostril. George Bush's cronies chew through the corpses of our dreams like so much wheat cereal, the machine would cease to breathe, keel over without him, but does anyone really want to look inside? I should have skipped to the funnies.

I have been to the Grand Canyon, can we call it quits?

Walking the trail to the Canyon...

I wake up sweating, Sarah snoring through those teeth that are barely English, let alone European: like I said, duplicitous.

Nothing in life goes where you expect. I remember her lecturing me that the opening lines to the top five greatest books ever written in the English language all make no sense till you'd read the rest of the book. They are teases that often make no allusion to the main character, and that's life too? What's her academic point? I majored in indolence, so...

"What about Moby Dick?"

A sudden flash of her once telling me about some guy she'd met who was writing a spoof on call centers and the linguistic repetition of call-scripts. It was called 'Mobius Diction', the first line was a text message plaintively begging for human contact, 'Call me... email?'

"You ever read it?"

She meant the Melville.

"No, but..."

"Fucking Americans... firstly, the start of that particular opus is also a tease, and anyway it's not in the top five greatest."

"Wah?"

"You only think it is because it's the only half-decent book written in America until after the First World War."

"Wah?"

"As a nation you had to go on spring break to Europe before you could write."

"Wah?"

"Wah? What is it good for? Giving you a culture. Even after the WW2 your best writers were Russian émigrés or Jewish outsiders. Try comparing Moby Dick with Proust and I'll knock you the fuck out, homie."

She'd lent me it, I'd got to the bit with the madeleine, and then… "…you wanna believe Moby Dick is great because white America knows in its heart that the first great art of America was the blues, and you don't wanna go there…"

"I don't want to call World War Two spring-break, either."

"I said World War One, and don't try and tell me what you know about World War Two, you weren't living in Europe."

No I wasn't.

I'm not yet thirty.

Then again, she's 24.

Or to put it simply. "Wah?"

None of us had experienced true tragedy in our lives.

It didn't stop us complaining.

Poor me. All I wanted was to forgive myself. Wanted the easy fix. Wanted the redemption that comes with knowing that your mistakes, every fucking one, had led you here. But I hated here too. Hated it almost as much as the mistakes. I didn't want historical context, and I couldn't forgive, couldn't let go, or whatever other bullshit it was you were supposed to do… Couldn't heal? Couldn't 'grow'? And the heat, this anger, this… what the fuck was it? What purpose did it serve? Maybe it helped Genghis Khan stab Chinese peasants in the face but I couldn't see its point now. Turn over, go to sleep… invade a new continent, run away, just sleep, sleep, sleep…

Did you know cats and dogs are the same species?

The reason cats in heat make so much noise at night is the discrepancy in the size of genitals- all cats being female, all dogs male. How would you like to sleep with a truly opposite sex?

I can't.

I can't sleep I mean, just keep chewing off more slipper than God can afford to lose…

Do you know how the novels she recommended ended?

I looked it up, god forbid I'd have had to read them all.

None of Finnegan's Wake makes any sense- not just the first line, and, come to think of it, since when was Proust writing in English?

I'm not going to sleep again, am I?

Ever?

I've got to get out of this room.

So I do.

The lobby, deserted, echoes.

I jog on, a boat against the current, borne back ceaselessly into the past, her voice telling me metafiction is dead, and that no great work of prose ever discusses literature… I run, run, run until?

When the sun starts to spatter the ground with splurges of broken light I start to slow my amble, consider returning. She's as far away as home. Poor Sarah.

Aren't we supposed to be alike?

Or do opposites really attract?

She had grown up, surrounded by the antediluvian kipple of two hopelessly bohemian parents, an unkempt tangle of wolfish locks and feral peepers of an impish, evil slant, left to run junk filled attics and crepuscular cellars in the barefoot dishevel of the hopelessly wayward.

Adorable child!

Garlanded now no more in daisy chain and cobweb but bonds of slavish graphite, ruled A4 and the clockwork disgrace of innocence lost, such a disagreeably slovenly wretch, her hair barely kept tamed by a plastic Alice band, her flesh scrubbed only as rubbery clean as a modicum of decency demands. Me I'm a prim flower, the kind of guy who should have been called Natalie, why have I surrounded myself with these filthy hippies?

Maybe I should bring her something back? A clump of nature? A leaf, a rock, a little piece of me- my dick in a box?

I get the SNL song stuck in my head.

I press on.

I'm winding down the shadow of a canyon wall, a worn sign and then a tunnel. My own breathing gets to fill my ears and then I'm out on a ledge about a hundred feet up a waterfall. This trail is far from elementary. I consider jumping, to be honest it's sheer luck I grasp the guide-chain and don't slip. When I first read Conan-Doyle I conflated the falls with the Rickenbacker guitar. Images of Moriarty falling to his death double-tapping the flight of the bumble-bee. Waterfalls and drowning also make me think of Wagner. Not Robert you sick fuck. Who would think that? Natalie wouldn't. I keep on walken'... There's a second tunnel ahead.

This is getting worse.

Like I don't want to make it back.

Like the landscape is bending to my ill will.

Rough-hewn steps, sand stained dark with the mist.

More chains anchored in the rock provide hand holds, I'm cold and sweating at the same time. By the time I make it across the wooden ladders I feel as if my heart's going to burst.

Instead I start crying.

I rapidly realize I'm going to have to cross the stream several times if I want to get any further and even Bill Murray wasn't man enough for that.

Beaver Falls is a long way off and I'm carrying no water. The sun starting to take effect. I'm going to have to climb back.

They sell 'I survived Havasupai' t-shirts back at the camp.

I'm not so sure I'll be buying one of those.

My left arm feels like the chicken drumstick that gets left in the bottom of the bucket and my legs... what are legs? A notion ill-formed of sawdust, splinters and regret.

I'm tracing my way back the way I came.

What a joke.

The only woman I've ever loved is a mirage, a fragment turned to dust in the fizzle of lizard heat. It's autumn but I'm sweating into...

It's tears, tears again staining my t-shirt.

Man up. What would a real man do? I can't help feeling he'd be back at the lodge with his girlfriend, watching her sleep, feeling her warmth, breathing in her bed-scent.

I feel sick.

Bile in my throat.

There's a fork in the trail and then two actual lizards scrapping in the dirt- a territorial dispute or coitus, tired of the metaphorical weight of the whole gecko-roman wrestling deal I press on...

I take the wrong choice, have to track back on my tracking back.

The lizards are gone, but there is one tail.

Savage.

It's bad enough I've had to retrace my steps.

If I have to do anything in reverse it confounds me.

I knew this guy once, a musician, who owned what was sold as a portable recording studio. It was all the studio he could afford, it never left his home. The cassette tracks were numbered one through to eight with faders. If he wanted to record a guitar that sounded backwards, he'd flip the tape over and track one would become track eight and vice versa. If you asked me what track would track four become I'd always guess track six. It's not, it's five. No spatial awareness.

Five more steps.

Steps in circles.

I'm counting backwards up to her door.

I'm trying to think of anything, because thinking isn't feeling.

I knew this guy once, a musician.

It didn't last.

My sister...

You can't replace your sister with a man. With a woman... With five more steps... I can see the trail becoming open space, you'd think I'd be out of the woods by now.

Keep going...

Landscape is never a metaphor.

It's just a thing you live through.

Ok, maybe it's a bit of a metaphor.

Just a shit one.

I've never had a metaphor give me a twisted ankle though. I've never twisted my ankle.

Like I said, if you keep thinking any old crap, then you don't feel, don't quite know what will happen next, until it's too late, until you've already done it, until you've already said the words.

"Sarah, I…"

Five more steps…

The trees are lovely this time of year.

Five more.

Just five more.

When I finally get back Sarah's already up.

The body I left with is broken, the spirit its twin, my thoughts blank, numb. Add a word to another, another, switch their places. Let the third become the sixth? Fifth? Five more words?

She's washing her underwear in the sink, and this is when I tell her?

What do I want as the setting?

A beautiful sunset, the Palisades Park?

Still, here?

I'll only remember her face? What else would you remember? Not even that?

Just the words, my own spilling like sick onto the floor.

'Sarah I love you but I'm…'

'I want to love you, but I also love…'

'Sarah, I've got to tell you…'

'You know that I really, really like musicals? Well, funny thing is…'

This is more than five words and actually I hate musicals.

I can hear Boyd singing down the hall, something about a girl who was only four feet tall and whose feet didn't touch the floor when they were fucking. I'm guessing it's not Rodgers and Hammerstein.

Is this going to be the background for a confession?

She turns to face me, perversely looking guilty somehow herself.

Has been crying, falls into my arms, that warm round sisterly-shaped blob. Like she already knows.

Like everything *is* in the wrong order.

First the Death Star blows up then Greedo gives Han a kiss.

Like there's a right order for any of this and I want to tell her but she's already speaking.

"I... I think I might be pregnant..."

5. Rogue Bleeder

The trench looms before me.

I'm wondering if I could borrow Boyd's chair.

I have no intention of making the jump, it's gonna take more than a big fucking ramp and a working knowledge of Midi-chlorians to get over this. You can't begin to understand the majesty...

Look, it's a cliché, you have to go. We hadn't really got there yet, but I already knew that the Grand Canyon is... well, grand.

That isn't why we're here though. We're here to try and find the caverns, we're here trying to delve deep into mother earth. Yep, right on cue, here comes that bile again. Let's swerve that slick morning sickness.

The original gravel road that formed Route 66 here, was placed next to the natural entrance of the caverns in 1928 so that the Peck brothers, who I believe have nothing to do with the famous Polish meat manufacturers of yore, could reel tourists into this long-standing attraction. I guess you could say an attraction that's been here since the Canyon itself was formed.

It's now a fifteen-twenty minute diversion to get here, caught between Seligman in the east and Kingman AZ in the west.

We performed a triad drive-by outside the Angels Barber shop already. Nerf guns cocked at unfeasible angles, Boyd half out of the window gripping the roof. It's the birthplace of the Route 66 Association, but we wanted to discover this road's charms by ourselves as much as we could. Never overly anticipating the next bend. How's that policy working out? Don't we all just love surprises?

For those of you who don't?

Well, there is always the Santa Fe railroad.

At least a hobo kinda knows where he's going, points his pecker down that track and rolls. He's got a woody to show him the way and it's not always Guthrie. Me, I feel kinda impotent in the face of the future. You could argue we should know our destination- given the nature of our quest, but life's such a little minx.

Mountain lions, bobcats, lynx, so much wildlife that I fear for Boyd's sanity- an abstract concept worn at the knees and elbows, just like our map.

We pull into a parking lot, before he leaps from the window to commune with the red in tooth and claw, slow to a stop before even William exits the vehicle- a new kind of maturity. It's a 60's Modinaire filling station, old pumps, new prices- oil well that ends hellishly expensive. After filling up and wondering when this Iraq business is really going to start paying dividends, we go in search of what turns out to be a big old black and yellow sign that says 'Caverns Inn'. This is where our money is to be, theoretically, well spent on staying in what is the largest, oldest, darkest, quietest motel room in the world, some two hundred and twenty feet below ground.

We know this to be true, and self-evident as there is a blackboard, with the yellow outline of a cowboy-miner scrawled on it, hanging from the dark wood ceiling. It also proclaims it's one of the ten most unusual places to sleep. This unsurprisingly provokes debate.

"Ron Jeremy's Jacuzzi."

"Charlie Sheen's nostril."

"The floor of the Taj Mahal…in Droitwich."-apparently, according to Sarah, an Indian restaurant that is almost as famed for its Vindaloo as its poor hygiene standards.

"Inside Motorhead's drum riser."

"Anywhere where the ants are this fucking big…"

They are fearsome.

I'm put in mind of the plaster statue of a T-Rex out front that we passed coming in.

Who captured that critter? The cowboy mannequins on the mezzanine above us remain tight-lipped. I even tried asking Betty Boop in the retro soda fountain in the lobby but she stayed silent, not one hyperactive squeal.

Inside the ants don't dare follow. Their society's greatest achievement is collective boldness, but here they falter.

What lies beneath?

Hopefully nothing too sentient.

If it was, it might join in with Bill and Boyd's latest heated and ill-informed debate.

"How dumb are you, ass-hat? Of course we've been to the moon, we've been on Mars since the eighties…"

Just whose side do you take?

Especially when you can never tell if William is just joking.

The staff that greet us remain impartial in a way that Sarah and I can only dream about.

Beer and scallops, more meatier meaty meat, a kind of bread?

The food is mammoth in both its scope and its willful disregard for the rules of traditional surf and turf, combining seaweed with the tear-spattered hunks of the prehistoric- no wonder the plaster T-Rex had looked pensive.

We go back into the lobby and next up is a little tour of the caverns- which mainly involves William and Boyd trying to find cracks in the rock, anything they can slip through in search of adventure. Do they need more thrills? I can hear them whispering, is this the Goonies?

"I farted blood."

"Was it pale or dark?"

And he tells Boyd?

Cancer doesn't usually run in our family, usually our livers give out first, but we are the first generation to occasionally spurn the demon drink in favor of more exotic pastimes. Drugs and craziness abide with me. You can only hope Boyd and William's stunts will take them before a more lingering death grabs them by the collar. I am so cheerful, it must be the thought of bringing a new little miracle into the world. Especially when I know I'm in a cave below the earth with no way out and nothing to do but discuss the situation with a woman whose hormones… I gotta calm down, she can't keep it, can't want to, surely?

"What do you think about Rupert?"

"Who's Rupert?"

"I meant as a name."

"As a name?"

"Oh, my God, I thought you were going to faint."

Slowly I feel the blood rushing back from wherever it had drained. "It's a bit gay..?"

"Gay?"

"Yeah, like me."

"Like you?"

"Yes!"

"If you're gonna get me, you're going to have to try harder…"

Can't she see what I am? Then I remember she's British, a country full of pop stars and clothes designers and camp media-cowboys who swim called Walliams.

We're contemplating the child she's about to terminate, let spin off into the ether, the roof of the cave glittering with colored light. It's dry in here, not damp at all. I start to cough.

"Would you, one day, I mean…" She wants to know what I think about children. I couldn't raise them here, not now.

She tells me she knows not now, she isn't ready either.

I say, I mean not in this cave, so, true to form, she punches my arm.

Our 'room' is built on a super large platform above the cavern floor. On a king-size couch, the boys are already comatose. Somehow a ton of complimentary candy bars, snacks and microwave popcorn, sodas and coffee, all this was not enough to counter the effects of this evening's pipe contents. There's a platter of Ferde Grofé's Grand Canyon Suite spinning low on the king size record player, Sarah wants to get to bed. I draw the covers up, vowing that I won't see another sunset without telling her.

In the morning we are served a made-to-order breakfast while the first few tours of the morning walk by. It doesn't matter when you're the invisible man, the shadow on the wall like me, but Boyd and William want to engage the interlopers, they run for one chair to cuddle up together.

"Do you mind, I'm trying to have intercourse with my life partner…"

"Yowsa!"

The staff are not impressed. We settle the bill with a weight of disapproval hanging over us.

Back to the road…

Shouldn't we be trying to find a doctor?

Two birds run smack into each other, a sickening crunch, the Tippi Hedron Collider.

WTMF?

Omens, portents. Not a good day to skywalk the Canyon. A kiss? Just for luck. We know it won't be enough, so decide to bail.

Later I find a review online moaning about the ticket price of standing in a glass box suspended above the Grand Canyon- how do you cost that out as fair- ask David Blaine? The difficulty of getting there, the banning of photography, a whole litany of problems then makes me think that we made the right choice. We decide instead to just walk up to the damn gulch and spend the day skirting the edge at Mather point.

Nothing much amazing happens except Boyd and William remain alive by the end of the day. What else can you say that hasn't already been said? The parking wasn't as expensive as I expected? Mark Twain thought it was Arizona's answer to the Waimea Canyon and that's a good enough appraisal of its breath-taking properties for me? I was just hoping my girlfriend would have her maternal instincts eroded by the warm desert wind. If not, she could always flush them back into the Topock Marshes.

Was that a little harsh? You think I'm straight right now? That panic isn't churning my guts to a smear on the blacktop despite her reassurances? I keep thinking she'll change her mind, no road is a straight story, even David Lynch knows that, especially perhaps. I yearn for coffee and a cop-out. If I get arrested will I turn into another character entirely, lightning arcing through my soul like the guy in Lost Highway?

I'm thinking about the Trails Arch Bridge, how it had to be higher than the one in Tallahassee, and considering what wrath has been visited upon my grapes that they have impregnated my future with such pregnant uncertainty, when Sarah holds me close and whispers in my ear that everything's already taken care of. We're ok. A magic moment. Like the Sermon on the Mount or when the guy invented that pill she's just taken. Stomach cramps, mine abating, hers beginning? Actually it was just a false alarm, no need for pills at all. Everything's fine.

Everything is finally fine.

Then I remember I have to tell her I'm gay. Well, when I say have to… It's a bit like Alan Turing's Lesbian Test.

Boyd has a theory, well more an idea for a b-movie, maybe Uwe Boll would direct? Anyway, it features an Artificial Intelligence which could trick men into believing a lesbian was at the other end of a phone-line. But could it fool a woman? Here's a review from a

Dutch hippy we met in a bus station and could clearly grasp all the nuances that Boyd was trying to impart with stunningly fried accuracy.

"It's fucking deep man, you know, it really gets to the nub of a lot of social issues, this conflict of the sexes..."

So I wonder, if we're so different, does Sarah even have to know? What good would it do? What were your first thoughts when you realized you had to tell your pregnant girlfriend you were gay? And how did that change when you found out she wasn't with child?

I thought about fucking another woman.

Why are my solutions to problems more complicated than the problems themselves?

Is bisexuality some kind of schizophrenic urge that clouds judgement?

I wish I knew, but I don't see myself so much as bisexual, more a full-blown homo with an unfortunate fetish for homely girls. That's what my good friend Jessie the lesbian money-lender used to say.

I believe my actions may be explained by my being what is technically known as an unflushable douche. Speaking of the vagaries of modern plumbing, the Trails Arch Bridge now just carries a pipeline. I carry on regardless, Topock isn't really here anymore, just a burn on the tarmac.

I'm looking for a metaphor, but nothing sticks.

On the side of a gas station in Golden Shores, the lake resort that has replaced Topock, we had stared at Annie Wildbear's mural of the map of Route 66 thinking about how far we hadn't come. If the Seven Eleven back home had this on its side would Boyd's fall, sorry, 'majestic flight', have been any more guided?

William is looking for God in his nose.

I presume it's God, the fervor of his dedication is positively Inquisition-strength.

We saddle up the compact and head off into the east.

I want Gene Autry, but I have to make do with the Belle Stars' Greatest Hit. It's not so much a compilation as an endurance test. My burgeoning love for womankind will have to take a back seat. Boyd even sings along for God's sake. Still at least back here you don't have to watch the speedometer.

Next stop Seligman- doesn't have the ring of next stop Flagstaff, but what can you do?

Seligman is not so much a tourist trap as the Black Hole of Camp Clutter. Angel Delgadillo will sell you every piece of Route 66 crap you have ever wanted. We leave his shop with a Cowboy Cactus Aerial Cover and the warm feeling you get from meeting a man who was instrumental in getting Historic Route 66 placed firmly on the map. Without Delgadillo, the road-Yoda, this stretch of highway would have been long gone- so I raise a glass and he raises his fishing cap. William raises hell, Boyd raises eyebrows, Sarah raises the Titanic. It's my new name for my Johnson. Many men went down on it- ok not many, but you'd never think you could coax it from the briny deep with a woman's touch..?

Like I said I like to think I'm gay.

The truth is I just can't keep it in my pants?

Besides, it's a week for miracles and resurrections. Did you know Jesus travelled Route 66 to get to some census? Of course, but did you really understand the Christmas story? No, neither did I till I met the Angel of the Mother Road and had his black eyes burn into my heathen soul. Don't say the name Delagadillo three times into a wing-mirror, who knows what may happen. On another note we had a burger. A good burger. A good burger with fries. It's like wow! You know?

Now I'm glad I came.

Except Flagstaff.

It has many museums, a zoo, a concert hall and...

We drove through.

Pressed on to Albuquerque.

We spent the night at the airport's La Quinta Inn.

Slept well as we couldn't hear the intermittent sounds of planes over the constant traffic noise. Everything smelled of regret and roach spray. My dreams were vivid if seemingly mundane- normally, though, I gotta say, they don't have dialogue. I'm guessing it's the roach spray... maybe it's the regret too.

In the first one I kept counting coke bottles in and out of an ice bucket and bleeding into this from the real world I thought I could hear Boyd and William engaging in a highly athletic verbal pole-vault to decide who should win the heart of a fair maiden, and then I was sitting up in bed, Sarah and I having one of those lovely conversations about our sex-life that only long-term partners could have with any semblance of calm.

"I like men..."

"I know."

"You..."

"It's why I started dating you, stupid."

"It's why you...?"

"It's not the only reason, I just also happen to like men who are..."

"Gay?"

"I was gonna say have an open sexuality..."

I think I'm gonna be sick.

"Come here, baby, it's fine..."

We're spooning, I'm the one on the inside, actually not feeling too bad, feeling better, knowing I've told her, knowing this is safe, just blanketed in sleep.

I look at her hands in the dark, her forearms cross my chest, the dark fine hairs.

"I want to make you happy."

She's twenty-four and I'm an idiot baby.

"You want me to buy something to fuck you with?"

Even now she can't stop joking, even in a dream- which is of course why I love her, why suddenly it's like she's a kid again too, adolescent, full of dumb fun, nearly as young as Alice when she left...

She stops grinding her pelvis into my back.

"Sometimes I wonder what it would be like to see you kiss another boy."

Is this a come-on?

She starts to kiss my neck.

Pedantically I want to point out that I'm barely in my twenties anymore and that if I kissed a boy it would be something that only NAMBLA, the North American Man-Boy Love Association, would approve of, but I don't bother as I can feel her hands on my ass now and I know this is the point where I'm about to wake up- a fail-safe mechanism that my neurotic soul developed in puberty to prevent nocturnal emission.

I wonder if when I wake I will sport the rictus confusion of a middle-aged man who's been promised anal sex as a birthday treat, only to find it was his turn to bend over. Through the curtains the day grows as hot as a teenager's damp sheets...

We're in the middle of the most blinding-white industrial estate the desert has ever known, the sun high overhead, and somewhere off in the distance I can hear Lynyrd Skynyrd- growing louder, a mosquito buzz, or a lone wild vibrator, or the rush of air across casters and already I know this isn't quite right. I want to fall to my knees but am frightened the tarmac will swallow me. We cave in, splurge, try and get a cell signal for a local cab company. The road roils like a sea-sick sea in the heat, eventually a black and white cab sails towards us.

We climb in.

Sarah slides around on the slick wet seat like it's the jelly from a Twinkie bar.

The taxi driver has an incongruous New York drawl.

"Who's the little guy?"

There's a baby in nappies sitting next to us on the back seat, she picks him up, tender, like a mother, a sister, and now she's French kissing him. She stops for air. She looks right at me like I asked the question, and maybe I did? Maybe the taxi driver just mouthed the words for me?

"That's our little boy, silly."

I've just started to notice that the guy driving the cab has a head like an Easter Island figure- but green.

When I awake from this?

Finally I decide I will be honest at last... won't I?

Boyd is banging on the door asking us who would win in a fight- Mitt Romney or George Takei? The image in my head is one of wrestling, just not quite Greco-Roman. If I feel nauseous I can't imagine how someone one hundred percent heterosexual would feel.

In the end? I keep my mouth shut. Boyd always loved George, so let's keep him guessing. I look at Sarah and think I want someone inside me, sure, but I want to be inside her just as much, and the person I want in me? That's Sarah too? That's what love is? Or something? Does it matter? Does any of this matter? Maybe I can learn to change, can move on. Become lovers again? Open her up to her true calling. Hey Sarah, don't you know that you too can have fun pegging a sissy boy? Is any of this really possible, advisable? People do tend to get too hung up on mechanics- I resist a joke about James Dean in filthy overalls, and wonder when have I ever heard my own voice in a dream before? Am I still dreaming..? I always used to know when I was dreaming.

Just then an alarm goes off in the next room.

6. Hot Dogs, Jumping Frogs

So I told her.

You knew I'd have to…

"It's Prefab Sprout…"

"Oh God, make it stop."

We block our ears, the king and queen of wishful thinking- like that'd end this easy racket, and then I finally let the pussy out of the knapsack too.

Told her outside a Krispy Kreme in Albuquerque- sugar being the great balm that it is, sugar being elemental, calms the mental.

And…

And she was ok with it.

Fine. Very European.

"…I'd be a hypocrite not to be, my last girlfriend was bi anyway…"- this is what is known as English humor or 'dryness'.

Of course she does cry, disappointment, worry, exhaustion, who knows… but it's a very English tear, salt in an egg cup, like I said, parched emotions, it must be all the rain over there. Don't cry, you'll flood the Axminster… again.

Speaking of precipitation…

So this really is Albuquerque?

It's easy to think to yourself what a wonderful world if you're walking on the moon, down here it's dusty and breathless, like, I don't know, the surface of…

Well, you know the rest.

Certainly I could do with one.

Sarah's holding my hand in her big fingers and I feel protected, then I put my arm round her waist and feel strong, we make a good couple, don't you think? At least till the sweat starts co-mingling.

Is this all too simple? Are we really going to "…work through this…"? I feel better now, I think, I feel like I don't care about the past, like it might just work. Just has to. Doesn't it? One step at a time? This isn't AA- though I did blow a pastor once who told me he could cure me. I've always walked the line- unable to fall one side or another. Just like Robert Downey Junior- it's just the faithlessness I need to work on. Or was that Rob Lowe? Neither of them? Really? They're both straight? They were both sex addicts though, right?

My desire to fuck anything had been making me impotent, now the truth was out I needed to be careful I didn't slip and start humping the sidewalk. I said once that the sex with her was ok? Did I also say I was a liar? Arch? Too much sincerity would just take the edge off of love, wouldn't it? Was it too much to admit I actually enjoyed fucking girls, the right kind of girls... Is enjoy too weak-kneed a word? Can't I think too much about Robert Downey Jr too? Or Rob Lowe? Actually the thinking has always been ok, I guess? I mean I can think about Frances McDormand, Starbuck in both the original and reboot Galactica or pretty much the whole male and female cast of NCIS- especially Season 5- if I want to, but I need to remember I've got a 'girlfriend' now, it's official, and morals apparently as well, it seems- which is somewhat something of a surprise, so...

So?

So Sarah kisses me on the neck and I smile like I just escaped a gulag. She'd just told me she was going to tell my brothers my dark little secret, and my sphincter tried to strangle my kidney. Seems I'm not really ready yet for that family meeting. Now she's grinning- this woman is evil, so evil, so I get a boner. Seems it's not just her smile that endeared her to me but also her lack of scruples. Just like Downey Jr. Damn, I know how to pick 'em. So does Boyd.

William had dragged us to the University of New Mexico because he's a devotee of the architecture of John Gaw Meem, a tuberculosis sufferer who came to Albuquerque because of its dry climate, if you believe my brother is a devotee of anything except women's BBW Beach Volley-Ball and Planters Teriyaki Peanuts... here he bumps into a somewhat overweight black-Hispanic girl in sweat-pants and a Donald Duck t-shirt who persuaded him to help her pick up some stuff from her tutor. Boyd's the fast mover though and while he's swapping spit with her, two of us decide to get lunch, the third taking the role of chaperone for the honeymoon couple. William acting as my other brother's keeper, is mouthing something about me 'owing him', but I feign deafness as he drives off with Albuquerque's most dispiriting advert for interracial harmony. The irony is, unlike William, Boyd doesn't even like them that big-built, he's just got 'Jungle Fever'- his words not mine, I think his taste for what he sees as the *'exotic'* started with a thing for Star Trek's alien women. Now it's an unusual accent or anything 'not Californian'. William was a science fiction nut too but his earliest erotic memory was Thelma in Scooby Doo. Solid. Though you have to say if you go back to the cartoons she's never as chunky as you remember. I expect that black girl's thick-waisted pizzazz is probably turning William's balls a bluer blue than any alien-slave-girl that Shatner shtupped. Warring brothers? We'll see.

Then Sarah kisses me, and now I can't remember my train of thought, even what we had for lunch- some kind of a first for my bliss? Maybe I can keep it in my pants, maybe I can love just one, swallow hard, woman.

How do I calculate this?

Time to do the math?

Albuquerque is divided into four quadrants. Pedestrians are divided into meat. We're rapidly discovering that everywhere there are four and six lane highways dividing the city and that getting anywhere on foot seems nigh on impossible. Still it looks beautiful as the heat drops, there's a big round building lit neon yellow and later we see in the distance the green glow of what we're told by locals is the Wells Fargo building. It's a bit like Vegas, but less tacky, which is to say in hindsight it's missing the point, but still we were young and the moon was a magic nickel that made promises we could not keep? Romance is not my strong suit. Actually it was only mid afternoon. So why the neon? Power fault? Hell, I don't know. I can tell you that Steve-O was born here though, that's gotta count for something. Speaking of jackasses, my brothers find us again finally and, would you believe it, no Donald Duck girl, instead a guy called Hench, about forty, smells of breath-mints and stomach ulcer medicine, he gets out of the compact…

"Hi, you must be…"

Handshake.

Walks off.

The boys fill me in with all the irrelevant details.

"My accountant."

"My doctor."

The two stooges giving differing reports.

Besides, there's no time for shilly-shallying, lollygagging and general tom-foolery. We're on another mission.

Boyd whips out... a flyer for once.

The American International Rattle-Snake Museum of Albuquerque.

William's offering?

Casa San Ysidro- a late 18th century house with a recreation of a 19th century rancho, a family chapel and a central plazuela and enclosed corral.

William, always the historian, can't wait for his own monument.

"Does the former have a petting element?"

It is dawning on Boyd that we are not going to let him play with the snakey-wakeys.

I blind-side them with small-talk about Albuquerque's old town, the charming adobe buildings and plethora of gift shops, but Sarah can't keep a straight face.

Three little words.

"The Sandia Peak Tramway."

Ok four, but it's the world's third longest single span.

Stretching from the north-east edge of the city to the crest-line of the Sandia Mountains. I can almost hear the wind stirring Boyd's wheels, the age-old desire to hang motionless above the void.

On the way there, William holds the wheel and some leaflets, informs us it's a 'double reversible jig-back aerial tramway' and I see Boyd's eyes light up with the uncomprehending glee of the four-year-old that's just been told that the Browning M2 50-caliber machine gun is an automatic, belt-fed, recoil-dampened, air-cooled, crew-operated machine gun which uses the M3 tripod and that by repositioning some of the components, the M2 is capable of alternate feed. Just like immortality he can feel the rush of life in his bones. When we get there it's closed. No, I'm kidding. That's just what William says as we approach.

"I think it's closed."

"Wah?"

"Or not…" He grins. The douche. Of course nothing is perfect. The cars hold 50 passengers so no ride to ourselves, no sudden nudity, no climbing out and recreating Jaws' fight with Bond in View to a Kill.

"This is kinda dull…"

"It's majestic…" I almost love that word as much as egregious.

To be pedantic it's actually the Domingo Baca Canyon and I feel a little nauseous. The highest I've ever been was the top of a Seven Eleven roof smoking that damn pipe. Down below the trees hide that snaking highway that no doubt delivers grinnin' Jack to the forbidding hotel owned by Messrs. Kubrick and King. It's like a hobo's belly, scratchy fur you could reach out and tickle, but then the stomach drifts away, the abs growing as trim as McConaughey's agent's intellect and I really feel I may hurl. We could have gone to an aquarium instead, I discover later. You can even pet a baby shark there, and that's gotta be even weirder than a rattlesnake.

William pulls me into a corner, away from Boyd and Sarah staring out at the tree-tops in silence for once, starts to tell me about the first guy who drove this thing, like it ever needed a pilot, how he was an epic onanist or the strangest suicide ever. It's not till we're halfway through his description of how they found him that I realize it's also strange, epic bullshit.

With his neck broken was how they found him, one of the tragedies of life being we don't usually determine our death, the tragedy here that this was definitely not how he chose to end his, but still it had resulted from his actions. Poised in the blue black fist of rigor mortis his naked body jack-knifed as it dived into the abyss, feet tensed against the partition wall, back arched over his twisted expression, his awful man-flesh, already stiff in his gaping maw, had grown tenser with the snapping of his top two vertebrae, a common reaction to hanging I've been told, and with the body darkening, death tightening the cliché of its icy grip, well, you could only pity the poor schlub who had to straighten him out; you couldn't nail the coffin down like this.

I thought of it as the hermaphrodiet; just eat a little of your most private self and let the guy in the black hood and cute little

83

matching scythe do the rest, puncture the diaphragm, let the rank gasses escape, and you've lost at least... What is a soul supposed to weigh? And after the worms have done their best? Except he hadn't *chosen* that plan, had he?

"He died doing what he loved best..."

Somehow we eventually end up back near the University in the back room of the Frontier restaurant, blue walls, Mexican rugs hanging from the ceiling. I hold down a Huevos Rancheros heroically, William has the Frontier burger and the Tortilla Soup, Boyd goes for bacon and pancakes, Sarah has a breakfast burrito. Afterwards we stop outside and stare at the roof which has too many pitches for anyone to be able to pick one to ride off of. It looks like a drawing of a dodecahedron Wendy's colored in badly by a small child. I start to feel sick again, want to lie down, we need a hotel.

The Westward Ho is flagged up by a neon cactus and that's where my desert moment happens, my vision in the wilderness, when finally I know I can't tell her, when I admit I can't tell anyone... what, like you really thought I actually had?

Damn you're even more gullible than Boyd.

I can't even tell myself, and so I get off the bus.

I let it all pull away from me...

Wouldn't it have been so easy?

Just to tell her, to end the lie, just a few tears and then it all gets washed away...

"Sarah, I'm gay."

But I couldn't.

I just couldn't.

Every time I got so close, but...

If I tell her the truth then that would never be enough, because then I would know the real truth too. The truth she couldn't even guess at. I would know it- just like, hell, I knew it already, but then so near the surface, carrying it with me like an open wound instead of this neat little scab, and how long before it came out too?

God Bless Amnesia?

It's only temporary.

Wouldn't it be oh so simple if I was just gay, but I'm not just that, never could be that damn predictable. This sickness, this fetish... What? It's got to stop. You know, it's like a biblical temptation, full of heat and dust and unbelievable plot twists and that bit at the end where we all die, only to be resurrected- a damnably worse punishment I cannot comprehend when all I really want is everlasting sleep.

I stop and I can't breathe.

I don't even know where the hotel is anymore, I'm leaning against something made of polished, corrugated steel.

The bus is pulling away.

It's a full ten minutes before I realize I'm on it, that the guy I'm watching through the window is myself ten minutes ago when I was swearing I would never just cut-out. I take another Vicodin and one of those red ones, wash it down with 200 proof mouth-wash and hope that when New York finally crawls out of the Hudson to swallow me like Godzilla I'll be a more palatable dish, a quasi-liquid entrée. There's nothing wrong with being drunk as long as you don't give someone the hiccups. That's just impolite, manners maketh the mangled...

I wake up, that's one thing.

But on a plane?

Hey shouldn't this be a bus?

There's a phrase going round my head.

It's not the one about the wheels going round, but it is just as catchy.

'After wiping his ass, Felipe stared intently at the butterfly print he had created.'

This would be less worrying if there wasn't a 300 lb Greek man holding my hand.

It turns out that this is Felipe's husband.

His fingers were growing tighter. "Imagine if this was your scrotum." Less advice, more a vice.

When Felipe came back he was wearing pastel jeans and a Louis Vuitton baseball cap tipped back on his head, he waved to me and then we swapped seats.

Swapped back again, I guess?

Now I was sitting between the two of them desperately trying to remember the last couple of hours.

Oh, yeah.

No, that wasn't good.

Still we'd be in New York in a couple of hours.

"We'll shortly be arriving in Paris..."

Fuck.

So this is jet lag?

Something more permanent?

Doesn't every malady feel like that till it's gone?

When I got off the flight I half expected to see my brothers waiting for me under a Californian sky, but that was another life... instead I'd called my good friend Jessie and she was meeting me. Apparently I hadn't made much sense. It was the promise of that car-crash entertainment we all crave that had swung it when she decided to haul her ass to the airport.

"You look like shit." Thanks Jessie. "...and why'd you always have to tell people we're good friends?"

"eh?"

"...with air quotes, you ass-hat?"

Ah.

She must have overheard me whispering my goodbyes to Felipe.

Where the fuck was his husband? He leant in close. "Let me tell you a secret, gorgeous..." Europeans, so theatrical. "He's not even Greek."

This is what happens when you get too wired.

I realize his husband is standing behind me as I turn, the 'Greek' grins and I feel kinda woozy.

Turkish?

Then they're gone and apparently I'm wanting to tell Jessie I've never been sure how much she likes me, hence the air quotes.

I don't have the will to get it out.

Instead she punches my arm and we're even. It's the left one, which proves she is in no way similar to Sarah in temperament.

"You wanna smoke?"

For a moment I think she's offering me tobacco, then I remember I'm back in California where we are far too health conscious not to smoke pot.

No, wait a minute, this isn't LAX.

"Is it legal here?"

"This is Paris, you ass-hat, not Amsterdam."

"How'd I end up here?"

We're in bed together.

I'm mostly naked and she's wearing Family Guy pajama bottoms and a t-shirt with a provocatively primitive cartoon. My head is resting on her thighs. She strokes my hair.

"You do know I fuck girls, Jessie?"

She looks down at me. "Out of choice?"

An interesting question. I let it pass. She doesn't look too worried.

Probably because if I got frisky she could snap me like one of Sarah's Twiglets. My brain was boiling anyway… and she had a cold too. Romance wasn't really on my mind, especially not with a muscular bull from the San Fernando Valley. See I managed to avoid thinking the word dyke. Oh wait a minute, no I didn't in the end. Besides was bull any better? Best not to ask, I already had a foul taste in my mouth without chewing on my own teeth. Something that wanted to be coffee but had clearly done something pure evil in a previous life. Welcome to France. She had a fruit tea. We won't judge, will we?

Wait a minute, France?

What time is it?

What year is it?

Even when I let my lizard brain take over it's just as useless.

Jessie's arguing that the 'like' button on Facebook is too non-specific. My rusty heart starts to grind with all the pathos of an empty shotgun shack's unbuttered porch as I realize ten years have slipped past…

"What if what they're typing is sad? I can't just reply 'like'…"

"Just, tell 'em you feel sorry…"

She interrupts.

"But these aren't people I know that well."

"So?"

"I don't have time to get emotionally invested."

"Then why comment at all?"

"It seems rude not to."

The essential politeness of the Californian comes up hard against the essential politeness of the Midwesterner.

"… I'd rather just have a button, so I don't have to type anything…"

"…I'd rather just give 'em forty pages of sound moral advice…"

The essential 'helpfulness' of the Midwest wrestles with Californian indifference.

"What would you have? 'Dislike'?"

"I was thinking maybe 'hate', or if you feel sorry for them, 'Yes, I concur with your nihilistic descent into drunken misery when faced with such grievous personal circumstances…'"

Neither of us consider emoticons, because…

Really?

You need to know?

:(

I despair.

That's not the only reason for misery.

I should have been reborn in shitting distance of Loch Lomond or under the tolling of Bow Bells at least.

Isn't that what planes are for?

How does France get me any nearer to *her*?

That was why I was in Europe, after all.

I mean sure, we're not in Kansas anymore, but France?

"You oughta settle down with a nice boy…"

There's no place like a homo.

Jessie was giving me her long-suffering Jewish mother routine, then got bored of using that accent and switched to a pseudo gangster drawl.

"Hey, did you know that in 1974, Margaret Schemenski, the first woman to be identified as lesbian- specifically *because* she liked big cock, was born in the Santa Barbara area…"

"Really?"

"I'm just saying if she could admit it, why can't you?"

"I have too much self-respect."

"Really?"

"Yeah, if I loved big cock what does that say about how much I hate myself?"

She almost does me the decency of a cheap laugh. "You could buy one."

Had she been watching old re-runs of my dreams?

I stared up her nostrils as she went through a Dave Sim Cerebus book with a highlighter pen.

"…Miss Schebibbleski the infamous one-legged Cuban dwarf spastic role-model did, after all, eventually 'marry' the 'lady' "- her air-quotes, not mine for once, "…who owned 'Dildos Are Us', but still, she didn't define herself as gay per se- preferring the term dyke-groupie."

She also said the 'D' word, not me.

Whenever Jessie got stoned she usually devoted some spare time to these rambling discourses. Sub-Waits-ian piffle, splurges of crypto-anti-pro-post-feminism delivered in a cod Edward G. Robinson impersonation that I never had the cojones to question. I was sure she only liked Tom Waits to prove she wasn't a girl. That's why she read Hemingway- let's face it, with the latter, there's no other justifiable reason. The monologue made me feel like I was in a bad play, the kind where all that the gay characters could talk about was their homosexuality. More pressing concerns? Did she know who Edward G. actually was, or had she picked up the 'accent' whilst tending bar? Enquiring minds had to know. This seemed less 9th and Hennepin and more ninth tumbler of Hennessy.

"You could say that you weren't really gay, just helping out when they were busy?"

"You know she knows, don't you?"

I wanted to stick out my tongue at her. Really you would think she and Sarah were sisters, except the haircuts and Jessie's truly unprofessional orthodontistry. That and she kinda liked my brothers.

"How's Boyd?"

I wanted to tell her he was still yelling "Yowsa!" in your ear at the top of his lungs, truth was…what did it matter?

What kind of American was she anyhow? Not the one we usually send abroad- army fatigues- yes, on occasion, but where's the shirt with the tropical parrots? This is an ex-line of thought, and so instead she asks me…

"You been keepin'..?"

"Busy? Oh you mean Xmas, Mardi Gras…"

"Yes, the traditional fag holidays…"

"…fleet week…"

"I think I need to roll another…"

"Oh, God the humanity…"

"What would you do with a huge manatee?"

What indeed? Even if the Navy were in town? If she knew the real truth?

Bestiality would have been less embarrassing.

It's one thing to want to suck another guy's cock, it's a whole 'nother ball-game to constantly rediscover that twisted need to grab the freckled thighs of nostalgia, to want to get real familial with what lies between the legs of …

"I can't roll with your head down there."

Weren't that the truth.

Apparently the big lezzer- thanks Sarah, uncharacteristically off message, for that one- hadn't taken the hint when she'd moved her muscular knees. She had legs like a stevedore- not my kind of woman, but not my kind of man either, to tell the truth.

"Did I ever tell you the one about the 'Eye of the Steiger'?"

Are all Europeans closet comedians? Even the naturalized ones? Sometimes the jokes are nearly as crude as Proust's but never as funny.

Fuck it.

Go on then, tell me, maybe it'll stop me blacking out.

And I paraphrase, "…to the tune of Rocky in her shaved noggin, she found the china eye in a gummy soup outside the Chinese Theatre, 300 yards from the wax museum. The tub was filling with rain, a glassy melody. Is this the eye of Rod Steiger, or the rheumy simulacrum of Burgess Meredith? All it needs is more Martini and we'd be set, drunk up to the eyeballs. Sorry, eyeball."

That was it?

What kind of a punch-line was…

Morning.

My arm ached from last night's left hook.

We stared out at another grey tower-block staring back at us, the place reminded me of Brazil- the movie. This was not the art nouveau élan I'd expected. Welcome to le projects.

"Bonjour, ass-hat, ouvre le fenêtre."

Apparently that's 'open the window', the only French she'd picked up in all these years, ironic given you couldn't pry up any of them in l'appartement de nose-bleed. Being this high made me miss the Seven Eleven. I missed William's pipe more though. Or rather I would have if I hadn't stolen it from out of the glove compartment... all those moments, fears down the drain. My brain decompressing? Would I give myself that chance?

Some missed calls from home.

To be expected.

My head felt like a Michael Bay film, long on explosions, short on... well, everything else really.

Tinnitus?

Oxygen starvation?

Jessie was making 'coffee' again and I was remembering how much I liked her, how easy it was, neither of us interested in jumping the other's bones. If she knew who Burgess Meredith was I guess Edward G. wasn't too much of a stretch. Finally someone a little more sane, saner than me at least.

Then she got this look in her eye and I thought she would cry, but she punched the wall instead.

"Fuck..."

Her hand was bright red.

There was a syringe lying half in a chipped saucer on the counter-top.

Last night I had guessed she'd merely done the fashionable thing and moved to Europe to take up heroin, so much more glamorous when travelling abroad. Or maybe...

Hormones?

OMG!

A real life transsexual?

How truly European, I can't wait to tell the folks back home, totes amazeballs. First chance I get I must ask her what her genitals are like, or maybe I could learn that my friend's junk was none of my business... who am I kidding?

"... you... eh, wanna..."

What?

Was that my voice?

I was offering to talk?

What kind of a pussy was I?

This was a real man, going through real trouble.

She picked up the needle.

I wanted to say surely not before breakfast?

Then I remembered again that I had guessed it wasn't heroin.

Suddenly she was aware of the situation.

"I'm diabetic...."

I still wondered why she'd punched the wall.

"Sorry about that, girl trouble..."

By which she meant trouble with a girl... but also she was 'on the blob'- thanks again to Sarah for that.

And then she shut up.

Just like real men do.

"I..."

"Ah, fuck her..."

Then she changed the subject. "Hey ass-hat, you ain't even seen the tower." For some reason I had an image of Pisa in my head. "You know you can't stay here..."

I knew that.

I knew where I was going.

Though why I'd flown to Paris first?

Heck, I'd known since I'd left California (here I come), behind.

Well, some part of me had.

I just hadn't wanted to admit it. Still I might as well see the sights whilst I'm here...

The Metro smelled of fiberglass and garlic- which was fifty percent more touristy than I had expected.

Unlike Montmartre.

In the silence of the Sacre Coeur I watched a thousand candles Klux Lux power the black shadows back, an ancient procession, flickering acceptance of a Catholic tryst. Some kinda voodoo. Outside cobbles and slanting rain, and a new kinda stillness, shallow. I was so cold I bought an army coat, double breasted but made of cheap green cotton, lined with rough wool, I thought I looked like Deckard but I guess the boho shone through, wore through to reveal the tramp beneath.

Then Jessie bought a couple of Norman beers and I found out Freedom fries just aren't a patch on the real French ones. The obvious stuff. I began to wonder what German food was like, now

I was such an expert on Gallic cuisine. I'd like to have seen the Rhine, as apparently the Seine was a mere piss stream but it looked grey and fierce and big enough for me, I'd never seen the Mississippi. What was I doing here?

No-one sends postcards anymore.

"You have the look of Joy Division."

A skinny middle-aged guy with a pock-marked face was calling me a fascist. Then I realized he meant the band and that I looked like a 1980's student. So I, Monsieur Anton Corbijn, and his somewhat butcher than Ian Curtis friend crossed one of the endless bridges, where a man with a rheumy eye made to get in our way but, as he wasn't really a Cyclops, and this was hardly an epic, we passed on by with ease.

"You probably think Walt Whitman should be part of a classical education..." I remember thinking, 'he's boring enough', and I remember not answering Sarah's taunt. I look at my phone again. I compose a simple text.

"Meet me in St Louis..."

Judy Garland, the wrong city, it had it all.

I deleted it.

Instead I thought, I had to go, I really did... I palm the phone.

Texts from the edge, never sent...

The rain has stopped but the streets are still wet.

So we wander for hours, isn't that what Paris is for?

Stop in a café. Black coffee of course, I watch people, or at least those too-stylish approximations of them that the French leave lying around to point out the crassness of tourists.

Jessie eventually puts down her book, a brutal twenties murder mystery, 'Straight on till Mourning' by Elmore Jeeves. You know the kind of thing that starts, 'Angel Maitland was found lying naked on the jazzy blue baize of a pool table in Queens...', or, 'Devouring a nymphomaniac through the night vision scope of a high-powered rifle...'

Well you gotta have a hobby, even if it's antisocial.

Me?

I've just been watching her reading, thinking about reading.

Reading. Reading Raymond Chandler. Reading Marcel Proust. And Gertrude Stein. Reading Chandler, Stein and Proust. Will probably. Not definitely. But certainly probably. Reading them together, en masse. As a block. As a Bloch? Proust joke, unnecessary? I digress. Where was I? Oh, yes. Reading. Reading in Sarah's beloved old British Library. Or on a train, or in a hotel. Reading. Reading Proust. Reading Chandler. Reading Stein. Reading Chandler, and Stein, and Proust. Reading them all at once. Dipping back and forth. Reading. Reading them all at once. Would probably. I say probably. Probably only. Probably only but here's the confirmation. Reading all three. Reading Chandler and Stein and Proust. Would probably make you think in very long paragraphs, full of short repetitive sentences.

That last one.

I'm wondering, just that last one, a little too long? Too much Proust? Can you have too much Proust? He certainly never thought so.

By the time the sun sets we're standing outside a club, the door is red, the music sounds red, the bouncer's called Jupien and his face is kinda... Greek, but apparently you never can tell.

Inside it's like a scene from Killing Zoe but somehow more squalid.

Music I know too well.

You'd play it on a soundtrack to indicate we've entered some form of post-apocalyptic future, middle America would wonder at the decadence, I'd wonder why the underground hits of the 90's were so popular in the year 2042.

There's too many people in here, so we push into the middle of them to try and forget that fact, till we get squeezed out like a spot along the bar, starting new friendships, ending them real fast, there's a girl's voice real close in my ear.

"This is Felipe."

It's a small world, not as small as my balls in a vice, but hey you can't have everything.

The girl who re-introduces us was Japanese, Thai once, maybe?

She's dressed like Noomi Rapace in that film where literally no-one was in charge of costume, but her friends think she looks like L.A. 2019, and here we have the proof, some continental Europeans really do think this is what punk-rock looks like. Here they can wear a slip-on shoe and carry it off, but a Mohican? Forget it. Still, how can one resist the call of gay Paree? Truth? Cheaper to get a plane here and then catch the Eurostar, under the channel, to England and then the bus to Scotland, rather than fly direct.

Jessie starts hitting on the Asian girl immediately, like it's some kind of requirement, manhood 101. She's not even a pneumatic blonde for Chrissakes!

Felipe oozes to the other end of the bar and I go with him, getting the feeling Noomi's not too happy about our retreat. Jessie always did come on strong with the ladies. That's why one of the funniest things I ever saw was a girl as butch as she was trying to get into her pants, I never thought a lesbian could be so homophobic. "...I just don't want some fuckin' dyke tryin' to grab my ass..."

I end up squeezed in the doorway next to a pale guy with the uncultured pout of a brutish bonobo, so manly, so Algerian French, who turns out to be from Hemel Hempstead, crushed here with me between the main room and, what they call in the European City of London, the 'snug'- just as Felipe is getting served.

There was a burlesque show on a crappy little stage, couple of big-built curvy girls, more Italian than local? On closer inspection, given the cellulite, I'd say perhaps even an exchange program from that scepter'd isle of the snug... maybe even Hemel Hempstead, what do I know? Sarah says all English girls tend to be pear-shaped, but what about Amy Winehouse? The girls onstage have fifties tattoos too, feathers and hooting, whooping, kinda dead in here- even with all the people. At the edge of the stage another Amy, a stick with kohl holes where her eyes should be was showing her friends her wrists. Felipe waves. Felipe's always waving. I zone in and out while we kinda watch the show and drink a clear green liquid which is as much absinthe as what Jessie makes is coffee.

"Where's the Greek?"

Felipe waved away the question.

Later he pulled me back into the main room, onto the dance-floor, through it somehow, a door next to the stage, under the speakers almost. It felt like somehow we'd slipped outside, the stairwell so cold, his mouth hot on my neck biting. Then he laughed and I followed him down the rabbit-hole.

The steps were slick as that old trope of shit sliding off a shovel.

At the bottom a crusted, rusted door with a porthole, bolts, cross-beam latches, looked like something Captain Nemo might use as a decorator's piece. I kissed him and he held me close. He was shorter than I remembered.

"C'mon, gorgeous…"

Moi?

I wanted to tell him you gotta be kidding, but he pokes me in the ribs instead.

He pushes on the door.

In the next room, the first of three it turned out, two African girls were sitting in folding chairs getting drunk and jabbering in Nigerian? One of them had a bowler hat on. A TV on a concrete block. Tom and Jerry. A black maid's carpet slippers kept flopping across the screen and they kept laughing. It was like we were in the ante-room to a theatre, reminded me of that bit in Escape From New York when Kurt Russell leaves that girl to get raped, gas-light dancing on the walls, submerged wallpaper, around the world under the sea…

The second room was more an ante-chamber, a vast corridor, red drapes and marble flooring, a sweeping staircase, brothel chic. Someone walks past in mesh speedos and I think of a game William devised around dictionary definitions.

Vestibule or Vesty-Balls: noun for any banana hammock made from a breathable weave, or similar mesh-based coddler of the testes, derived from the string vest, or Aertex, proto-type. Original meaning? Archaic, probably Sin Francisco in origin. The kind of under-crackers that a human porcupine, or more than airtight adult industry avatar from the San Fernando Valley, would wear.

Musicians, junkies and punks, skunk-drunk defrocked monks in tight leather trunks sunk in the funk of despair and quasi-religious ecstasy, the lost, the beautiful and the damned, all the flotsam and jetsam of a new millennium, as, on a bed of peacock feathers, a perfumed boy now proffered his velvet slipper, filled with something approximating champagne, to the carmine lips of an impressively mustachioed cavalry officer dressed in nothing but an antimacassar and Polish riding boots...

I'm not European so it's probably easy to impress me.

I devour the bodies and sink into reverie- '...when I am gone and the boy awakes, in the hung-over whimper of a broke-backed dawn, the greasepaint smeared across his breasts, the drummer boy's tattoo pounding out its dreadful reveille in his delicate temples, then, as sunlight turned to dust, the feather-cut military wag would be straightening medals, pulling on his riding britches, wiping away the last vestige of that painted moustache from a dewy upper lip and stifling a yawn hidden surreptitiously inside a belch, then, and only then, will the boy wonder, just like in the song, "...is that all there is..?"'

The officer's lips, transformed to those of a young maiden's, like bruised plums, like plump crimson cushions, pouted, as, suddenly enticed, the boy leant forward to kiss his forehead, only to become aware that someone was watching them in repose from the comfort of an over-stuffed chaise-longue.

Silver lightning across the crimson field, the argent streak in an immaculate Titian coiffure, a world-weary ease, and the lacquered proboscis of a jet black cane- these it transpired were not Halloween props, not a young girl made to appear old but a travesty who had retained the first flush of his considerable beauty and added to it the allure of a wisdom that so effortlessly ensnared the poor blonde ingénue.

Citrine prey and carmine carnivorous.

Cleaving the smoke, with cheekbones of glacial ice, Monsieur Scarlet, as 'she' chose to be known to all her 'acquaintances', was an enigma that transubstantiated upon the wind, the low voice book-ended in the authoritarian boots of Teutonic consonants so intent on trampling the cloying caress of thick French vowels that any blood-stained Flanders field would be so, so proud. Here the fireworks, the thunder flash high above the battle, the flame red of phosphorous curls relit by dying embers in the eventide's collapse, here, right here and now, just as he inclines his stance and...

Eclipse.

Now, I've stopped dreaming...

Just a little, more? Oh drummer-boy! Was he already on his knees as the vision spoke?

"Will you come home with me tonight? Allow yourself to be forgiven black and blue? I'll milk the skin from you with a crystal whip and wear it as a supple opera cape, only a simple slip in decorum will leave my name carved upon your eyelids. In code though of course, the police will never have to know, or your mother..."

In the slick leather black of a speeding automobile, in the breathless fug of a private plane...

Normally my fantasies aren't like this.

I left ersatz kink to William.

Mine usually involve moonlit walks by the ocean or meeting the young Charlie Sheen's parents... or, being honest, sometimes Rickie Lake's- a touch hefty for one not of William's persuasion I know, but, my God, those teeth, they make anyone proud not to be a European.

A voice redolent of garlic and Gauloises cuts in, "They wanted to film part of Interview with a Vampire here, but..."

Felipe the tour-guide.

I really can't pin down his accent, so instead I compose a short poem to capture the scene.

'I'll never be as decadent
As old Lord Byron
I should know, I nearly killed
Myself with tryin'.'

Incidentally Byron wrote better poetry than this.

Just.

Then we kinda stumble through, not so much a door but the curtains parting and we're actually in a theatre after all, baroque, small I guess but after the corridor the space feels large.

In the center aisle, 'the Greek' stands and slow hand claps.

"Finally, Mr. Bond."

Felipe is behind me, his arm around my waist.

So, what can I say?

"Did I ever tell you the one about Nelly?"

7. Scotland's Dreaming

The train is late?

We can't be in Germany then.

I'm travelling in the opposite direction, waiting to be under the ocean, crapping my pants.

Last night was... not what I expected? Greek love is difficult to understand?

Is this the Midnight Express? Wasn't that Turkey? Some of the things we did last night seemed Turkish. Certainly a delight.

But I still miss her.

Even after all these years.

Even with a tin-man's heart.

So... I need to stick to the plan.

On board the St Pancras-bound express this chic little brunette takes off his brand new chapeau, a fedora of a mauve hue, reveals a page-boy cut, falls into a continental sleep, starts dreaming the rest of the passengers with such savoir-faire that I feel I'm sub-par and should be there on the platform waving goodbye, and there a better me would be, perhaps with shorter hair, perhaps already nodded off as the train pulls out, entering the dream myself, and then who can tell who's making this up anymore, as another big old iron horse rolls into the smoke's foggy belly, with a chuff, chuff tune, coughing hoarse... falling back into a very British past. The electrics shot, the diesel frittered away on oiling the pomaded crowns of hard-bodied land gals with tattooed axes, stars, pin-up maidens, lover's names writhing under the itchy wool of pre-war auxiliary uniforms, till I guess we are left with just that good old steam, after all. Now all we need is a carny mirror to trick us into thinking that there could be land-girls before the war- but who notices continuity with a headache like this. Clickety-clacking along at so many thumpety thumps per hour, your heart's locomotion rattling the trilling pace- always a terribly thrilling prospect, because we are already on board Sarah's beloved Thomas... and off!

Now all we need is an excuse to chat to a young man who... has already nodded off. I move on past my sleeping self.

In the dining car, the lights flicker as the pressure drops, at the bar the plum countenance of a professorial bore blurs with his neat whisky into a mad scientist testing his latest liquid death via a process of sour-faced trial and error, and at a discreet distance from his achingly strong breath, despite his attempts to traverse the points, he fails to bring a tobacco-stained finger into play as probe, rather than a mere tool of emphasis, upon the shapely figure of a somewhat scarlet lady, a Mediterranean film actress? High eyebrows, low cut dress, the roman cleft of her mountainous cleavage a biographical summary of her ambition. This acting lark of course, could be fancy on my part, I have a tendency for this.

Already I'm sketching in the details of her awfully gauche brand-spank-me-new Frenchy friend with, now her beret was removed, such an a-la-mode wave. This Parisian- the smartly attired travelling companion of the stoutly upholstered matron in the Tyrolean hat and dark-rimmed glasses from the next carriage, it turns out, was definitely taking more than an academic interest in the comely curves of Miss Italy- I do not require evidence to make my accusations, after all they will come to nothing, I jot them down above the eyes, file them for Boyd and William who just love a lady who loves ladies... and then lose them in the time it takes to say hello and dispel all the preconceptions I had so lovingly crafted- don't we all?

So busy ascribing traits to the central players I almost don't notice the mouse in the corner.

Ah, I give up!

I can't make up another's mind.

Who is this silly boy?

The truth?

Now he's awake he's not a boy at all, he's just me, a middle aged roué with a bob, rickmanning his saucy tongue round a mouth made loose by liquor and from what I can overhear... does he really think he's such a wit? And still, still it all is a little dreamy, a bit murder on the express, I myself am in such a sleepy muddle, as we set off, that, who knows... where this may all end up?

He had pointed to the seat opposite me.

I had nodded.

"Smoke?"

"It's a train..."

Felipe shrugs.

Maybe we're still in France after all?

I once watched a Japanese girl smoke in a Scottish hotel, so really I've seen it all...

The 'Greek' touches his nose.

Till they both sat down I'd only noticed Felipe?

And when was this the livery?

I can't remember changing trains but I take it I haven't fucked up yet.

Oh, that really is a good one.

Why is no-one laughing?

"What's your name again, cowpoke?"

"Cowpoke?"

"You look the type."

"The last time I had sex with an animal it was still fairly illegal..."

"A long time ago then, my friend."

"Last night, maybe?"

Felipe nods. His friend grins at me through mortgaged enamel. I begin my tale from last night once more.

"So, then they discovered pachyderms were the only sentient being other than man..."

"Is this the one about Nelly the prostitute, again?"

"You know it?"

"I wrote it, gorgeous."

"Why'd you keep coming back Felipe?"

He pauses.

"I'm a recurring character, baby."

The 'Greek' leans in. "He's like crabs."

More like herpes.

Not so much like Sean Connery. Unless they're both from Spain rather than Greece? I decide it's time to unleash Nelly, whatever the zip-code.

"You know I'm gonna tell it, anyhow?"

"It's your choice."

"Really?"

"Ok that's a little… optimistic? Just get to the bit where Nelly tells you she doesn't mind having sex with you as long as she gets paid…"

"Oh yeah, of course now she could do dirty-talk she wanted more peanuts, maybe a bun, but when I tried to get her to live with me she just laughed "Pack up my trunk and leave the circus sugar? You know it ain't like that, let's just keep things simple…"

"And that's the bit where she shits the bed?"

"Trumpety, trump."

"I don't get it."

"What do you know, you ain't Greek."

"Who is these days?"

Christ, you're better off being German.

"Are you following me?"

"The world does not revolver around you."

Patently that's a lie.

Would you like to check my passport, Herr..? Names didn't matter, that Luger in his pants looked promising- why had he said revolver?

"I'm going to see my Aunt in… Leicester?"

A poor liar.

"That's a long way from the Acropolis."

Felipe butts in. "So? When I take a shit I like to think of a mid-price Swedish hotel."

Who doesn't?

Wait a minute…

Maybe this is getting lost in translation? Perfect English changed to whatever it is I speak?

"I was born in a box-car, I ain't ever going home…"

I try to correct him, but he swears it's his quote in totalis and not a mangled citation.

"We are all travelers off the world, and the comfort of stranglers is to be cherished…"

Isn't this a little coincidental?

Bumping into the two stooges again.

Wait a minute, what did he say?

"You keep turning up like this and what should I think..?"

"Trust is important. I was born on Christmas day but I sure as hell ain't Jesus...

"He just screws up as he pleases..."

Thank you Felipe, but let the 'Greek' talk.

"My Italian-American parents called me Noel, Noel Grassi, and I am now one of this world's premier conspiracy theorists. Which is to say... I can't tell you anything more, not with them watching me like this. So leave a message, I probably won't get back to you..."

He tipped up his hat, fell asleep? This is Europe? Actually it's Birmingham, but we'll let that pass. You see even I don't get that joke, maybe Sarah would explain it to you, after all?

I'm on the fast train to Scotland.

I wonder how things would have turned out ten years ago if we'd just caught a train to Chicago. Life is a series of odd left turns, coincidences...

"You do remember telling us we'd be on the same train?"

Felipe grinning.

Fucking theatricals.

They do more lines than you but when they have to remember them...

I guess they sharpen their brains with the dialogue of others, a curious version of intellect. Merely recitation. Dead parrots again. It's like Latin and public schoolboys- perhaps the shared passion for buggery and political intrigue?

Then I remembered that it was me that fell asleep when the 'Greek' tipped his hat, perhaps before?

Am I dreaming again?

I can't still be stoned all these years later...

Later the train is dark, table-lamps loom like phosphorous mushrooms, my neck is a broken gosling.

How long is this journey? Where is the heart of my darkness?

"I used to distrust black people because I thought it more likely that they would steal from me."

A heavy silence, thick as tar. I've woken in another country. A cough.

Felipe and the 'Greek' are nowhere to be seen. I'm eavesdropping on the table in front, three seats ahead, a white guy who sounds like Billy Connolly's posh aunt is chatting to a thickset black guy in a wool overcoat. I wish I could wrap my head in it as I can hear every damn word. Why can't any of these fucks speak a language other than the only one I allegedly understand?

"It's a matter of mathematical probability." This should be good. "More of them are poor."

Percentage chances are, this is a hole he won't be able to dig himself out of. "I thought that is why more blacks were in jail." Perhaps he'd never met a cop, ergo he'd never met a racist cop, ergo... "Now I realize, that due to my social circumstance, most of those I will meet are honors students with a future..."

So now they belong to what Sarah would have called the same 'class', so... "...so, I'll be back in a moment, David. Lovely to have met you, by the way..." He left the table, and you wouldn't have blamed David if he'd wondered whether to steal his phone or his iPad. You wanna know which? For shame. David sit down, don't get up, don't leave before he returns... now they'll never kiss, it's just like Before Sunrise.

But without Ethan Hawke... which is a shame.

Why am I so horny?

I stumble to the john, dowse my privates in Virgin Trains tap-water and get off as cool as Yuri Egalitarian.

Why do people always look so glamorous getting off a train? Is it the stark contrast with those struggling masses heaving their trunks on over the metal sills? I guess you could use the disabled ramp when you got on. Steel bolts, miniature mosques with overly endowed minarets holding down a substantial slab of flat, bookish plate, a biblical weight, dense with the accumulation of metropolitan muck. Stand clear of the carriage doors please... but you're still pushing uphill and that too ain't ever suave.

Look up and down the platform. No sign of Felipe, or the Greek. My chorus is gone. To be honest I can't even remember the first line...

There was a couple arguing, finally in German. Blissful garble.

I haven't come all this way just to learn Scottish. If I wanted that I'd have stayed in Hollywood with Mr. Connery.

I really need to stop obsessing and just decide where he should live.

And honestly, no I wouldn't... well, maybe in 'Zardoz.' Scotland's as good a place as any to live.

Down the platform the kraut opened the lady-kraut's handbag, prized apart the Gladstone's soft leather lips, I guess he spanked aside the plump behinds of Babybels and a single rubber ball- clear speckled from the inside with glitter, swirls of gilt dust and there it was, underneath, the deep blue treasure, the papal edict which gave him ownership of her soul. Again. He opened her passport, the photo pin-sharp and blurring the truth. In the here and now she was heart-meltingly pretty- never really his thing (or mine, as I've often said, well not with the ladies). Perhaps he had always desired striking, that combination of beauty sacrificed on an altar of quirk, the angular, the irregular. Perhaps he knew nothing about teeth?

She had a smooth oval face, not too round, not too gaunt, it was only her heroic attempts to ruin her charm that drew him to her, the hair like an overstuffed pillow of cotton candy, the glasses too big for her pretty, pretty, pretty prettiness. God knows what she saw in him? Large hands, his undertaker's smile? She wanted to be buried by him that was for sure.

I bet he just said, "You won't need this..." as he took her papers. It was only her identity, hadn't she already given him more than that flimsy thing? I was day dreaming again, in shades of grey rather than black and white. I guess I didn't want to think. Dumbing downwind of my reflection. Look, there he goes again, back down to London... Couldn't wait to slip through the gaps.

I'd been drifting in and out ever since I'd left Sarah behind.

Alone.

I'm alone.

If you're alone then at some point you're going to start listening to that stupid fucking voice in your head, you're going to start imbuing strangers with lives- a ridiculous notion, you're going to start tearing yourself up into little collages of yourself, you're going... lots of people spend years struggling to live a life that seems effortless. I have always found it natural to veer towards the self-consciously complex. You've got to have a plan. If you are not the author of your own fate then you really aren't a person at all, just some piece of scenery that I've made up to help my own story along and what does that make me? Essentially, I'm saying that girl over there should be grateful I haven't given her a wooden leg just for color.

This loose miasma of events isn't even advisable anymore. Life does have a beginning and an end, but a middle? That would imply a way of locking this together like a jig-saw. Let's hope I can get out of this station and get things back on track.

Sarah once said that being inside a train was like an old ad slogan for Cinzano, you could be any time, any place, anywhere. Just like the Bible or Iggy Pop's European car insurance ads, people you trust will claim this is stuff that happened, but do you actually believe? Where are we really? The passing of time could be verifiable, sure, maybe it's ten years later than our trip to Chicago, but how do you really know? Like all of life, there is no turning point, just one long graceful glide into the curve before our hands are taken off the wheel and the inevitable crash...

Well, looks like this'll be sooner than I thought.

Happy, happy, joy, joy.

The bar should have been closed, but this is Scotland where alcohol is just about more sacred than profane.

I sit wondering how anyone could get drunk in a museum. There's a painting above the urinals for Chrissakes. I keep waiting for the locals to start playing traditional folk music. Given my mood would that be appropriate? In times of woe there is nothing like a banjo, but failing that? Music will suffice.

Then I see her.

Forty inches of uncut plasma.

It's not even showing sport, what is wrong with these people? Where's the tradition?

I try to follow the plot, no sound. Familiarity breeds contempt? I carry on drinking, hoping that as real absinthe makes the heart grow stranger, my lip-reading may suddenly blossom under the caress of the regal shivers of Chivas Regal.

I look to the left of the screen and we see him. Let's say his name is Tom Collins. It sounds believable till I remember we're in a foreign country. Shouldn't he be Hamish? Is this film American? Dubbed into English?

Tom Collins was a restless man. Kinda guy who couldn't sit through a good short story. So we won't bother with him, he'll be dead in a couple of minutes anyways. You just know it.

Let's look who's next to him at the bar. Gingham and a bitchin' tattoo. A good look for a schoolgirl assassin. Not so much for a plumber from Queens. The skirt's a little short for a guy called Joe.

Lucky her name is Hentai Yakuza.

Not her real name, that'd be ridiculous. What kind of father calls their little girl Hentai? Kind that lets a fourteen-year-old hang out in bars? She's not really fourteen, just looks it. Asians have that trick down pat.

That's why when she walks in, sits on a high stool next to Sam, asks him to buy her a drink- all before the barman has noticed her, well, Sam gets nervous.

The barman has turned round now, is about to speak. She's already opened her legs, just a little, a little more. Sam more terrified than aroused. Still he can't help but stare, just like in a bowling alley. She lifts the hem of her pleated skirt, just a little, a little more. He can't hear the barman asking for her driver's license, can't hear a damn thing. Shining like the moon and just as hairless...

What?

As hairless as a bowling ball?

And you thought she'd be wearing panties?

This is Europe, hence the dreaminess, and I'm drunk enough to believe anything, even that they're showing porn in a bar?

Like I said, you can't help staring, it's the light bouncing off her cooch. Is my obsession with the phallus... malleable? Getting floppy?

'Course that's when she pulls out the gun, and I get real, real excited, even though it's a little thing, a child's toy?

Bye, bye Tom.

Hello brain stew.

Hot blood on her face.

Seeping through the pores, into the cardboard and glue like sperm through a Kleenex.

She's just like Tom really, no more alive, just more fun to watch. Tom Collins was a restless man with a terrible beard.

She gets up.

Let's follow her.

She'll never know. How could she? She's just an object of some other fool's desire. A trick of the can't tell wrong from right.

I look to my left.

Damn, lost her...

"If you want to remain alive you'll follow me..."

"Felipe?"

Of course it wasn't.

All the real guy in the real bar really said, was, "...are you ok, buddy?"

Why do Europeans all think we call each other buddy?

I blame cheap movies, cable TV.

These aren't even my fantasies, just a stupid B-movie someone made up to deflect from my truth, drunk, lost and lonely, the voices in my head... so I flip the barkeep a Shanghai Gesture and go in search of noodles. Ramen, there's something you can believe in.

An absolute, un-malleable truth.

I end up eating chips.

8. East Of East Kilbride

You want geography?
Buy a map.
Local color?
Here's a crayon- they make them in Perthshire.
That may not be true.

I'm outside a laundromat looking in, holding meat wrapped in *battered bread?* Hitting rock bottom, tasting flesh, looking for a hotel. I must be a racial profiling clairvoyant… because there's a real life anorexic J-Pop girl with a sports bag and big 70's headphones, basketball tall. Is this East Asian thing becoming a theme? She's wearing a velour track-suit and has one of those t-shirts underneath that splurge stuff for TV programs or films that never existed, but this one with the requisite Japanese twist and sooo many words, 'Queer Today, God Tomorrow- will Big Ken convert to Jesus or will he stay an openly gay tetsu itamae eiyuu?' the boy looking so cute, so unthreatening. I start to wonder if it's a real TV show or even a real translation. At least it's not a band that she's never heard of- Def Leppard or Motley Crue- you wanna wear the crime you oughta do the time.

It's even worse if you see them wearing some band you actually liked, though with me so far only Motorhead seems to fit that bill. See, I told you I really don't like musicals. All that pesky melody. At least they're not selling Heroine Sheiks t-shirts in the Gap.

The girl comes out holding a black rubbish sack full of clean clothes and that warm biscuit smell of electric dryers. I bummed a cigarette, started talking. She was nervous, kinda young around the eyes, old around the mouth, and frankly if you can't hold two opinions about someone at once… broken English, odd accent, she looked like a squashed kumquat with acne, an upturned saucer of a face, oddly concave. She said she'd been staying in London with her adopted sister who was originally from Korea. My fellow American by accent. Her sister coming from Korea makes me think of Mr. Tham, his endless attempts to capture the sunset over Kristie

Kenpo's, then I look up at a leaden black sky, feel dizzy. I got the impression that this girl thought of me as some kind of project, but she couldn't stay upright either.

She told me I had to try Scottish Fish and Chips.

You're battling through a dense cloud. Like you're tumbling into sleep or one of those pesky wire-frame asteroid fields my brothers were so fond of, these memories again like beers in the brain, the déjà vu from hearing your dreams retold to you by someone who knows the landscape so much better, as weeks drift by, Sarah's voice, that constant companion of mine, delineating cadences in the local color, bipartisan, a tartan weave sewn from English wool, filling in the moth-strewn weft of my tin ear...

The smog shifts and it's not you fighting through the smoke, it's someone else, are these your hands really? Then it's the door closing, the fruit machine belching and farting out the theme to Star Trek IV. A girl with an English learner driver's L-Plate and no sense of direction staggers to the counter and out of its clutches, while the gang of 'hen night' harpies pressed into the only booth are giggling, giggling louder, louder laughter. If you think a bachelorette party can be scary, the British 'hen night' is on a whole new level. This bunch? Turns out they're English rather than Scots.

"Get us a can of..."

A cackling scream...

The girls are up from Kant- a state named after a German philosopher, or lady-junk, the mob of reprobates here to celebrate their friend's imminent nuptials, and what better fuel for the night of the hen than a deep fried stupor? The heat inside me, at my face, my neck, it makes me feel as if the steam is somehow re-condensing, is ashamed at its timid attempt at heat, is crying, frying in contrition on my volcanic brow before evaporating once more, leaving me behind...

"Fuckin' 'urry up."

"Calm down lassies..."

Did he really say that?

I'd express sorrow for the guy serving, if I wasn't practicing my very best attempt at inconspicuousness.

"Come on, no knickers."

One of the girls is patting the torn orange vinyl next to her, whilst leaning a plywood tray against the thick chrome stand beneath the table, as the bride to be plumps down four cans of diet carcinogens, looking like she's surprised that no-one had tried to trip her up, but only long enough for that small bubble of relief to be burst with a, "Get your tits out, get your tits out, get your tits out for the lads…"

I look around, hoping to spot some lads, or at least anyone to take the heat off me, Tanaka and the spotty guy in the hairnet.

And that's a mistake.

"What you fuckin' lookin' at?"

The girl opposite flashes with an anger which subsides into a kind of fitful amusement no less intimidating, her top teeth bared, tongue fiddling with the diamond stud above her glossy lip then pushing out the flesh beneath her lower, her eyes crossing, the guttural whine turning to a bellicose guffaw joined at once by hyena cackling again.

"Fuckin' 'urry up…"

"Yeah 'urry up, I'm fuckin' starvin'…"

First the ketchup and grease stained stripes of the top half of the apron sink like a skewed barber's pole behind the greasy 'TV screen' framed in steel, displaying dubious pies, warmed-over saveloys, cod and- 'huss'- is it? Then a blotchy sunset of heat-bloomed flesh rises, a heavy gold rope at neck, a shockingly pallid neck, the face not exactly human, but then not lost completely to resolute hardness either, and though the tumescent zit on his chin would refuse to be hidden if there was any point to make-up at all in all that steam, he has still tried to oxycute himself into cuteness. What a brute. As for mascara in all that fug, well that would have given him the panda eyes of a junkie or made him the kind of emo one of these wedding party harpies would have 'goz'd' on from three floors up.

One green eye gives a wink and now he goes down again, doing the splits, his party trick from what I can only assume is at least eleven years of ballet-modern-tap- because the Scots are nothing if not unpredictable, and two of the girls at the table are waving their cellular phones in the air, the same tune out of synch. Then, once the pinned and tucked straggle of ginger cotton candy and the constellation of blackheads sucking light through the smudged bisque at the hairline, all of that disappears behind the deep fat fryer once more, then you can hear him sneaking about, first the apron like a toreador's cape appears sans the chef, then whipped back, whipped out, back, out, tossed onto a box of burger buns and a skinny white butt, lost somewhere beneath voluminous sweat pants, pokes out from behind the powder-blue Formica, as he winds it, bumping up against a physical Jamaican slang in a flat-footed butterfly stance, trainers squeaking on Lino, wanting the audience to just kiss his fuckin' backside...

The guy is a toreador with balls of steel.

Still if he wants the 'lassies' to calm down he really isn't going the right way about it.

Surprisingly though, this doesn't produce a riot, instead the bride drops her chin into her neck, gazes at the four cans of loco cola in front of her, gets half up, spins a chair round, flops back down onto it, rocking fore legs and aft, she's facing its back, scraaape, jockeying it, scrape, scrape, scraaape till it's rammed against the edge of the table, chatter, smokes, the girl in the corner wakes up again.

Kiki?

As a name it just doesn't fit her.

Kiki it is though. Kiki too drunk to lift her head, too intimidated by peer pressure to carry on, is slumped down in her chair. With her hair scraped back tight, from the neck up she has the sharky threat of a lightly freckled Kate Moss-bulldog cross. Not as bad as you might think, if that doesn't appeal, but not quite as good if it does. The XL men's padded body warmer she is clutching round herself stops halfway down her thighs exposing an expanse of sporadically bruised flesh that leans towards the lean in the sharp glow from the neon blue fly zapper above. She slips down into her seat further, two taut arms which perhaps should have belonged to a wiry fairground lad and therefore look strangely blank without a heart or a dagger. Now she's heaving herself half up again with a mighty burp, a combination I'd guess of Messrs. Lambert and Butler cauterized with pickled eggs.

She pokes Chantelle in the ribs.

"Oi, oi big tits..."

"Fuck off..."

More group laughter.

Chantelle is acutely self-conscious, despite the bravado, especially of her shape. Perhaps it's become something of an unreflective habit of which she is *almost* unaware, but she cannot help cross her legs when someone mentions her cartoonishly ample bosom. A low-heeled hot pink sling-back slips half off, is nervously jiggled by frosty pink varnished toes in a contra rhumba to the gold anklet's cold tickle as it slithers on her orange-olive skin.

Then she can't help ruin the rhythm by pulling down at her mini, the jangle of gold bracelets, another set of beats cast in light. Oddly her discomfort never stretches to the saucy seaside curves of her chest. Remaining still, her locket, her initials, various charms, and her name in Diamonique, which lays off-center in the deep V of a luridly patterned knit, which carries its golfing DNA with the same understated élan as its wearer carries the genes of all those British pin-ups, down, what to her, would seem millennia.

You can bet her mum's mum loved Monroe and saw that in herself, rather than the curious mix of Elvis and Diana Dors that is nearer the truth. She would have her dad's side of the family to thank for her thick black brows, her wavy dark hair- spilling from a black and white checkered flat-cap fashioned from some poly-vinyl compound, and the subtle flaps of skin that turned down the edge of each eye-lid. The thick liquid cat swipes of eyeliner she used to deflect that would have given her, with the help of arcane knowledge of this sceptered isle, the epithet of, "Oi Sugababe, Sugababe", on a regular basis some ten, fifteen years before, even without the ball piercing above her pink pearlescent puffy lips, that her thick dry tongue is now, once more, idly teasing in between drags on a coffin stick which contains only 1% more fat content than the skinny bitch with the simpleton grin slumped next to her, who then rests her head, but somehow not her razor parting or the tight oiled pin curls of her hair on… was it her sister's shoulder? Chantelle's shoulder, because sisters don't fight forever do they, even half-sisters, blood's ficker innit?

"Get off you silly fucker", a rustle of *almost* flame retardant tracksuit and the girls' head lolls upwards with a stream of afro-Caribbean vernacular which is as obscene as it is quasi-racist.

The food arrives and the girls start to tuck in with plastic knives and forks, paper plates, it's a children's tea party.

"What do you fry in?"

My newly minted Asian friend is asking the wrong question. A look of stupefaction in thick Scots brogue.

"A fryer?"

"No, fry in?"

"Oil."

Was he being sarcastic?

"What kind of oil?"

"Cooking oil"

"Is it lard, I don't eat…"

The galloping gourmet interrupted, "It's that…"

He was chewing gum, pointing to a drum of liquid corn effluvium.

"Two Mediums then."

"Open or wrapped?"

"Open."

The girl in the checkered cap shrieked, one of the others nearly fell off her chair. This time the one in the corner repeated it louder so even the dick behind the counter who was now grinning inanely could hear.

"I bet 'er fuckin' legs are."

In my own country we only let dudes be sexist, believing it to be men's work.

Over here everyone's a trainee comedian.

My new friend froze, and of course the pack could scent the fear.

She already placed a couple of pound coins on the counter, every tiny hair on the back of her neck waving like an electrified forest of kelp. She could smell the chip shop guy now even through the clotting fog of the fryer, smell everything bold as brass, the cigarettes of course, some kind of peach or apricot cream, hand wash?, the dull tang of his sweat.

"'Ere Miss, Miss." They were back at school now, back three or four years ago when they sometimes turned up, as if they were identifying the muted tones of dress, the unruly plait of wavy brown hair, the flat clunky shoes, and thick woolen tights of their standard prey.

This though was a risk.

They were after all abroad, north of the border, far from home and the 'chinky-cow' was wearing lime green.

"'Ere Miss?" In between fits of giggles two of them in a rictus of embarrassment tried to shush the voluble girl up, but the big mouth wasn't going to stop, not when she could smell blood, so she shot them her fuck off look.

"Miss, do you wear a thong?"

Just how old were they?

At least ladling on the salt and vinegar was one of those tasks you can do relatively easily with shaking hands, I guess? Surely I should be their traditional victim? For heaven's sake I was wearing jodhpurs and a trench coat.

Words came out of my mouth. God knows why.

"Why don't you grow the fuck up?"

They mimicked my accent...

"Why don't you grow the fuck up..?"

"Fuckin Yank."

Really, people still said Yank?

Fuck you, limeys!

My new friend finished sprinkling her thick cut fries with salt, vinegar, salt, then stopped as if in a daze, put the greasy shaker back onto the counter, slow.

Took one step towards the girls who kind of flinched, then she grinned, grinned big and somehow we're already out in the sodium haze, the 'warm' Scottish wind redolent of curry, vomit and candied apple. Faces pressed up against the glass, one of them shouting through the half open door, "...what you doin', you fuckin' mental?"

Keep walking...

Keep wandering off, like dissipating steam... oblivious.

Feeling like vapor, so dark, dark...

Does that make any...

Sense going, bye, bye, bye, bye, proper sleepy bed bo bo time...

Almost.

Hotel bar, a little later. Took me a while to work out it was my hotel.

Ayaka's sister now taking notes? It's not like she lost her notebook, not like she ever had a notebook, just a weird distance that kept falling down between us. How much she missed her dad, then clammed up. Wasn't Ayaka a Japanese name anyway, not Korean? I want to know more about her sister. Tanaka put her hand on my leg when she got up to go to the bathroom. I nearly went with her I was so drunk, obedient, following the mommy bird...

We didn't exactly talk when we found ourselves in my room, she just asked me questions about what I was doing here now the festival was nearly over and I just kinda grunted, kept it short.

Then Tanaka leant in to me, trashy kohl-rings of eyeliner that, like savage ants marshaled themselves round boiled eggs, "You stare at me like this I cannot breathe. Knowing all my thoughts, my feelings even as I try to tie them to me, hold them to myself, impossible..."

Then she laughed, her hand over her mouth.

She *was* reading from a notebook, did she have a notebook after all?

For some small time my eyes kept following the rings of the spiral binding, surely they led somewhere...

She kept talking.

Poems?

Thoughts?

It's easy to be profound when you're young, when death is just a call-back to the joke of your birth, intangible really...

"You would pull them from me, take them against my wishes if it wasn't that I give them so freely, my will, whilst never weak, never my own. You take what you want, when you want."

The room was spinning, her English getting sweeter, more cloying but somehow making just a little more sense with every swig. Or was all this just in her eyes...

"You took my hand the first time we met, my hot child's paw, all fingers and thumbs. You were wearing gloves, black kid, softer than I had expected. We had hardly spoken, a bar in the west end of Soho. It seems odd now that you came to me, that you would walk over to my table. The next day, the next, over and over the

116

words you said, your eyes, the movement of your lips, but now, now more and more I remember how you held my wrist…"

She held my wrist.

"…turned my palm upwards…"

Ditto.

"…how I thought I knew what you would say, how you would tell me I mustn't cut myself. And you did. 'You shouldn't make marks upon your skin…' You paused, gripped my arm tighter, '…leave that to me, my dear.'

I looked at her wrists, little ruby charm bracelets, or strawberry laces tied in a candy kiss bow, I couldn't focus.

Deja vu?

Again?

Really?

It was like I was reading from a book too, I didn't know what she was saying, the words weren't that long but still I couldn't quite get it, I don't mean the meaning exactly, just I was lost and I remember she did tell me she was a poet, whatever that means? Then I could see lines of text rising up and down like a bumpy road, she was touching the floor, a soft, slow caress where her brow was a mother's arms and the pavement her children… When it was over, my head was locked, trapped into staring at that yellow star in a blue orbit, my neck pressed against the cold flat plain of a fire escape strut, morning battering in.

How had we got out here into the dregs of night again?

Where was this?

Apparently this isn't Scotland at all.

This is Edinburgh and once a year there are nothing but pretentious fuck-wads littering the streets, shivering beneath blankets of discarded invitations to choreographed rape and balletic mugging.

Usually their own.

The fire-escape turned out to have been advertised as a balcony.

I wanted to find a note written in Japanese on my hotel bed, instead there was a girl curled round the toilet like a fetus, her Juicy Couture sweat pants round her knees.

I go to the sink, pick up the Hello Kitty wash cloth.

When she opens her eyes it's just as I realize I have her panties pressed to my face.

Later when we're trying to hold down some orange juice she accuses me of being typically Japanese by which she means I'm a pervert and I try to figure out, given the state we were in last night, how she took her panties off and left her sweat pants on. She pulls out her note-pad and starts reading me another one of her performance pieces. She'd written this earlier? Or had she been inspired by my mistake with her undies?

When could she have written it then?

Have you ever thrown up raw alcohol, clear as a mountain stream?

I was still as pickled as last night's eggs in the chip shop.

Her voice somehow stopped the world from lurching, cool, comforting, like a young girl's wet panties on your forehead.

Of course this is just my translation now, though I try to keep to her words.

"'She'd taken to stealing the poor girl's underwear. Fogged as if under the ache of flu, breathing through cotton and her scent, the off-white clamped to the mouth, touching herself and dreaming not so much of her, as more the sense of being her, of eating, sleeping, walking home as her, home to herself, watching herself sitting on the sofa with the panties 'cross her face. Somehow knowing before the key was in the lock, at work, late on the bus… this other her would be here. Surrounded by books and biscuits, knitted blanket, loose and hot, wrapped round, falling into pleasure, half sleep, falling into fever and sudden guilt.

She'd get up maybe now? Cup her hands under the faucet, ring her mother, her boyfriend? It was hard not to fold them neatly, but still she always just balled them up, dropped them into the pink plastic mouth of the open-weave basket.

The door did open, a blast of cold air.

'Hi, honey I'm home…'   A joke, same joke at least twice a week.

'You wanna biscuit…' She offered the packet, her fingers still hot from herself.

Long legs, gawky, sliding under wool next to her, too close. The television was on like always, no-one watching.

Her thigh felt like a furnace, heavy, the other girl's legs cold across her lap. They sat there awhile, talking about work, and she watched the girl's tiny ill-spaced teeth, the darting tongue licking the sugar off a malformed bourbon cream, mushing its edge. A small mouth, cupidinous, the thought of kissing that mouth made her feel sick, she had the mouth of a boy. Her own boyfriend had the mouth of a girl and this symmetry made her a little dizzy.

A plane flew over.

Quarter to six.

What do you think?"

God she was like a demented puppy. Talking incessantly about her career in Tokyo.

Her 'career'?

Spoken word was a career now?

I didn't ask if the panty-stealing theme was coincidence. Or if the story was personal or true or whether she liked guys or gals or if she'd lied about when it was written and knocked it out just for me whilst I was taking a shit that was less mid-price Swedish hotel and more murder on the Orient Express- (as it powered through the Channel Tunnel.) I'm trying to say I didn't care if she thought I was a pervert or fucked up or... I couldn't remember what I'd told her about me under an Edinburnt moon. More than I wanted to know? Last night had blanks, and you had to wonder why she was still here? So obliquely I asked her.

"Everything you write about is sex?"

"Why'd you think it's about sex?"

Oh she was good, I kept expecting her to punch my arm.

"Because it made me hard?" I grin like the ghost of a jock, buried over there on the forty yard line.

"You are a bad man."

Was that a question?

I'm not really hard, in fact I'm eager to please, even girls, weak I know...

That's why she wants to leave? It's the decent thing to do. Of course she stays and we were even going to start drinking again but then we start smoking that stuff instead which, given how we feel, is more heroic than fun.

Fun?

For a while…

She starts to tell me about her boyfriend Veen, who is a soccer player, a Russian goal-keeper. I think about Sarah's big hands, so I start telling her about a girl I knew in Queens- though the nearest I've been to being a resident in New York is watching Seinfeld.

"Please pay attention, I'm delivering this as a sermon."

"A sermon?"

"From the mount." In my head I kinda climb on top of her, like I'm getting playful, and what am I trying to prove? I imagine she squeals, tickles me, and I'm hoping she succeeds in fending me off. If she didn't I'd have nothing to give her, nowhere to go. That dead feeling again so it must be time for me to preach. Did it go like this as I lay flat as a board by her side, or was this what I dreamt I said as I swam in and out of a dirty drunken fug?

"Now listen brethren, they will try to imply there is good morphine and bad morphine. Old man saintly morphine administered at death bed's head and bad junky morphine that slithers through the streets on non-stick tires, up the grade schooler's staircase, into the dreams of stainless steeled nuns…" I have no idea how this pours out of me. I've never created anything in my life except a feeling of ill-will. Perhaps it's the deluded belief I can make her stuff sound like shit that is so inspirational? Prose is like that. Authors are either narcissists who want to tell you about themselves via a series of masks and that is literature, or they're people who write pulp fiction because they want to escape their lives, which they consider to be the worst, most awful lives ever… because they are narcissists. Trust me, my brother ended up a kind of 'writer' eventually, and we all know how much he loved waving his willy around.

I stare into the eyes of my audience.

Her eyes are gummed with mascara, her pimples not so lucky. I guess you could join them up with eyeliner? What would that shape be? A wendy house like the top of an old-fashioned toy wooden arc, or Leonardo's last supper?

Which Leonardo?

I think DiCaprio would opt for a Wendy's double whopper, the fat little fuck. Ass like a… well, a girl.

I practice pick-up lines for Leo.

"I don't want to *butt* in on your conversation."

"Exsqueeze me?"

"I just thought you'd never *ass*?"

"Ask what?"

"For a light... still can I just *bum* a cigarette off you?"

I always imagine he smokes like a train.

Tanaka lights up. And I steal it from her little claw.

"They say, my sister, that with drugs it is actually a matter of the bullet killing you, not the hand on the trigger, and, my lord, Oh Hallelujah! Kitty had veins like..."

"Kitty..?"

She says it like, 'there always has to be a woman', right?

She was right.

Even with a fag like me.

Kitty was actually the name of my sister's cat... and yes, there always has to be a woman.

This is pulped fiction, so a dame, a doll, a devil in a dress... essential.

"Kitty's veins were beautiful, perfect, a whore on all fours begging for the shit-smeared kiss of a conscience-free hypodermic. Who's to blame? No-one. She resisted. Good for her. She got great grades. Well, good for that school. Left the neighborhood. Stopped hanging with Lenny before it all went south, and hey, Lenny's not a lovely young girl with skin like cinnamon and a cute turned-up nose. Lenny was an ugly fuck, a complexion like loose meat, and with a mouth like a slit open fish. Poor old Lenny."

"Amen."

"Thanks, now shut up."

I once saw a burlesque of a band where the frontman said kind of the same thing. 'This one's an oldie, so, if you know it? Please don't sing along, you'll only fuck it up.' Something like that. He thought he was funny. Don't we all?

Lenny wasn't even amusing.

"Curse poor old Lenny for not being... well, much. To tell you the truth he wasn't even that ugly. That would be cinematic, it's not like he weighed more than a house, or had an inner peace and wisdom that he could regale middle-class white folks with. It's not like he became a junky and then was redeemed. Never even dealt.

121

He just got hit by a Greyhound bus when he was twenty-two. Like I said, it all went south. Except his left leg. That went north on 23rd street. Loss of blood. 911 is a joke..."

Typical.

"Poor Lenny."

I'd stolen the name from Of Mice and Men- I thought it went well with my Kitty cat. Does anyone really know someone called Lenny? The rest was just...

"Kitty wanted to be a dancer. You gotta have legs for that. It's also a short term occupation. That's why she stopped fucking a bouncer at a titty bar four blocks from where she roomed and started seeing a guy called Mike who had a computer repair shop on the lower second..."

I paused. This wasn't supposed to be an anecdote where a moral would no doubt spill out through God's grace- you had to avoid that with something made-up, or people didn't believe it was real. And soon as they lost faith then it would have to actually be some kind of truth to justify its telling, so...

No. That's too neat. Too venal.

All my tall tales are told to strangers, family just gets the ugly truth...

That's why I could spend a long time with my brothers never uttering a word...

"No. That's too neat. Too venal. Actually Kitty fell in love with Mike. You shouldn't judge Kitty so quickly. He was a real looker? Not bad. Big cock."

She bit her lip, like this wasn't the bus she had signed up to get on, so I veered, even as I personally couldn't stop thinking about my made up Mike's big cock...

"Seems she was freakin' shallow, just not an addict or a gold digger..."

Then veered back.

"How'd it all fit in? Kitty was five foot, minus two inches. So by my calculation that's at least up to the bottom of her breasts." I put my hand out flat like a shelf, up at Tanaka's neck, across the distance between us as I squint one eye. I wanted to tell her that the human body is a miracle. Certainly as long as both legs stay together. Kitty's must have been almost as far apart as Lenny's to get that damn thing to disappear inside her. How come Mike was blessed and Lenny wasn't? Do I write the rules? No. I have a bladder infection. So clearly I don't. Still, I don't have a tiny penis... well, not tiny for that Midwest school, and I still have both my legs so...

All the while I'm thinking this through Tanaka just keeps staring at me like an angry bunny.

"This is about sex?"

Isn't it always?

I ignore her.

Pissed off.

"Kitty gets a beer from the fridge."

Odd statement. The present tense? She's intrigued.

"Kitty wears a long t-shirt with a generic football franchise, bare legs, bare cooch somewhere up there."

She frowns, but still she can't help but join in, "Peter and Jane play ball, run Spot run."

She's spotted that this doesn't sound like the truth any more. So now she's probably thinking maybe it is?

"As Kitty gets her beer I play with myself under the woolen blanket. Same old tricks. Wish I had a pair of her panties 'cross my face, but she doesn't seem to wear them much. Do you think she'd notice if I held them to my nose while she looks for a Bud? I'm not saying she's dumb... but she is. Still if I had a small penis maybe she'd notice what I'm doing, so I guess it's lucky I haven't got one at all. A plane flies over. Quarter to seven."

"Nothing like my stuff." She's lying next to me on the bed, turns away in a huff.

Then she spins back round.

"You wanna go get pizza?"

For a performer she doesn't have much of an ego, can't stay annoyed for long.

Pizza?

A beer too?

I have a picture of the Eiffel Tower pop up in my head. "Sure..."

Edinburgh takes it out of me, too many hills or not enough tartan? I'm an American, I need more tartan, stat!

We find a Polish 'Indian' that sells what Domino's calls pizza, I'm reminded of the fall of Rome. She sucks the cheese they put in the crust- don't ask- through a retainer. I wonder how I could possibly have not noticed that before. I think of my brothers fighting James Bond's Jaws high above Albuquerque. The guys behind the counter are arguing about a cousin of theirs. I chime in, asking them to slow down and the surprisingly friendly Niko Bellic-a-like gives me the low-down. It goes something along the lines of Vladimir Putin's father being cuckoo.

What kind of a Pole calls their son that?

Vladimir Putin Walesa? No wonder he turned out wrong. Wrong as wrong can be. Well, his father thought so. His neighbors too.

Ever since he was a small boy all this particular Putin dreamed about was penguins. On his wall not second-hand pop-stars, no faded Stallone, or peeling Cantona- no, I have no idea who that is either. Anyway, it was penguins. One specific dream.

To tango.

To waltz.

To cha-cha-cha with this most formal of fowl.

The boy was touched, and not by greatness. One day the world will freeze over and he will walk north, only to fall through the ice, said his cousin.

A big joke.

Little Vladimir, under the ice. Maybe then he'll meet a penguin.

When Vladimir was twenty-one he joined the ambulance service. At least the van was black and white, eh? Keep him out of trouble? Stop him from visiting the zoo. Now only the weekends. A flask of hot stew, sandwiches wrapped in paper. What year was this?

After the flood? Tupperware could be had. Who still wrapped their sandwiches in paper? The boy was a fool. As cuckoo as his dad.

They shrugged like the French at the end, a habit which they'd picked up from one Scottish customer who was a fan of Gerard Depardieu- I made that last bit up, but I had to sit through that entire bullshit story about their cousin Putin, so it only seemed fair.

Was it some kind of a wind-up, a traditional joke?

"Hey, do you know the Greek?"

They shrug.

I remember he's not even Greek.

"Doesn't matter."

Later on midday hit me like a hammer. I'd started to accept vinegar on my fries as the only way- if you're going to go native you might as well go with the flow. Miss Tanaka wanted to know if I wanted to go somewhere fun.

Why not? I'll try anything once.

Besides if I didn't like fun I could always go back to what I was used to. She took my hand and led me to a place called the forest, or wood or something?

Old collapsing Edwardian red-brick. Inside again the condensation is rife. Dreadlocks, dirty nails. Bubbling on the stove-top, hot unidentifiable stew- with a distinct lack of gristle. Oatcakes and fair-trade Wi-Fi. Kind of place I felt safe. The building seemed bigger from the outside.

Inside most of the tables are taken. They sit chatting, equable, some even in love, college librarians with shoes made for pacing away the days, the blue flicker of phones reflected in their glasses, on their heads scratty nondescript wool that mimics a haircut or maybe they wear it longer, dye it henna red or green. There are a few older women at the bar, those twins, matching spiky hair, work boots and key-chains, dockyard matrons too tired to do anything but drink. Then the pretty girls. Pretty normal, pretty drunk, pretty highly strung. Ten, maybe fifteen of those, some are even wearing skirts, would you believe it? They're all chasing the same three adolescent boy-girls. Maybe one has a motorbike? They sure look tough don't they? They've got Marlboros in the top pocket of their check shirts, they got thick lips and bad attitudes! It's like they're auditioning to be Jessie but they don't quite have what it takes. So this is a gay bar? I think I'll go back to being homosexual instead.

"Can I have a drink Daddy?" Tanaka has an evil sense of humor after all.

I'm not actually the only man in here, but there ain't a lot of us, and those that are really do exemplify an aversion to testosterone or at least a kind of resigned acceptance of our evolutionary futility. The punk behind the counter rolls up her sleeves, stares in despair as I nod sheepishly. It's a bad day for politics, a good one to feel that hot fever of comic shame. I want to squeeze Tanaka's leg and call her doll-face, but instead she pulls out her own twenty.

"Just joking hot-stuff, I'll have a beer and a cocktail for the little lady." Tanaka looks at me, I wince, and the woman serving us grins, almost laughs. Somehow Tanaka's pressed real close to me, got her finger in the waistband of my Vivienne Westwood pants.

I feel a little out of place… it's not just because I've got a cock and tonight it's apparently spoken word poetry. It's I'm always out of place, is that it? That's the fun of it, though, I guess?

I sipped my soya milkshake and then Tanaka led me downstairs, felt like waving goodbye to the couple of guys I left behind. A paint-spattered staircase and a Nevada-dry basement.

Seven or eight hippy girls were trying to prop a wardrobe up and I thought I'd better help. Tanaka looked almost as out of place as me. Gold hoop earrings and stacked trainers were not de rigueur- everyone else here made me feel like I was back in San Francisco again, but that this time the rumors about not bathing were true. That's not being fair, but the girl closest to me did stink. I wanted to tell her to smoke more marijuana, she'd have done us all a favor. You're wearing head to toe hemp so why not smell like its most popular by-product?

Sudden nostalgia for the West Coast, all those crazy tales of big-foot spotting Thomas Pynchon loping through the pines of Big Sur- like I said, I really need a map sometimes, or a nap. Still those golden nights and local characters… Everyone remembers Sancho's Panzer Division, don't they? Sancho had been tilting for windmills in Texas under the name of the Cosmic Cowboy, but then became known locally as Don Kyoto, one of a handful of green activists wanting to uncouple the Texaco Star from the Lone State, and then place wind power center stage of its energy policy. By any means necessary? Perhaps. When he'd been chased out of Kinky Friedman's backyard he headed to the fake approximation of San Andreas we call home, where he'd worked a scrap-yard; he would provide the plate steel and the rusted but sturdy iron that they would weld to the hybrid vehicles donated by a wealthy benefactor known only as the Condor.

Do you think this'll fly?

An attack on the pumping crude heart of the homeland?

All's well that ends oil?

We recycled our jokes too back then, and this one was brought to you by another ghost of Tom Clancy. Stay in your homes. Vote Republican. Never look up at the skies. And now the National Anthem.

I was humming the stars and stripes remembering swapping bullshit with real old Greenpeacers as I 'helped' with the wardrobe.

The denizens of the basement were looking at me like I was nuts, and then it kind of dawned on me that Tanaka and I were actually the audience. Or supposed to be. I let go of their performance piece and it listed violently to one side. I thought of Stan and Ollie and that piano rolling down the stairs. Boyd nearly got killed trying to help them shift that thing. They were supposed to get Don to connect it up to a solar generator, but then... Did they ever play it manually? They were more bongos and kazoos kinda guys were Stanislav and Olsen- like I said- golden nights, my friend, good times, a great couple. I'd roll another but I'm stepping back, collapsing into what I thought was a plastic chair but turned out to be a bin and then Tanaka giggled which just produced more frowns.

Tragedy slipped into kabuki, a big death-rocker, counter-culture-goth chick climbed out of the wardrobe. At first I thought that maybe she was actually just another average, straight down the line hippy and the face-paint was just a hark back to awful 1970's encounter theatre and not teenagers in awful 1980's shopping malls. I waited for a lion to follow the witch but I'm guessing these pagans weren't too fond of C.S. Lewis.

I take in the scene.

A Halloween flash of Boyd in a long white gown and a wig, the taste of pumpkin.

She was wearing an ankle length tasseled skirt, dingy green, not quite tie dye, like they used to wear way back in that awful bit of the eighties that the U.S. almost missed. A New Model Army t-shirt and a German army parka, Doctor Martens. My first impression had been wrong. She had a large black folder covered in a Wite-Out liquid paper scrawl, full of loose papers in clear plastic covers. Her hair was messy but not quite dreaded, lots of those big silver rings that not even losers wore since steam-punk got too big for its brown leather booties. It was like she'd been frozen in time. The past is another country, and from what Sarah had told me I'd guess Camden had declared independence in '84.

One of the neo-hippies broke open a glow-stick and that was the signal for someone to press play on a CD of... wind? Northbound traffic? Something someone had actually paid good money to listen to under the misnomer of it being ambient?

Punk had been and gone and cross-bred with its arch enemy in the festival mud more than a few years back now. I thought back to the burning woman, remembered Sarah lurching towards it yelling, "Burn Thatcher burn…"

There was so much mirth to be had if you only embraced the positive side of life, and so many dreadlocked anarcho-punks are so very full of life. The witch's accent, someone told me later, was an upper class version of something called 'Bristolian'. I kept thinking of Benny Hill and Sarah telling me that 'bristols' was English slang for somewhat humungous ta-tas.

The witch started to speak and no-one laughed and believe me this really happened. You can't make this shit up.

Thank you Tanaka for delivering me into the arms of poetry.

First the goth matriarch started with some rural bullshit about ploughing fields and how the seed of love, the fingers caressing the soft, fertile soil was so much more preferable to the harsh plough of man tearing at the land, I guess maybe she was fucking this one girl she kept kinda half looking at, who had just stopped dating guys recently? Heck, I'm no detective. The rest of the stuff was much angrier, topical, less purely socio-political in tone? It was sometimes let's say, 'more than a little hectoring' which reminded me of Sarah berating me about Americans not understanding how much Mrs. Thatcher was fond of berating the English working class… look the argument was circular, I forgot how it didn't end.

There were some bits I didn't mind. She could laugh at herself, which was a little refreshing. Though I think if *I* had said any of what she did I would probably have got a good kicking. She's talking to an imaginary kid with a voice like treacle running fast up-hill.

"What is a lesbian, Mommy?"

Then she's herself, "Have you heard this?"

No-one nods, except her, then she shakes her head, lifts her arms in the universal shrug for Jewish confusion.

"Well, there are two old ladies…"

The treacly voice returns.

"Like you?"

She replies, "…maybe like Grandma."

"Oh."

"And one says… My daughter's dating a lesbian."

"Mine too."

"But that's impossible."

"Why?"

"Because your daughter's dating my daughter…"

She pauses.

It's almost comedy, and that never stopped Jay Leno.

"Do you want to know what exactly is a lesbian?"

"Yes, Mommy?"

"Well, there are three types…"

The routine ends with, "Still, it's two more types than straight men." And the little girl telling her she's funnier than her other Mommy. That, it turns out, is because she's got a shorter haircut and more men's shirts- ok, that last bit was me.

Like I said I don't think I could have got away with that. It was like the time I told Sarah that concentration camp joke.

You know the one that finishes… with my ass in a sling.

The witch-poet ended with a dedication.

"For… all of those, who've realized; all the doctors, builders and bus-drivers, all the knitters and bakers and especially the candle-makers!" She laughs. "All the strong and feminine, sensitive and butch, all those that society decides are pretty, or plain, or coarse, or too old, or too young to have their own mind, the mothers, the young mothers too, all the clever and brightest and best, the jokers and travelers, and those who never left home, and those who never wanted to come back; all of those who've realized, that really, truly… We don't need a man in our lives."

If only *I* could believe that.

I'd wanted to think that this dyke thing was becoming a theme but that would imply they were a homogenous group, just like East Asians or the kind of racist shit who'd make a joke like that. Which box am I supposed to be in? Bitter? Sardonic? White? Middle aged? Atheist? Drop-Out? Dope-fiend? Father? Faggot? At least the dress-code was easy, all the above wore checkered flannel shirts, or was that lumberjacks and old Nirvana fans only?

Afterwards Tanaka, the poetess, a few others and I got chatting and actually she was really nice for an awful bore, but maybe that was because I told her I was gay. It seemed like the easy thing to do and don't I always take the easy route? Perhaps it was because we were her only audience afterwards, that she seemed likeable? She was so attentive to our need to listen to her.

"When I was twenty-one I used to travel each day on the same bus to University, listening to Sheffield synth-pop, reading Camus and eating a Gregg's Leek and Cheese Pasty. Not all at once, necessarily. Not perhaps every day. That's just how I remember being twenty-one."

It was still a performance, you imagined it was the same old stuff shared again and again. Apparently headlining over the cirque de wardrobe was only a warm-up for tomorrow night, a very mixed bill, supporting Kevla the Grate- a gap-smiled conjurer whose main claim to fame was his abortive attempt, at the 1973 Milwaukee World's Fair, to catch a loaded revolver between his teeth.

I had a flash-bulb epiphany of meeting Kevla in Miami in the twilight years, a one-legged drunk with a wheat allergy whose greatest feat had become making a bottle of malt disappear in under an hour.

I guess he didn't need a firearm any more.

He was loaded enough.

The lens of the camera becomes a high-powered scope, every pore in every face a crater, then my vision tunnels, flattens, reverts to normal, are they still talking?

It was going to be one of those prestigious post-festival gigs where far-from-near legends go to die and the up and coming are finally revealed for the never-will-bes of their fever-sweated nightmares. She mentioned the venue and I could tell Tanaka was envious, maybe there'd even be seats.

"… oh, that, and that a lovely old lady once told me I looked like Julie Christie. I was wearing a midi-dress, still wearing them can you believe, just above my not too bad knees, and flat shoes, oh, and those dense, dense tights that are almost wool that you used to get from C&A, and for once I was just as plump as you would want to be, which is to say, half as plump as you remember your best friend was in school."

A guilty aside, "My best friend was quite plump..."

She laughed at herself and I was surprised again by what a warm smile she had.

"…still, I tossed my long, mid-blonde bob and brushed the crumbs from off my lap, and even though I really ought to have been thinking more serious thoughts- given the political climate- I still couldn't help but conclude this will be a good day. A very good day, thank you very much. When I got off the bus, the driver got off too, though this was not unusual. Not for them, anyway…"

She already told us how she had ridden this 'stagnant-smelling heap' every day, nearly every day, for quite some time, and yet somehow she had got off at the wrong bus-stop this once, even though she'd had time to make up her mind not to.

The driver had sat waiting for their colleague to show, then exchanged some banter with him, picked up their broadsheet and got off like they always did at this point, and rather than waiting for the journey to continue on its way our semi-celebrity poet did too.

"For some time the driver and I had been exchanging pleasantries. First about the weather, then about me sleeping in and almost missing my ride on several occasions. Then they'd say something about one or two of the books I had juggled with my change and the Gregg's pasty, various keys. Most bus drivers read the Sun or the Star, this one read the Guardian and it turned out, as I got to know them a little over the weeks, they'd also already digested a fair slice of the stuff on my course."

Tanaka handed me a glass of organic wine.

"…It was weird seeing their legs. Little blue cotton-viscose pistons. I'd seen them before, of course, at the end of their shift when they'd got off at this stop, but now we were almost walking together, somehow. I remember their saying to me, 'You don't usually get off here...'"

Was this going anywhere?

"I was quite a little taller than the driver. Never noticed before. Their hair was as cute as a little gelled hedgehog when seen from above. They were asking about how I'd liked a book, some book I've forgotten now. If you told me the title I'd remember the plot, but without it... I was going to peel off, over to the shop across the road, we'd reached their little gate. Their index finger like a chubby Walls sausage curled on the paint-chipped wood, opening it. I can remember the writer, of course, but never which one of her books." She paused. "You know, up until then, I'd never even kissed a working class lad... much less been fucked by a bus driver from Essex... he was such a brute."

Like I've always said, the English- absolutely bloody filthy mouths.

Wait a minute, she's straight?

What the fuck!

After a while I stopped not listening, the shock abated.

I wonder if when she repeated this story after her next show, twenty-four hours later, she'd finally find someone who was shocked by the way she phrased that. I carried on nodding.

"He was educated working class, in his early forties and I was twenty-one and Daddy was the Member of Parliament for..."

I guess I was shocked too. The English have no taboos about sex or money, but class? They liked to talk about that a lot but only as an abstract concept applied to others.

"...so you fall in love don't you. Fall in love with a strong butch beauty you want to bend to."

Christ what a ghastly phrase. Butch beauty? No wonder I'd kept thinking she was gay.

I imagine Bob, a grumpy dwarf with dirty fingernails discussing the merits of posh pussy whilst sharing Tunnocks bars with some tea-swilling mates at the bus depot.

"Bob would have been mortified by how I thought of him, back then... and rightly too."

Poor old Bob, I wonder what happened to him when she left?

You never know what's gonna happen when you get off the bus... driver.

9. Between Calls

I'm back on the bus, but not the driver... though he does have nice hands. Edinburgh falls away real fast, along with Tanaka, slips into villages and concrete sea defenses, rotted planks too, a half empty mouth, wooden teeth sloshing in the salty froth, a landscape of power stations and strange hard beauty.

If Scotland was a face it would have far too few pimples, the map you drew would have to make do with freckled heather, high boned mountains.

"That's my wee boy."

I want to show granny a picture of Elvez and claim he was my husband but I haven't the will to break her wee heart, and her toffees are real nice, so I show her someone who is clearly only old enough to be my son.

"Ten."

"And does he take after his father?"

"No..." I say, "...he's more like my wife Sarah, you can see it in the teeth."

He also liked girls.

Which is not to say we could ever prove she did.

Though Boyd and William would have liked to have died trying.

At ten I can't say whether that means the little fella will take after his father or he's just suffering from precocious heterosexuality.

I often wonder if I could have turned out just a normal healthy homosexual if mother hadn't died when I was so young and my sister had stayed home too. Dad did his best, but how distant can you be when you're raising three boys alone? Granny looks out the coach window at the damp fluff of Bonnie Prince Charlie's realm with hope perhaps for a less perplexing companion on her next jaunt. Why doesn't she just sleep?

Has she been mainlining shortbread?

I've never wished I owned an iPod before. I mean I used to own one, but actually wished? I'll leave that to Stephen Fry.

I wish Frank Oz would stick his hand up my ass so I could be as wise as Yoda. Or Hugh Laurie at least, who I think of as Ernie sans Bert.

And yes I would, but as Wooster not House. If we keep sharing box sets the Atlantic will disappear entirely and this sceptered isle really will become the 51st state. It all started with John Cleese hosting the Muppets, and… the wheels on the bus go round and round.

Yesterday Tanaka and I had said our goodbyes at Edinburgh's main terminus. She gave me a big hug and a kiss on my nose and told me her favorite painting was of a shoe that was a foot, or vice versa. It's in the Brighton Museum if you wanna go see it. I think back so many years and wonder what size it was, whether that dwarf animator we'd bumped into had seen it growing up? As I was momentarily gay the kiss on the nose was acceptable, allowed. Miss T. was midway through telling me her earliest memory at the time. It was an inconsequential doozy.

She said she had found 'it' just when she was old enough to know already that this was to be what she was to remember most about her childhood. Perhaps she knew it in her bare feet or scraped knees, not yet in her head where, lying in the shallow dish of her upturned face it would curdle, turn sour here, here upon her back, here beneath her Uncle's porch. Drip, drip, drip, spider web water, eight-legged dew. Back, far back looking for the bright red ball her little brother had kicked, kicked so much harder, so much further back than… Had she ever played with the red ball?

I wondered whether she'd not yet read that thing by Nabokov where the red ball goes under the table? Was it a short story, part of a novel perhaps? She assured me she had not read anything by him yet. Was waiting until she was old enough to not identify too strongly with Lolita. A definitive answer. She did half recall a mangled quote from the text. Her father had underlined it, part of a crossword clue- perhaps mother would be able to solve?

Today the greatest conundrum? How the ball had got so far, rolling, rolling, one heroic object against so many determined leaves, also a hose-pipe of a startling orange faded to pink, damp earth and the little belly, there it was, that moment.

With the curve of first trimester, the ying to the yang of her concave features, somehow she wriggled over through the muck to it, and to think she had almost not changed- the sailor suit collar and pleated skirt of her uniform folded neatly on her bed. Folded? Yeah!

Her mother wished, she'd torn it off to throw it on the floor in a heap, still, it wouldn't be muddy at least. Now, in tatty jeans and an old t-shirt, she was a great explorer, possibly even the inestimable Dora, still a child despite the missing tooth and the love bite her best friend has given her on the back of her wrist.

The leaves brushed off easy, why wouldn't they? The dirt? That required her to sit up and scrub, scrub, scrub, what was above her? The crawlspace no longer so tight, instead a box cut up into the house? Beneath the boiler? Her attention was focused below. First the thick, thick glass then the bolts, some more bolts, the handle! A door into who knows where? A hatch into the earth. She squatted over it and then flew into a panic as her legs lit up with ambient light. She had the impression of an old man with long, long brows staring up her skirts at her, looking like the creep at the railway station. Then she remembered she was wearing trousers and that somewhere she had read, somewhere more pertinently she had retained, the idea of lights that came on automatically, a timer switch, proximity? It didn't matter. She would have to get Father because surely the... it wasn't jammed, but loose, slippery with thick, thick grease, the handle turning, the door moving, no great weight and below? A ladder, metal rungs into half-light and then darkness.

Her breath came back at her from the walls, steel not concrete, metal tang. She was small then, but still a tight fit, again she thought of the little man at the station, how he always folded his paper to sit on, like a child uses a cushion to reach the table in modern homes. What advantage were these millimeters in height to him? No more rungs, she almost slipped and fell. And then she did. When she awoke, another house, another day, her head in the trash and bigger than twenty years and quite old enough to tell her own story thank you very much. Meniere's is a condition of the inner ear that leaves you prone to dizzy spells, fainting fits, she never had it seriously, maybe that one time counted, but...

"My sister. You should meet her... she's a medical oddity."

"Ok..?"

"She lives for the moment, because any second..." She closes her eyes, fakes passing out and I catch her.

"So that's not really your memory..."

She answers at an angle, avoids, reminds me of myself.

"She's nothing like you, Mr. Gayman."

I look blank.

I don't think she's trying to be offensive, and even if she is? It's just endearing, which I guess is patronizing enough to be offensive on its own.

Then I remember she'd told me last night that I look like Neil Gaiman.

"It'd be funny to watch you have a conversation."

"Why?" I had to ask.

"You are a bad liar, and my sister isn't."

"I'm a bad liar?" As she nodded I realized that perhaps I was so good she hadn't even begun to realize how wide of the mark she was.

"I don't get what you mean…"

"A bad lie is easy."

I stayed quiet.

"You a bad liar, your life's easy. You a bad liar? People catch you out, you don't have to lie for long…"

I smiled.

That came easy enough.

I guess she was right.

I wanted to take her home, bring her up as one of my own but I wonder what Sarah would think?

Best not plough that Farrow.

You can't help but like the way she covers her teeth when she laughs, social foreplay, forbidden fruit.

Boyd once had an Asian girlfriend whose parents were originally from Hiroshima. Our grandfather was a Canadian who served in the American Airforce, and was stationed in Hawaii during World War Two.

Boyd never mentioned he'd seen the film Hiroshima Mon Amour.

She never mentioned Pearl Harbor.

I'm not surprised.

It's a terrible movie.

I catch sight of Ayaka's sister still hugging me in polished steel.

The first time I saw two boys kiss was in a mirror image, when I was thirteen. My best friend Jake bent towards him, leant his forehead against the other boy's, and then in the silvered font of Main Street's Soda Fountain window their lips just met and I would have been terribly, awfully, heartbreakingly jealous of that reflection if the other boys lips hadn't been mine. But, as they were my lips, instead I spent a heartsick summer, so damn jealous of that memory of a chaste little peck. He never kissed me again, some big fucking joke.

She lets go.

She presses a book into my hand.

I don't know why but I expect it to be something by the witch poet.

Jessie once delivered a pastiche of lesbian poetry which now half-echoed in my head.

'I'm knitting another horse.

The last one was cardboard, got soggy, paint ran,

Disintegrated, mulch, eventually damned.

Wool you can get wet.

But it does stretch, and yet...

I've never met a man who could stretch a horse.

Or indeed one who could stay the course.'

Too phallic?

I'd actually read worse, delivered more po-faced. There really were some very bad lesbian poets. Even the ones who were straight.

The kind of girls Jessie dreamed of didn't write poems, they worked in biker bars or maybe a mythical version of Hooters where they really were working their way through college- a course in hot-rod maintenance perhaps, and sporting bodacious ta-tas and preferably a Runaways tattoo? 'Wow, she's really, actually, very feminine *and* she can ride a motorbike...' We all have our fantasies and our prejudices. It seems that there are those who still don't make passes at girls who wear glasses, well, unless they're wearing biker momma mirror-shades.

The 'book' Tanaka gave me wasn't poetry.

Instead it was a collection of short science fiction stories.

Do you think there is a pattern to the universe? That all this is interconnected? Ask Gene Roddenberry. He once said, "We must question the story logic of having an all-knowing all-powerful God, who creates faulty humans, and then blames them for his own mistakes." Ah, what does he know? He's just a writer. Ok, at least he's not a novelist, but still...

This was not a book so much as a boutique fanzine, a thick, slick pamphlet whose graphic design far out-stripped the contents in terms of artistic merit.

"My sister draws commercial manga, but what she wants to do is write stuff like this, that's why she came to England."

An hour had passed and now granny's toffees had run out and what the fuck else can you do on a bus? Heck, they were only a page long. The thing was called 'Between Calls'- designed to be read by call-center drones whilst waiting for the next enquiry from a customer. A noble gesture of pity? A canny marketing idea? Or perhaps an accurate reflection of the short attention span of the author? If Ayaka was anything like her sister I pictured someone... a little flighty. As she lived in London, that would explain the pseudo-post-pretentious feel but perhaps not the poor grammar? You just knew as well that once she had enough of these stories they would all link up and become a novel, that the format was a blind-as well as a dead end.

To me it read like Kurt Vonnegut for the very generation who needed him least. Surely mankind had evolved to a point where morals had sloughed off like fur, we didn't need reminding of how twisted we were, did we? It was just salt in a wound, not even salt but the ironic, low-sodium equivalent. Don't get me wrong, Kurt was fine by me but that was the trouble. I'm old. What wisdom could he impart when humanity was already this devolved? You could show a teenager footage of a man being kicked in the nuts and what would he do? Other than ask his best friend to kick him in the nuts? Film it?

I thought then, about the times I had kicked my brother in the nuts- golden nights, good times. Pity we never seemed to have a camera. Really there is no hope. I missed Mr. Vonnegut. Slaughterhouse 5 was such a forbidden text back then. Heck, when I was in school they wouldn't let us read Frankenstein in case we went and lost our religion down the back of our desks. Most girls lost theirs at the back of the sports field. I wish I too had the sense to realize how stupid I was, and then actually try and do something about it. Like I said, no hope.

I look out the bus window at concrete and blasted heath.

No life?

Nature has no life?

These aren't thoughts so much as their stunted ancestors.

I look at the cover of the pamphlet and its claim to reveal 'The Truth!' in a hokey 'Astounding Tales' font and wonder how many times you could reveal 'The Truth!'.

It's once in Planet of the Apes and that's it.

When I got off the bus I left the stories on the wooden window sill of a pebble-dashed toilet block. Everything smelled faintly of biscuits and the rain was of an angle only God could forgive. I turned up the collar of my what I had now decided was a fully Deckard-esque army-coat and started walking, trudging towards a golden land of opportunity and adventure, past low white-washed walls, down the road named on the battered postcard in my pocket.

10. A Missionary's Favorite Car

"Have you read any of his stuff?"

I frown. Not really one for fantasy... if it sucks.

Just a guess, just putting it out there...

A strong, hearty and handsome Scot is singing the praises of a Christian science fiction author, one fond of cosmic coincidence. He was not going to convince me that someone with that many initials was capable of writing anything except the fabulous arabesques of his name in urine... maybe. Even then I'd need to see his cock first. Didn't I always? The handsome Scot hands me a Kindle with this genius's last one loaded onto it and bumbles outside to the log pile.

"I'll read it tonight." His wife frowns- and I wonder how she knows me at all let alone so well- but somehow she does?

"I mean it." Who does this convince?

She pulls her cardigan tighter round her and the kettle whistles.

Whistles! Can you believe it, it's like Harry Potter or something. I ask her about the cottage. It's attached to the church, over a hundred years old.

"Attached?" There was a lean-to between them, but also a wall, tombstones.

She means it belongs to the clergy and that's when she first tells me, "He's a preacher."

She married a preacher?

Don't sit under the apple tree, they don't fall far and you're liable to get hit on the head- though apparently this doesn't guarantee any sense will get knocked into you. Newton was an anomaly. Apparently even if you run away from the apple tree it's like in Tolkien, they'll follow you or something...

Just then a dirty-blonde kid with a smile like... well like hers, runs in. She's singing the theme tune to 'Treme' but she's changed the words, just like Sarah does for our kid, "Down in Botswana the frogs eat bananas, they wait till manana, de-da-da-de-da-da and hope to grow a soul. In Tierra Del Fuego the worms have lumbago and..."

She stops, already at that age where embarrassment is felt keen.

It's like looking at the past in a smudged mirror.

I almost hadn't recognized the woman who'd sent that postcard, but the little girl... there was Alice.

I feel like I'm wearing a mask, wondering why I'm here, why I had to come.

"This is Sarah, our oldest."

Sarah? Maybe there is a God after all, a trickster, a bladder-carrying holy fool.

"Hi..."

"This is my brother, your uncle..."

The air hangs still. The kid looks nervous but kinda smiles and I'd know that smile anywhere, been searching for it most of my life, and then the real Alice smiles too and it's like the first recording in stereo, that fledgling moment when sound reached all around you without any musicians in the room. I don't know what to do so I reach in my back-pack for my wallet, pull out the pic.

"This is Billy, he's about ten."

"Two years younger than..." She kinda nods at this new Sarah, her Sarah. "And where's his mother..?"

My sister was never subtle, maybe she got that from George Lucas, who knows?

"Sarah's back in L.A., thinking about another one maybe..."

She smiles at the coincidence with the names as I mime a large belly, start telling her about little Billy always claiming to be a native of the windy city because his Edward G. Robinson is so Chicago perfect- but inside I wonder whether we all got the dates wrong?

The kid butts in. "Who's Edward G. Robinson?"

How'd you explain that to a twelve year-old?

It'd be like showing them a road-map of life. Look, here's the point ten years ago when my own personal attempt to live out 'On The Road' became the lynch-pin of my settling down, you can just about see the point where I nearly ran out on my girlfriend but then decided that maybe only a primo-douche would do that, so, well I didn't, and then...

"He's an old actor."- So my sister knew what to do. That doesn't mean I over-complicate things.

"So, a preacher…"

When she left home she hadn't wanted to escape so much as find something to compare it with. That was what she was now telling me. The great adventuress we'd all admired so, was just a frightened little girl who wanted to know she wasn't crazy for maybe thinking that this was right, that home was all right. Was the place to be. So, anyway, she decided she needed to know it was. So she left. Just to check? Which makes even less sense than anything I've come up with for hiding the fact I like touching cock, but hey…

She ended up in Boston and then the West of Ireland, Amsterdam and finally here. For most of that she'd been running with one church or another. She had her wild times, had even claimed to be a Quaker before she'd realized just how close that was to just letting go of your faith. I told her I was still Baptist, it was easy, wasn't like I didn't know the lore- as my brother William used to put it.

Don't know why I lied though.

Habit?

No?

Really?

She's asking me about Boyd, now. "How is he…?"

To tell the truth I didn't see him so much, not since he'd moved to Seattle.

"He's fine, still skateboards now and again." The measure of sanity. At least he didn't do it in freeway traffic anymore, as far as I knew.

Telling her he's in advertising now?

That would have just undercut that claim to stability.

Then I remembered she'd left before he'd even bought his first board.

"I can't believe I'm here…" To be honest I was off in the clouds, thinking evolutionarily.

"You'll stay for dinner." It wasn't a question.

Her husband did seem nice. I wouldn't have said no.

I wondered what Felipe was doing now, but then I thought of my wife and the kid and that old fake Baptist guilt really harshed my mellow.

We had rabbit and roast turnips and I thought he was going to tell me about the Church Roof Fund but actually he knew a lot about motorbikes and politics which was just as... hmm, yeah, fascinating. I really need to get to bed, yeah, just so tired.

"... you think Animal Farm is an attack on the principle of revolution? If that was the case then life under the original farmer wouldn't have ended in the slaughter-house as well..." Listening to Alice nearly drunk? It felt like getting a lecture from Sarah, like I wasn't really on holiday at all.

Once they're gone, of course I can't sleep.

Let's dive in to the third can of Spartan, (the lager choice for those who want a taste of old grease and a hangover like three hundred men in leather battle shorts have just stormed the cerebral cortex).

I remember something dark my sister said over dinner, that look she got in her eyes just before she left was still there. Maybe depression is a family trait.

I change the subject and think about Boyd.

The only person in my family that I ever actually told. Ten years ago I'd figured he'd die before he'd get the chance to finally throw me out of the closet. Fat chance. Yeah, he lived near Seattle but suicide wasn't really his style, not after the shit he's seen, but surely the drugs? But no, not even an accidental overdose. Indestructible? Premature death just didn't seem likely now. He was chronically middle-aged; well, middle-aged for a Boyd. Riven with a cowardliness that was something I expected of myself, not someone who just over ten years ago had once surfed an office chair off the roof of a Seven Eleven. How do you street-luge when you live in the middle of a forest miles from any hills? I'd have to ask, then he'd hide the fact it was just an excuse not to even try.

In the morning I wanted to ask Alice the same questions all over again.

Apparently her answers last night weren't to my satisfaction.

Could you give me meaning to my life please?

After all you're just a human being who knows as much, more, or less than I do as we float on this damned rock through cold, forbidding space. I'm beginning to sound like Keith Urban in the reboot of Star Trek- a movie Boyd managed to send me twice on Blu-ray- a format I don't even own a player for. Perhaps she could just explain why I have children? Because I couldn't admit I was at least fifty percent gay? Maybe, because I wanted what I couldn't have, a mother, a sister? And now that I've admitted that, if only to myself, isn't that enough? What am I supposed to do? How am I supposed to live my life? Anonymous encounters with random men is no way to feel fulfilled...

There's a joke somewhere...

And this is?

This is a way to feel fulfilled?

I look at her on the step. I remember how when she was very little, and I was even smaller, how fond she had been of torturing other children, and the thorough disregard she had for the lives of the defenseless creeping and crawling creatures of this world. No wonder I'd got so hung up on her. I never once saw her offer herself up to be the victim, not even in games of cowboys and disciplinarians. It was not that she was wicked per se, it was more she was naively unable to empathize; an old soul, yes, but somehow despite her wiles prone at times to fall into the trap of a kind of uncompassionate gullibility.

Her husband is waving, grizzled and windswept.

She holds the hand of the five year-old, a baby on her hip, that adorable girl next to her too, the one with the not quite believable smile.

I get on the bus.

I eat another toffee.

Granny shouldn't have waved me over. She's almost as bad as Felipe.

Sitting down, waving to Alice's husband I think of the old joke about a missionary's favorite car being a convertible. Granny interrupts my thoughts.

"Are you off back to Edinburgh?"

Not after those teeth... I need to head home to my wife's doppelganger smile, to LA, home of quality orthodontists.

For a second I think I've spoken out loud, then I do, my voice sounding directionless, like my last words somehow too.

"No, I mean yeah, that's where I'm heading first, I think…"

11. Back For Getting Kicks

I get off the bus.

To tell the truth I haven't even got on...

"Are you ok?"

I'd forgotten how perfect she was.

How dumb I could be.

I'd only been gone ten minutes.

That's all.

The bus had pulled away and I watched some kid with a cocky expression wave back at me from my seat. Let him have it, I ain't goin' nowhere, buddy.

Sarah gives me a hug. "We thought we'd lost you..."

I smile.

So this is Albuquerque.

"I'll always be here."

She looks at me like I'm crazy. Sincerity isn't my strong point. Neither's geography or dates.

"I got lost."

"It's still Albuquerque."

"I'd figured that much."

Just then Boyd and William roll up arguing about which Bond was the second worst and all seems right in the world. I'm guessing in ten years' time none of this crap is going to matter, but for now Boyd still won't let go of his childhood, still wants to believe in super-secret agents, zombies and rocket-ships, glamorous exotic bi-lesbians riding on the back of giant space ants, maybe even God-who knows, he's that gullible. We are living in Fortean times, my brothers, going round in crop circles... scared of the edge of the village.

"You wanna get something to eat?"

Sarah is insatiable.

Boyd, who in the absence of both chewing tobacco and spittoon still manages a passable Confederate salute, looks down with pride at the latest humectant blob he's blessed the sidewalk with and then flags down a passing obese and asks it for directions.

We decide to splash the cash and invest in the Kiva fireplaces, brick floors, 17th century hand-carved Santos, and copper-topped bar of the High Noon Restaurant and Saloon. William orders steak with his steak which seems reasonable given the setting. I have the San Felipe Burrito, Sarah likewise, Boyd the burps. I guess that's a step towards heaven when you think of where it usually comes out of him. We sit outside on low stucco walls that abut traditional western blacktop, dreaming of Edgewood before deciding that Santa Rosa sounds more exotic.

Where else to head than Bozo's garage.

I was hoping for a chimp tuning 50's Chevys. Instead a motor museum with the kind of checkered floor that would have made One Eyed Jack's proud. Outside there's a yellow hot rod twenty foot up a pole, inside more flame-jobs than the inside of Boyd's pants.

We don't stay long, just enough to not quite buy the t-shirt.

James Bozo Cordova is a Latin guy who looks more like a Samurai, thinning hair, indeterminate beard, welcomes you to the museum, apologizes for his wife not being there. Nice guy. We wander past Joseph's Bar and Grill a little later, the sign above looks like a picture of Bob Hope and we speculate on whether Bing Crosby ever stayed here.

Then it's time to fire up the twat-mobile, as Sarah calls it, and we drive out into the desert for a date with the one true false idol.

God.

Here he comes again, here comes the mighty cross.

It is big, don't get me wrong, girls. A massive boner for Jesus. But somehow it's not worth a tree full of shoes; a hill of beans maybe?

Though William does think it's at least, "...pretty cool..." But he's got a hard-on for Jesus' great escape. Always thought the resurrection was a Blaine-esque trick where he'd managed to pull the wool over his stern old Dad's eyes.

Is it concrete?

The pure white dominates the landscape.

But it doesn't dominate our hearts.

That's not to say you can't see it coming from twenty miles away.

"It's freakin' huge."

"It's a bird."

"It's a plane."

"It's a bird-plane thingy."

"God, please don't make it a bird-plane thingy."

"Why?"

"They're the worst."

We park the car in the shadow of a leaning water-tower whilst William takes a piss.

"Asparagus?"

"You want me to sniff your piss?"

"Only accidentally, I don't want it to be weird or nothin'."

This would be a good time to renew a discussion on the habits of flies, as there are a few more here than giant crosses or water-towers. We spit our fair share of the aeronautically challenged and get back in the jalopy.

When we finally make it to Shamrock, the Conoco gas station's U- Drop Inn is bathed in the unearthly light that only masterpieces of neon-clad architecture can manage in the baking noonday sun. We bask in the glow and its art-deco beauty shines through. Stucco, gold-glazed terracotta tiles, ridges of sandstone colored sandstone? A delight. Only Boyd can truly capture its majesty.

"Ribbed, for extra pleasure."

Conoco sounds like the Japanese oil company that broke up the fab four. Texaco, Exxon, BP and Shell have been creating spills on their own for years but can you imagine the kind of ecological disaster you'd get if they worked together?

Maybe something as greasy as what William's shoving in his mouth.

I'm reminded of how he used to have a bikini-clad poster over his bed of Summer Knights- the then holder of the record for the largest number of blow-jobs in one twenty-four hour period- that he'd put up *ironically*. *Ironically* over his bed. Whatever. Maybe it was. She wasn't a big girl, not really his type, so maybe we'll let it slide, his pride appearing almost paternal, nearer admiration than lust to be honest. He'd eulogize on how she'd throat-fucked her way to immortal glory and that no-one would eclipse her achievement in his lifetime, how those other porn stars just weren't '*really*' trying. Or as he liked to summarize, "One swallow does not a Summer make."

I look at the corn dog in his mouth. Slight nausea is sometimes a prerequisite of life.

He takes two more bites and that lowest of metaphors is gone. Finishes chewing his snack.

The Conoco café itself is now a chamber of commerce and community center so we decide to eat at Mitchell's.

I can't decide what about the interior is more charming. The food splatter on the wall next to our booth or the light fixture right over our table that had captured at least half the bugs in Texas with the promise of instant frazzle only to let them starve to death beneath the dim fluorescence of its strip lighting. The lazy fan can't do anything to entice the smoke and old fried smell back out of our clothes.

I didn't use the washroom. It seemed here they bring the toilet to your table instead.

"I can't believe you ate that."

"It was fried."

This is William's benchmark for hygiene. He may have a point. Five Star Salad will give you food poisoning faster than grease slides down a glutton's gullet. You want to eat fast, never eat the 'washed' greenery.

It's late afternoon, we need to press on?

I can't imagine sleeping in beds made by hands this oleaginous. It'd be like housekeeping was an army of Summer Knights.

We floor our way 'cross the county line, Erick just a blur on the way through, faster than Sheb Wooley's "one-eyed, one-horned flying purple people eater". Someone told me that he was born in Erick in 1921. I don't see a memorial passing through. The country star Roger Miller, who wrote, "King of the Road," "Dang Me," and "You Can't Roller Skate in a Buffalo Herd," was born in Fort Worth, Texas but grew up in Erick from the age of three and when asked by an interviewer where Erick was near, Miller wryly replied, "It's close to extinction."

So I guess that's where we're all headed.

If I was a Republican there'd be a joke in that as the next stop is Clinton. Which of course is famous for its cigars... or not.

Clinton is home to Water Zoo, Oklahoma's first indoor water park and overridden by popular demand we decide to stay the night. I look at the pipe in William's fist and curse the way all the best laid plans can go up in a puff of smoke. Then I puff at smoke and...

We decide to stay at the Hampton Inn, mainly because Sarah can't stop laughing at its name- it's another English thing.

I still don't believe they bowl al fresco.

She decides to test my gullibility anew with 'Tin Pan' Bolan the glam rock celebrity chef, citing recipes whose grimness could only come from that doughty isle, the tinned meat and crackers of 'Jelly-gram Spam', the '20th Century boiled', 'Chicken of the Revolution' and the incredibly feathery, 'Thunder Wings'- which contain an exhortation to divide a white swan.

I wonder what's stuffing our pillows.

I guess bowling shoes...

It's a genero-style sleeping factory but when Sarah finds they have what they describe as a clean and fresh Hampton © bed, she once again dissolves into fits of giggles. She's still giggling when we start doing the big nasty in one. It goes well, we have fun. Good times.

Afterwards she tells me though, that she feels as if she has eaten green spuds dipped in motor-oil, an oily slime like a sea at night, bouncing the eggy moon back off its heaving stomach.

We go for a walk, across the way in a pool of half-light from a security beam, dangling the bottom half of her bare legs over a little plank jetty that formed the floor of a 'veranda'. She was just beginning to feel the night chill, but she still just sat, kicked off her flip-flops, letting the tall grass tickle the bottom of her feet.

In the morning Boyd comes down barefoot and gets cold shrift from the staff. I don't blame them, no-one wants big toe with their free oatmeal. I haven't slept so well in weeks.

"It must be the Hampton in my back."

I know what I'm doing.

Sarah turns purple, sputters out her juice.

153

Next stop water-world; we can't have a worse time than Kevin Costner, can we?

Surprisingly it's another dose of what I need.

Sarah and I sit by the pool watching the wave machine do its magic.

I even go for a swim- which for someone who lives in California is as close to sin as the state recognizes. Ok it's not the beach, but this place does have waves. Did I say waves? Indoor waves goddamit! I'm always impressed by man's attempts to mimic the moon. Keith Moon, Yung Sun Moon. That guy from Twilight who looks like the moon.

Sarah's wearing Bermuda shorts and a Little Steven t-shirt, which is her attempt at being more American for the day. I find myself staring at her curvy legs. Have they put something in the water here? Maybe I'm getting straighter as I get older? Perhaps it was a Greek thing, an adolescent phase. A Greek looking guy in speedos walks past. Maybe not?

Somewhere I can hear screaming.

William walks by without a hat.

In a swimming park heated to 80 degrees this should not be an issue.

However I know that means Boyd is now wearing it in a concerted attempt to get us thrown out.

It's at that moment a plastic hamper on casters that is full of float toys hits the water with Boyd riding bareback.

I look up at the 'Big Splash', a tribute to Mouse Trap on a massive scale, and wonder how he'd managed to get a plastic hamper on casters that is full of float toys inside a 600 gallon tipping bucket thirty feet above the pool below. The police in Oklahoma are very nice.

Two days later Boyd tells me he's over jumping off of things, he needs a new challenge.

Dear God.

We're sitting in a park in El Reno wishing it was May 4th.

That's El Reno's fried onion burger day.

William is eating a fried onion burger.

Fuck your schedule, man.

Boyd takes a wine carton and cuts a hole, pushes his lips, his whole mouth into it, glugs from it like a tit.

Fuck your rules.

He's drinking inside the box.

Sarah starts to sing an old English folk song. "Who's the twat, who's the twat, who's the twat in black?"

He's not really an umpire. He's actually a coach for the Hibbett Sports and El Reno Soccer Club called something like Trevis Blickle?

Both my brothers have beards. They watch the lithe young boys playing soccer. Moms and dads get nervous. We move on.

There's one sex offender to every 1288 people in Reno. Which is roughly the same as the percentage in the Bronx- the worst borough for this activity in New York.

Just sayin'.

Just moving on.

And now just before we get to the city that is oh so very pretty the absolute highlight of any trip.

Yukon.

Sister to Krnov in the Czech Republic.

Home of the Yukon Mill and Grain Company.

And most importantly the inspiration for the children's monster-piece, 'Grady's in The Silo'. The only American work of fiction in Sarah's top ten favorite books.

I've read it, but the real tale has something more.

February 22, 1949, the Mach's six-year-old Hereford cow, Grady, gives birth to a stillborn. A veterinarian, D.L. Crump, is called to help. Dr. Crump ties Grady to a post and then, once treatment is finished... she is untied. Freedom is a founding tenet of our great nation, so Grady span about and started chasing Bill, who jumped on a pile of cottonseed sacks to escape.

From the small opening to the silo came the shed's only light which Grady dove for. Mach and Dr. Crump stood in frozen abject horror as Grady was now in the silo.

Cash money, ya'll, is also enshrined in the constitution, and so as they couldn't tear down the silo- it being too valuable and the opening could not be made wider because it was encased in steel, this was cow-tastrophic.

Bill Mach did what any American would do and asked for help through his local newspaper.

This great nation rose.

People all over the United States offered solutions. Phone calls, telegrams and letters, people started showing up in cars and planes. Grady was featured in *Life*, *TIME* and newspapers all over the country.

Solutions included mining under the silo; bringing an attractive bull to lure her out; helicopter air lift....

Three days after Grady's leap, a real man answered his call.

Ralph Partridge, the farming editor of The Denver Post, where men were men and the cattle were safe.

"I'm coming to Yukon to get Grady..." was probably what he said on the phone or something.

Partridge had a ramp built from the floor of the silo to the door whose edges were then coated with axle grease. Grady was given tranquilizers to make her relax. Ropes were attached to a halter and the heroic Partridge, the now legendary J.O. Dicky Jr., and to preserve scientific integrity, a Yukon vocational agriculture teacher, all pushed. Grady came through! A few scratches maybe.

She went on to become a mother several times, and she was such a tourist attraction that Mach put up a sign on Route 66, keeping her in a special pen by the road. Grady the cow died in July 1961 and the old silo was torn down in 2001 to make way for a regional hospital. The legend of Grady lives on in their work. God Bless America. Hey, you don't like my attitude? Don't have a cow man.

We stare off into the grainy haze.

This is why I came on this trip.

That and the great music.

Tonight it's the Bohemian Knights at the Yukon Czech Hall. Where we can 'Enjoy popcorn, peanuts, candy, hot-dogs, klobasy sandwiches, and ice cold sodas and beer from our bar and kitchen areas.'

It's only five bucks.

I can't make my mind up whether this is a genuinely legitimate off-shoot from his love of oompah, or just another way of Boyd sharing 'the love'. God knows how he knew about the place...

Of course there's a girl. Marsha. Freckles, braces, and way more meat than a baby calf that's been stuck in a grain silo. Is he just trying to upset William or does corn-fed start to seem exotic when you've grown used to being surrounded by plastic surgery's uber-bland? I daresay if Boyd lived in Hong Kong instead of California I'd give him three months before he swore off Asian girls as being way too obvious. Always after something new... I'd like to say the farm gal was red-headed too but that'd be stretching credulity. The smiling faces and open warmth we're met with here already seems like a tall tale anyways. It's simple down-home fun. We're made welcome. They even offer to take the klobasy off the bread for Sarah and me, till we explain we're not actually vegetarians, just suspicious.

"My uncle Frank was suspicious, he went out west..."

You had to be there to understand how good a Yukon anecdote that was. Meanwhile Milo Shedeck is tearing it up on stage, kids are doing the chicken dance to the weaving tones of his saxophone. His ancestors came from a small town on the Czech border during the potato famine and started farming wheat. You need to know more? No, you need to dance. That's what Boyd said. He's drunk on happy, his arm just about around his sturdy girl, whirling, turning, William kinda worse than jealous. I think back to where we'd come from, how we like to look down on where we've come from, but then again home was never like this.

Still nothing's perfect.

There's a Garth Brooks boulevard.

And I have to watch another one of my brothers smooching a fat girl.

We head eventually to the Yukon Motel, thinking it will have the sign I saw in a book on Route 66 signs and finding nope, that's gone.

Boyd and Marsha are in the shower a hell-ass long time but then there is a lot to wash.

I think back across all the road we've travelled. Wonder about how far we have to go. Should we start robbing stores, banks?

I'm reading an account of the Filthy Thirteen who they based the movie the Dirty Dozen on. Hollywood always did love alliteration, that's why Kong was King and the Blues Brothers weren't twins. The thirteen were part of the 101st Airborne Division, or "Screaming Eagles". They parachuted into Hitler's Europe during D-Day and got their name for their bath-dodging antics, shaving only once a week during training and rarely washing their uniforms. Hello, Boyd.

Like Boyd they were also fond of stunts.

Mainly they blew up bridges.

Led by Jake McNiece, a part-Native American Choctaw, his brothers went into battle styling Mohawks and war-paint.

I'm chewing on a quote from one of them describing D-Day, "We landed near a hedgerow, from which the Germans were firing at us, and the guy I was with was killed. I got hit in the right shoulder, which broke my arm all the way down into the forearm. The bullet was lodged in there for a year. I was able to get away, though, but could not hold my rifle."

You can hear the disappointment.

I wonder how many arms of mine they could break before I couldn't carry out my duties as a first class crazy son of a bitch war hero and decide it's probably in a ballpark figure of less than zero. Evolution may be a fact but is it necessarily a good thing?

Boyd waltzes past with a shower cap on his hairy junk and I'm not convinced. Eventually we all sit eating nachos and watching a documentary about Yukon Men on the Discovery Channel. It's not the same Yukon. It's the one in Alaska. Huskies, snow. I'm not paying much attention and the sound is off after a while, but the second episode we see has them trying to relocate a 'fish wheel'. There's a guy who looks like a low budget Ryan Reynolds and another with a ponytail, older. For all I know they could be father and son, but it looks like a NAMBLA recruiting video. The room smells of farts and for once it isn't William or Boyd.

Jesus Sarah!

I pass out at one point and wake up to see my brothers wrapped around each other like limpid lovers, snoring. Marsha is playing Go Fish with Sarah, telling her about this guy she used to date and why 'he had to go…'

She just keeps on bitching.

His feet were too small.

He didn't have cable.

He wanted to be a stock car driver... at 34.

I jump in for a couple of rounds of cards until I can't count them anymore and then I guess I must have been snoring too because suddenly it's sun-up, or noon as it's known to us. Marsha is kissing William. Then over her shoulder he mimes the literal tongue-in-cheek sign for sucking cock.

12. Make Your Own Pet Food

"I think she might be slow?"

"You're saying a retard gave my brother head? Which one?"

"Which retard or which brother?"

She knows what I mean, is just being pedantic.

Pauses, then she continues at a slight tangent...

"...takes one to blow one..."

Thank you Sarah.

I don't see how that helps.

Maybe the 'retard' blew both?

We're moseying into Oklahoma City, Boyd spending the day in bed with his farm girl, William's in a sulk.

"Well she is Czech... wait a minute, that's the Polish who are dumb..."

Sarah tells me that tonight the part of Jeremy Clarkson will be played by brother William.

Who?

I can't feign ignorance. Top Gear is a global phenomenon, like herpes or police brutality.

I could do with what Sarah refers to as a truncheon as Bill skates past us on his brother's board trying to out-offend Sarah.

Where's a twelve inch klobasy nightstick when you need one?

William does a kick-flip and his junk drops under the frayed edge of his shorts.

"No pants again? Really?"

Wait a minute, isn't that Boyd's job?

"I'm an American." He stares intently at Sarah, daring her to take the bait and deny him his freedom of beach-wear.

I change tack.

"Why'd you think she's a 'tard?"

William so quick to judge, as he scoots past again "She can't pronounce 'molestation'."

That might be a dig at the girl's taste in men or at Sarah's snobbery, or... With William, meaning often falls second best to

mystery. Like the conundrum of not being able to wear under-shorts.
It's timeless, enigmatic... icky.

"She..." Sarah pauses.

This is not like Sarah.

She considers. She presses on regardless.

More like Sarah.

"She looks like one..?"

"Good call."

I decide to stick up for the poor girl in her absence.

"You two are assholes."

William spits into the gutter.

"... and..."

"It's just she can't follow..."

"... what you're saying? Neither can I, toots."

'Toots', William? 'Toots', really?

Wait a minute, wasn't he agreeing with her a moment ago?

He's on a roll now, no stopping...

"We are all pygmies in the dark, the long shadow cast by your English education leaves us breathless, deafened by the ringing clarity of your wit, ask not for who that bell tolls because you'll only have to tell us it's for whom..."

Aha, her reply is the universal sign for fuck ya'll, accepted at all the world's finest roadside dust-ups.

Shall we eat instead?

Oklahoma City is big.

With big attitudes.

We're at Captain Norm's Dockside Bar where public smoking is actively encouraged. Outside though? Skating is frowned upon. So we go in to see just how big the portions are and whether perhaps, if we can't skate outside, we can at least pull tricks across the tables.

The waiter has eyebrows like the Hoff and a general ambience of Dolce et Gabbana Est. Like he's been schooled in being gay but has no practical experience- so how can we fit him with a position? That's what my brother speculates. Why are straight guys so obsessed with it?

I remember what it was like to be gay, the tightrope mélange of bitchery and regret. Never again, sugar. Why become embroiled?

That's what I say. You know what you can cure? Athlete's foot? Even that's tricky. Shall we just assume that nothing is immutable? That I'll just keep making up these notions of a sexual permanence until the cows come home which, as Oklahoma City has one of the largest livestock markets in the country, shouldn't be that long... So should we try the beef? Corn dogs?

"I want to..."

Boyd is back in the house! Trying to get us to drive to Amelia Earhart Road for the 99's Museum of Women Pilots.

Though he's less keen when we tell him there has never been a female zeppelin captain. Boyd gathers most of his understanding of history from movies, and as he'd never seen one which denied the possibility of Beatrice Dalle, in riding boots and an eye-patch, shooting flaming flying robot monkeys from the heavens, he was banking on something like that having happened sometime.

William twists-pours an awful lot of pepper on his fries. Stares at Boyd.

Boyd shakes his head.

I shake my head.

Sarah shakes her head.

None of us produces salt.

We shake harder.

Not even dandruff.

Eventually Boyd admits having screwed with the pepper-pot.

This means he forfeits any right to contribute to the day's itinerary.

Sarah gives me the edge of her smile, it's more than enough, she tickles me and I don't resist, I just telegraph back a genuine squirm of fun. Life feels buttery for once. I smile and she looks guilty like she's stolen some of Bill's fries.

"You think he likes batting or catching?"

I almost don't feel defensive, like William's attacking someone else's baseball team, but hey fuck it, we all love a fight and the one we started outside never really ended, so...

"Bill you're a douche."

"Don't forget and an ass-hat as well..." Thanks, Sarah.

"Bill you're a..."

Bill looks down at his fries again.

I feel pity.

No man should have to lose a plate of fries.

He starts to brush the pepper off. Eats one. It seems to have worked.

So fuck him.

"I hope your dick falls off."

"Yeah, but what am I?"

A family joke.

We pause.

"I just wondered…"

"Why'd you care?"

"…makin' conversation and I get castigated."

"Big word."

"Big word for a man whose dick's gonna fall off…"

"Where'd you wanna go?"

A deflection.

We woke up in Stroud about an hour later.

It's hard to explain.

All I know is that my head was under the front porch of Mamie's General Store and the sun was high in the sky, Marsha long gone. I thought I could hear snow melting, a dog had taken a leak and it was dripping, writhing, seeping towards us from the porch above. I thought I could hear a rattlesnake too but it was the wind whipping the cord on Sarah's cargo shorts as she rolled over, scrambled up. Turns out that Boyd and William were 'tap-dancing' above our heads too and a small fire was behind my eyes.

"Tequila?" Too simple.

I kissed the underside of Sarah's chin, freckles and jam? Strawberry?

Too simple?

"I love you…" It was simple, easy to say and easy to mean it too.

She held my hand in her big paw and I felt safe.

The four of us crawled and soft-shoe'd our way to the Rock Café.

It reminded me of the food I liked as a kid. Even simple dishes need love and attention. Balance is important. Flavor, texture.

Cat-food on whole wheat just doesn't cut it.

And while we're at it, 'dolphin friendly'?

Like the cat gives a rat's ass.

What about the tuna that got sliced and diced?

Dog food?

Horses, bear meat? That's what I heard.

Maybe even prairie oyster, but we'll see if that theory bears fruit.

Bear fruit? You shouldn't be surprised. Nothing's like Momma used to make. People forget that.

No-one makes their own pet food anymore.

Everyone says it's hard to kill a dolphin.

Try maximum velocity at both ends… That's hard, ask Boyd.

When Gene Roddenberry died someone told me he had two hundred tins of cat food in his kitchen. And no cat. No dolphin either. I think he may have had a ranch, so horses perhaps? Nothing strictly domestic.

It's not all doom and gloom. At least I haven't tried to swim with the fuckers yet. I'd probably touch them inappropriately or something. Don't dolphins have enough trouble being trained to blow up ships? Do the U.S. Navy still do that? A truly live round. Point and shoot. Can you imagine the smell?

Unremarkable cheese fries, bacon cheese burgers, omelets, buffalo steak and outside walls made of… burnt toffee in stacked briquettes. Inside a massive range called Old Bertha and a sign above the hatch warning us not to trust skinny cooks. The waitress was kinda surly and the décor the kind of depressing brown clapboard of a thousand greasy cafes but the food was cheap and filled the hole, so at least it ain't cat food, or even worse PEK beef.

My dad used to buy it from a guy who owned a plough but no horse.

I'm not saying it was horse.

It was tinned, European. But I defy you to know it was beef either.

PEK.

Came in a can, in a sauce… well, more sewer effluent really, from Poland.

Poland in the early eighties? Poland in the early eighties exporting minced 'beef'. Weren't they waiting in line for basic goods then, over there? Why were they exporting PEK to us?

Thinking outside the box?

It was like thinking outside the box if you're a cardboard storage solutions consultant.

Outside the box.

Inside the can? Who really ever knew?

A whole brave new world.

Of grey slurry. Abattoir gristle.

Was that what PEK stood for? Some kind of Polish acronym for reclaimed effluent, after all?

Or could they be trusted?

Was there a Mr. PEK?

A titular head of PEK industries in a red waistcoat and top-hat like an Eastern European Mr. Peanut?

Keeping his firm cartoon hand on the tiller.

Or an actual individual. Someone's brother or uncle?

What kind of an uncle pours milk onto cereal in the morning, kisses the blonde crown of his favorite niece and then goes off to shove horses in a meat grinder?

Don't get me wrong.

I'm not saying it was horse.

Absolutely not.

Categorical denial...

But I also really do defy you to know better.

I really do.

All that meat and I'm reminded of a chubby girl walking past a swimming pool, carrying a water fowl under one arm. What does it mean? Can I draw something from this? A duck-billed platitude?

I reach in my pocket. A plastic whistle that says Route 66.

I blow it and William slaps me.

"Ass-hat."

"Douche."

Am I turning into a brother, finally?

"Only twenty-four hours to Tulsa..."

William has a fine baritone, if by fine you mean coruscating and by baritone you mean bowel-wobbling brown noise irrigation irritation.

"What's in Tulsa?"

"Sex?"

That wasn't my reply to his question.

That was what the guy in the Speedy Carpets van was suggesting as a fair exchange a few hours later.

Sarah and I hanging on the curb.

Van draws up.

It says Speedy Carpets on the side.

Fat man, sweaty like an incidental character from Hill Street Blues.

He'd laid some carpet, got paid in white powder.

"I don't touch it myself…"

No shit porky.

We asked him what he wanted for it.

"Sex?"

With whom, me or the girl?

"I'll give you two twenties, Mr. Speedy…"

Even if it was baking powder, it had to be worth it for the story.

So ten minutes later Sarah said to me, "…and then my mother was never going to come back it was a disaster she left with him and I thought I've lost her I really have and you just don't get over that ever do you it's a blow that can't be accounted for or is that too imprecise if you look at it it's only like being left without a limb or like God has drifted away from you and damn I might feel good now but let me tell you it's a long time coming to get to know someone new and to trust they won't abandon you though right now I couldn't care less because I feel like God, like Jesus I really do you have to understand that and I'm nominally Jewish even though Appleyard's not really a Jewish name is it and you know I could really do with some fries lots of them perhaps we could share and anyway yeah my mother what a piece of work is man but that woman no wash-cloths? This is a woman who I once saw attempt to wash herself with a sliced white loaf anyone knows, it's hard enough with a baguette ask the French…"

Firstly why does everyone tell me about their mother when they're speeding and secondly is Sarah the only person on the planet to whom amphetamines give the munchies? Thirdly, damn the English can't stop attacking the French, can they?

It's like they stole their girlfriend or at least helped her to get away from the abusive relationship by providing a naval blockade...

Still it's hard to get annoyed at racism when it involves such whimsy.

Anyone knows if you want to wash without a wash-cloth you're better off using a croissant.

It's stickier but the pointy ends make it easier to reach those tough-to-clean places.

I watch with cool indifference as she tucks into the veggie plate- hominy, corn, butter beans and fried okra in an apple sauce at the Western Country Diner: Sheridan at 21st Street. Black vinyl chairs, a lot of varnished wood, simple, comfy. A wax dummy of possibly John Wayne, but I never saw the Duke in a t-shirt, stares in disapproval at us. 'Where's the steak you bums?' I can see my face all squiggly, reflected in the steel-topped table. When we leave the boys are huffing something the wrong/right side of being tobacco. The car lot is half empty, a vast stretch of black praying for tennis nets or at least a solitary hoop. I wanted to stay for the Green Country Troubadours. One guy just brought in a double bass. Instead the car park has a lone cowboy in a 'Mother Truckers' t-shirt. I want to ask him why he's performing in a half empty car lot but he's already curtailed the end of his song, is bending my ear for ten-solid-minutes... real time.

"...and that's how I wrote 'Achy Breaky Heart'. I ain't seen a dime. Billy Ray Jewed me out of it, no offence."

Sarah half-smiles and hates herself for it.

Actually he's looking straight at me.

We climb into the car, stubbed cigarettes, feet, a far off fecal reek of spent gas and hot dogs.

We're only ten hours from Chicago.

We still stop at the Claremore Motor Inn.

We could be anywhere.

Maybe not Paris, France.

Over there you can get a decent croissant allegedly, and I'm told they come with these cute little bars of lavender soap.

However I have just seen a near life-size blue plaster whale in a snake, leech and mosquito infested mud-hole pond, and that's gotta beat the Seine, right? Blue concrete actually, now I'm closer. You can walk inside his belly, dive off the side? Not at night. Boyd starts to climb the fence and then loses the will. Getting older? The chairs in our room are worn. I have had trousers that were a worse color, but not for a few years.

We're in a double room with two double beds.

Sarah and I go looking for trouble- maybe it was the heavy, cloying... mildew, not quite mildew smell?

William's sleeping more and more these days and Boyd just wants to watch cable, so they stayed behind.

Before we leave though I catch Boyd perusing porn.

Well, when I say catch.

"Hey man, you gotta see this."

He holds up a magazine called 'Paddock Pursuits', a centre-spread of a girl and a horse.

As well as a tide of interspecies-ist disgust I also start to wonder what the horse is thinking. Given the decade in which I presume this was shot I wonder if he's put off by his co-star's wardrobe, or maybe that's what horses like?

A gingham shirt crudely knotted in the middle exposing the stolid midriff, the deep valley of heavy cleavage, the denims cut off at thigh and raggedy-assed, the work-toned grace of strong lengthy legs and then those big old farm-gal feet sinking in the mud. A real tan, not today's porn fake but a honey glow overlaid with the red raw burnish of a farm hand who's had to do take after take. They didn't have Viagra back then and how do you measure the dose for a horse, anyway?

She lifts her battered hat, all ten gallons, mops her brow, thick curls, darker than chestnut, lighter than Elvis black, slow, so slow, the laid-back come hither, and perhaps Mr. Horsey's thinkin', really thinkin'...

'I could do with a wrassle.' Not the roar of the crowd, the mat and the bell, maybe not even the ropes, just a pin her, pin me, who cares who wins tussle; but, you see, he says to himself, '…it's like this, I'm a horse.

A real life horse.

Not a porn-epithet, but a real-life, leg at each corner, (but last time I looked I ain't no gosh-dang table) veterinarian-certified, genuine, un-gelded, genus-equine son of a bitch…

Horse.

Now I can hear all you neigh-sayers, and like a bad pun you can't wash the stable stink off.

Believe me, though, I've tried to be humane.

Gentle with her.

You can tell I'm a sensitive soul.

I even wrote an article about the stigma of my southern accent, sent it off to the New Yorker. I should have tried the Kentucky Post. Did they write back? Ok, my hoof-writing's atrocious… The point is though, is that it's just prejudice. I ain't ever gonna get a bite of that Big Apple. Live the dream of becoming the horse of letters I always wanted to be, instead of an adult star.

I guess, you just gotta accept that when you gonna get right through to the bone, I'm always gonna be a down-home, oat-eating, fence-leaping, sugar-cube snaffling, county fair rosette winning, electric fence jumping, thirty-five mph galloping stallion of steel who's bucking to be accepted in a race I can't win, and well, let's just get on with what life has given me, heck that dark haired mountain momma, she's a big girl, big for a human, but…

Like I said, HUMAN. Only human.

It's no contest. None at all.

Over before the first round's last bell.

No need to get ready to rumble.

In a fair tumble, let's be real here, this kinda horse play is always gonna end with me on top.

So you gotta ask, if the seduction is over already? If I've batted my eyes and we're already flying, like a log flume floating you down fast to frolic in sin's frothy foam…

Oh, heck,, don't judge, I understand a woman's needs… it's just foreplay ain't such easy work for hooves either. This woman-horse malarkey does have to have its downside, but I guess for her the ups are pretty big too, hell, way big... I guess with most girls, too big!

I expect with most girls it's enough just to see *it*, to touch *it*. And she's got a good grip I bet. Like I said. Farm girl's hands. Mountain momma's mitts. A big girl all round. But boy, with what I've got? Still she's young and strong and determined, and two hands are better than one, and then, oh lord, oh lord, even though she's never had children neither, well, she's giving it all she's got, so...

Somehow, somehow, with half a pail of rancid buttermilk as lube and a lot of words I didn't think no country gal should ever know, well, somehow, somehow we ease it in. Not all the way up to the testicles, mind you, Reverend.

Christ this isn't the parting of the red sea, or nuthin' like that, but still, still it's mighty fine, more than mighty fine, tighter than a photo-finish in the closest derby! Even with just the half of it you can best believe I'm nearly up for knockin' the stall in it feels oh so natural and good, and- even though that puts her eyes to roll back in her head, even though that should be more than any gal would surely want, would ever need, hell, could even stand, well, afterwards, if she can stand, after she's done all her kickin' and brayin' too, well, she promises she'll be back to try and get me *all-in* next time!

So no surprise. Like a lovesick sappy soul she's down to the paddock every day. Sometimes just to watch me gallop round. Dang, eventually she even knitted me a new nose-bag. Of course, come evening though it ain't just animal welfare I'm talkin' here. Come evening...

Come evening, Sir, it's a bag of apples and a rubdown and down and even though she's walking like she's been riding the trail all day from last night's fun and games, well, let me tell you, that still doesn't stop her bedding down in the hay for one more gallop round the range.

Eventually it all falls apart.

These things always do.

Like I said, you can't win every race.

Heck, I even hear she's been sucking a donkey off!

You know, I could have handled her descent into total depravity, expected it maybe. After all, it's everybody's God-dang

American right to get more than their fair share of fun every once in a while, man, woman, and horse all equal, and I ain't no prude, but shee-it!

With a donkey? It's like Christopher Robin had chosen to forego the camp, easy charm of his little bear for the suicidal allure of Eeyore. What have those miserable mealy-mouthed mokes ever done for us? They say we're related, but it's hard to agree...'

Am I not being fair? Am I the one putting words into a horse's mouth?

Talk yourself, horse.

The truth? What do I know?

I'm just glad my brother was wearing pants when he showed the clip to me.

I'm sitting on the toilet now, daydreaming still, regular as an ill-wound clock even when I'm a little sick, three times a day, sometimes two. When I push down, and at my age I really shouldn't, then the endorphins kick in, an element of fantasy. When I was very small, if I was playing outside, I used to hold back going to the toilet, hold it in and my play became heightened, my fantasies more real, till finally I'd have to go. Run to sit there. I'd look at the patterns in the linoleum imagining myself soaring above the canyons of some far-away planet.

I've tried on occasion to pick up my old toys, the few I have left, and I can never lose myself like I did then. The nearest I get to that feeling is when I'm sitting on the toilet, the actual moment it hangs half in, half out of me as the muscles clench, and even then my dreams are more parochial, I always seem to dream that same dream now, that I am in a mid-price hotel in Sweden...

The wood is exquisite.

By the time I've shat it's too late for the Will Rogers Memorial Museum otherwise I'd have expected to see Boyd naked behind him on his steed Soapsuds- the statue is on a plinth outside. The Will Rogers Inn? What else does Claremore have to offer? I know there's a gay bar that's been here since '57 called the Bamboo Lounge, but... I'll leave that family outing for another day.

We eventually find ourselves not far from Will Rogers Boulevard at Spirits of 66, a generic wine and beer shop, chasing the teenage dream. Brown paper bag and some kind of wood alcohol that tastes how you imagine Hadacol would have.

"And this is the morning?"

"This is…"

Light.

Always the light.

Boyd is standing up. Quite a trick in a Chevy compact.

We're driving through the home of Gene Autry and Doctor Phil.

Also past a wedding cake they like to call the Chamber of Commerce and the Old Randall Tire Company. Remember when cars had tires? I wish ours did. But William's always been cheap and Boyd just loves sparks, so…

"Fuck 'Doctor' Phil."

You know it's not an argument if everyone agrees.

"And fuck Gene Autry."

William can drive one-handed. I know this because he just punched Boyd harder than one of Sarah's left hooks.

We're going to Clanton's for 'breakfast'.

At Clanton's no-one tells Gene Autry to go fuck himself.

It's a family restaurant, it's been one since 1927.

Green brick, green awnings. It looks like an old Italian place I used to go to in Sausalito. Inside wood paneling- what else? A waitress greeted us at the door and showed us to our table. Red leather booth seating and a boar's head on the wall. Two of us had the famous chicken fried steak. Sarah had fries and chicken strips. I had coconut creamed pie and a black coffee, regretting the burger I'd eaten earlier. Then I ordered some fried mushrooms. They went well with the coconut.

In twenty minutes we're in Afton. Sarah tells me there is a river in Scotland called Afton. You can see how the last two weeks have on occasion flown by. William thinks I can only satirize the people I know, that my ire has no moral purpose. Like jumping out of a car at 20 miles an hour serves the greater good.

Afton station we pass by, it's only approved for Packards. That's what the giant circular sign says. William just doesn't want to stop. First time I've seen him with any energy in days. The building is generic Oklahoma architecture, white walled and terracotta roofed, like it's been restored to the point of losing all character except the two red gas pumps out front and even these could do with a bit of tender, loving rust.

Miami, Oklahoma gets the same treatment.

The Coleman theatre is a beaut. The days of the Raj brought to the desert. A confection of white icing and fruity excess. They do like their cake buildings round here.

William wanted to press on but then I said they might serve slushies.

They didn't, but Boyd did buy a CD of Lyn Parson playing their Wurlitzer. On the day it was Dennis James accompanying some Harold Lloyd shorts. Even Boyd had enough respect to keep his pants on until the interval. Then the grandeur just became too much. Was it the gold leaf trim, the silk damask panels, the stained glass, the marble accents in the plaster, the carved mahogany staircase, the Wurlitzer pipe organ itself, or the decorative plaster moldings? I will never forgive William for keeping his foot down as we left, I wanted to say a slow, languorous goodbye to this gem, but when you gotta go...

Still, at least he had the good grace to pay tribute to the locale by playing Free Bird full blast in all its vinyl-taped-to-cheap-cassette glory. No version of this classic compares with the one William owns. Its wow and flutter perfectly in symbiosis with the historic tone of the original piece. God rest Steve Earl Gaines. God bless my brother's ass mooning from the fifth row of the balcony. God bless William for keeping his pants on, we all know he's commando beneath, but knowing and seeing are two different things- a good Christian upbringing teaches you that. We'd only missed the Eagles tribute by three weeks, I think Boyd might have made a leap for one of the chandeliers if 'New Kid in Town' was playing. I wasn't afraid he might fall. I just didn't need to see his wang dang doodle any more this trip.

Doh!

I just hit my head.

And we're in Springfield, Arizona- where a surprising number of the locals have three fingers, given that none of them are bright yellow. In the time it takes to slow-mo scream "McBaaaaaaaaaain" we now find ourselves in Lebanon. There are only around fifty to a hundred Jews in the Lebanon of the Middle East, which must make it pretty much neck and neck with Lebanon Missouri.

I'll ask Sarah.

We hadn't enough time to visit Nancy Ballhagen's Puzzles, a mecca to the lover of all things jigsaw- and I don't think Sarah will ever forgive William for that. Instead more highway and the slow burn caress that is William's digestive system. Why can't he do the decent thing like Boyd, hurry up, and just get on with fouling his shorts?

We roll into Rolla and keep on rollin' with the windows wound down.

In Edwardsville Sarah's gotta piss... so somehow we end up in a nondescript flea market. It looks like a bargain basement hellhole, from outside, but it's much more than that. I would have gladly swapped Sarah for the shell of a vintage Battlezone Arcade Cabinet or the intact 1960's drop coin 'Challenger' shooting range but instead have to content myself with a pair of zebra print shades and a vinyl copy of the Mel Brooks History of the World Part One album I lost in childhood- to have it back means it's now, '...good to be the king...' once more. Boyd sports a brand new 'Titanium Sports Necklace', Sarah clutches a teddy bear dressed as a red and black striped bumble-bee with a heart t-shirt bearing the moniker 'Love Bug' to her ample bosom and William is finally persuaded to sport a 'Devon Traction Engine Club' button and to wonder how it found its way here.

Go on wear a button...

What that one, really?

Wouldn't you rather have the 'Al Gore For President' one?

Eventually we leave.

Though I regret that lack of room in the Aveo meant I didn't grab the box set of Uncle DVDs, all the way from 'To Trap a Spy' to 'How to Steal the World'.

"I preferred him in Colditz."

"I preferred him in Ben 10."

The first one of you douchebags to say NCIS trumps UNCLE is going to get my foot in your stinky ass.

Speaking of THRUSH the car is now waist deep in moldy candy wrappers, extruded corn flavored holy relics and the bitter salt tears of all these lost days.

In contrast Staunton is clean.

We move on.

Jumping the gun by three years, the Ariston Café in Litchfield has been a family run business since 1924- originally in another town before being relocated in 1929. We all plumped for fried artichoke hearts just for the novelty. It turned out to be an excellent choice. Manicotti, liver and onions, fried chicken, it was all good. Probably the best I ate this entire journey. Sarah said the decor reminded her of a Chinese she used to go to in Kent. A silver sheen to the wallpaper, a hint of deco in the general ambience but the architecture was more a hodge-podge of utilitarianism and the quest for a friendly family ambience. We liked this place. At no point did Boyd drop his trousers. William cried. He was in the toilets, he denied it, he wouldn't tell me why. The artichoke hearts were very good.

As good as a cozy dog?

William was unsure, Sarah was with me in favoring the 'choke.

But Boyd? In Boyd Town nothing beats a corn dog on a stick.

Not even Lincoln's tomb. And Boyd did become an expert on it. Ever since he saw Night at the Museum 2. Back then I still had the sight of Sarah going dream- eyed over Robin Williams as Theodore Roosevelt to look forward to. Coincidentally my brother had just started to expound on the philosophical grace of Amelia Earhart.

"If God hadn't meant us to fly he wouldn't have given us skateboards."

Sarah butted in again. "God gave you skateboards?"

"Yeah", I replied, "last Christmas."

"All I got was a rampant rabbit and a 3-D picture of the Pope."

"I didn't know you had such Catholic tastes."

"It was God's will- his choice, not mine, he's very conservative."

"Like Mitt Romney."

"Who the fuck is Mitt Romney?

"Just you wait and see…" William as ever the cryptic fortune teller.

"God is…"

"Like Mitt Romney but less religious?"

He was scanning an airport true crime about cult leaders, we all assumed Mitt was a Manson wannabe.

Sarah couldn't wait to expound on the nature of our Lord and Savior.

"Yeah, like someone who believes in one of those old time religions, Buddhism, Hinduism…"

"Fire worship, cannibalism."

"Yeah, anything made up before 1830."

Boyd perks up at the mention of cannibalism, more so when we move on to what's for lunch? Then again he is always hungrier than the Donner Party- which Sarah thinks is a group of students living above a kebab house.

We're still here in Springfield, Illinois where even the cannibals have at least three fingers after all and appropriately, given this is where our sixteenth President spent twenty-four years of his life, it is a multicultural melting pot- with a 75% white population like much of the state. Once upon a time we left California…

"Mommy what's a China-man?"

Well, you may be able to get one at the Pottery Barn but… wait a minute there's no Pottery Barn in Springfield? That can't be right. I can't tell whether William is lying or not.

We drove on through Lincoln, the heavens closing in, the darkest clouds, wishing for rain, praying for a reason to stop, to slow down our inevitable arrival at our penultimate destination. Bloomington is the home of the beer nut but instead we took the longest diversion in recorded history avoiding Towanda and hitting Gay hard before Pontiac.

Gay.

What can be said about Gay?

It's not on Route 66.

It's most famous for a two-story outhouse built in 1869 for apartments that were attached to a general store. The top floor was used by the apartment dwellers while the bottom floor was used by patrons of the store. Although the store and apartments were demolished, the outhouse remained. Each level has two seats, so the outhouse could be used by four at a time. Waste from the top level dropped behind a false wall into a pit, but from outside it looks as though you wouldn't want the bottom seat. Gay was also home to Hitler's Bicycle. Placed there by a prankster, the bike with the sign saying it was Hitler's was eventually stolen in 2005.

"Will, why?"

"Why Gay?"

"Yes, Will, why Gay?"

"You ever been to Towanda?"

I didn't think he had. "Nope."

"That's their town slogan..."

"What?"

"I'd rather go Gay than go through Towanda."

"That's Gay's slogan?"

"No, Towanda's."

He was looking at me, daring me to? What? Disagree? It was like glass, a windshield between us now, had been since... when?

It matters not, we're nearly at the end, aren't we?

We eschew Pontiac's swinging bridges, partly in respect for the Chevy; we just slow drive past their majestic match-stickiness. They're servants of foot traffic and to abandon the car so near Chicago seems like blasphemy. We finally park up as close as we can to the Illinois Route 66 Hall of Fame and Museum. It fills a couple of bays in Pontiac's old firehouse. The building is also home to a military museum, the old city jail, and antique shops.

Boyd falls to his bony knees in front of the Cozy Dog display and I hear William urging him to lick the glass but Boyd believes this would be to worship false idols. The scripture may be here, but his lips will only pucker for the real deal.

I wouldn't want to give Rose a heart attack. She's a lovely lady and a swell guide. White fluffy hair, a body warmer and a no-nonsense approach. She shows us the entry in the visitor's book from an Iraqi tourist from Fallujah: "Thanks for liberating me." Boyd is touched- mainly in the head, Sarah amused, I want to be both liberal and patriotic at the same time, William scratches his nose with one finger. Like I said I don't know where he is right now, maybe he's pissed at Boyd, that last girl was pretty hefty. Had he crossed a line?

We ponder our great nation's involvement in the Middle East by sitting in a booth from the world's first Steak and Shake, which closed in the 1990s. The place is crammed full of the finest clutter known to man. All I want to do is keep asking, "How much for the…"

The VW Hippie van doesn't seem to hold the interest of Sausalito 'natives' Boyd and William but Bob Waldmire's School Bus Road Yacht is a classic of the counter-culture gas guzzling genre. Bob rode the Highway we've tried to stay true to, for years, drew sketches of what he saw, and taught a love of all the meat that once dripped from this road's bones. The damn thing is immense. It's got its own sauna for Chrissakes.

Boyd wants to paint a mural on the side of a building, it seems everyone else has. There's an old Police Station shaped like a gun so I warn him that they probably take their job seriously round here. It's almost midnight by the time we cruise into Chicago. There's only one place to stay, and it ain't the Palmer House Hilton. Not in these shoes.

13. Chicago

Welcome to the Chinatown Hotel, Chicago. From the outside an Imperial Palace. From the inside? Not so much. But the Hilton wouldn't let me wear golf cleats, so here we are. Breakfast? Not quite yet.

Instead a skinny Polish girl, with legs like strips of chewing gum, dusty yellow white, stippled by goose bumps, stretching slow then jogging fast with each step, as though the technique would save those calves from snapping, the legs popping off, just above the kind of flat orthopedic pumps that nurses wear. She's lugging a Numatic Henry wet and dry vacuum, its happy stretched face (an advertising ploy that aesthetically left you in mind of the Master Control Program from Tron) smiling its pumpkin grin, up a flight of stairs into the moribund murk of a windowless landing.

My brother's gaze is impudent, relentless and I wish I could have had the earth swallow me up just that little bit quicker, close my eyes.

The girl's response is a little more direct.

"What are you doing?"

"Watching an angel ascend to heaven."

Jesus!

He could have tried "Staring at the legs of a hot Polish girl. You really know how to work 'em luv..."

Well, that was Sarah's suggestion, delivered with all the grace of the lesser spotted Statham. Though I guess we didn't know then that the girl was Polish, so...

Would she have been offended?

She didn't exactly recoil in horror at the corniness of Boyd's actual approach, just was pleasantly dismissive.

"I think the piss you are taking, yes?"

A reasonable response.

From where I sat, beneath the ever so, ever so, slight doubling of her chin, as she loomed over me, her pinched features, the pallid anorexia of her face half shadowed, even with her hair so tightly scraped... well, it's just another kind of exotic for Boyd to pursue. Around the world in eighty lays. At least she's not fat, William's toes will remain un-trampled.

Then she grinned, a snaggle of off-white, one badly chipped tooth.

Certainly not my type either.

Boyd asked her where she was from, gave her his phone number, she never called.

Shall we get breakfast? Finally? The dining room smells of kiddie poop. Not the hotel's fault surely, there is after all a young family with a kid that's soiled itself. On our second morning there is no child but there is still that smell, like sorry Chicago that's it, you're forever the home of the filled diaper, Chicago- that toddler's town. At the moment though we don't know that, think it's just the brat, and so Sarah still manages to wolf down some buttered toast and expound with assured clarity on a city she's never been to before.

"Chicago is the old folk's home of the blues. Where blues was sent to the electric rocking chair to slowly die. Where the sound that invented rock and roll played catch-up with its offspring, denied its acoustic roots and played at Chess like so many old men do in their twilight years…"

Sarah doesn't like Muddy Waters, B.B. King or the Chicago sound but she will give Howling Wolf a free pass when she's feeling generous. Old grumpy black guys love it when little white English girls let them off for bad behavior… something like that, this argument goes nowhere. William won't come out of his room until he's taken that perfect dump he's been dreaming of since Gay, Boyd is… Where the hell is Boyd now? Not a good sign. We'd all said no to his offer to set the alarm early and head out on his post-breakfast search for a lunchtime karaoke bar, but still that doesn't mean all he's doing right now is singing. Sarah did decide we needed to get out of bed early anyway, but not for choir practice, instead we just head into the City where the Love Song of J. Alfred Prufrock was first published, looking to get almost lost.

We're leaning on a rusty chain link fence near the Chinatown plaza, trying to find Joy Yee's noodle shop, which someone in the hotel had recommended. We're staring at a public mural of unremitting positivity and ugliness and the crappy concrete lion-dragons that denote that cheap plastic crap, tin-ware and paper-lanterns are available just around the corner. Maybe we'll get to buy a taxidermy puffer fish.

"Is it taxidermy?"

"Hmm?"

"Well I don't think they're stuffed precisely, I think they just shove a tube up their butt and blow them up."

"Hey that's taxidermy enough for me, if they're willing to do that... it's like professional Thai lady-boys- if they're willing to get their schlong chopped off, it's only fair that we as men do them the good courtesy of fucking them."

"I've never heard of prostitution being a moral imperative."

"Oh, Sarah, so young, so naïve..."

"Yeah, I'm a real peach."

We give up on Joy Yee's and then of course find it. There's an outside service area that specializes in smoothies, 145 flavors, but still we go inside instead.

It's big and yellow and kinda heaving. A smell like unwashed socks. Bare ceiling, harsh bare bulb lighting. Massive wooden box shelving with raw produce stacked in them. There are glass cabinets displaying sushi, big woks full of food frozen in time. I feel like we're in a Museum of Noodles.

The chairs look like something from Space 1999. Grey plastic geometric mesh, the table's utilitarian, that single bottle of soy huddled next to the squeezy chili sauce. Standard as Sarah says. Everyone who works here wears a brown baseball cap.

The front of the menu looks like the kind of website seniors set up for a traditional jazz club. White background, white-on-orange lettering, comic-sans, kinda harsh lit photography you always find above the counter of a fast food joint.

It is not the high standard of literature I normally expect.

It's blunt and yet opaque. Then again some other menus could be criticised for being a little florid.

I guess there is always a battle between eloquence and brevity which cannot be resolved. Even when they meet in a divine confluence there is still a tension as old as mankind. That is the echoing tick and tock below the gears of Twain's prose or Wilde's epithets. Every thought that attempts to grasp the human condition has already been thought. Civilization is just the piling up of words in an attempt to build a temple to protect us from the harsh rain of that realization. We've already reached high-tide. Now we're just rolling back towards the grunt of the hash-tag hominid and the sign language mysticism of science, shouting at the dark, and that's a shame. Almost as much as using that font.

Sarah is shouting out a collection of her favorite prime numbers in the hope that one corresponds to a more culinary delight.

This atypically voluble display is final evidence that the road has claimed another great mind.

The Bobba bubble milk tea was excellent, the portions huge-good, solid greasy Asian food. We wobble into the street.

We toddle down the most nondescript road ever to grace the earth. Sarah tells me we could be in Slough and apparently this is not a compliment. She's got a doggy 'bag'. Her plastic spork is delving in a polystyrene tray of grey noodle mush, when I kiss her, partly to stop the squeak, her cigarette and chip breath is somehow peppered with peppermint and egg. I never knew a human tongue could reach so far back into my throat, and I can't breathe, the dead tail of a river of raw alcohol, the coconut schnapps now too, from when?

At the end of the street we take a left and then a right and we find ourselves next to an overpass. We walk for what feels like forever, bloated. We're supposed to be near the river but all we can see is concrete and steel, then it kind of opens out into grassland and... is this really the Ping Tom Memorial Park? It's supposed to be a romantic spot, pagodas and general hokum, obvious Chinese tourist stuff, but I guess we're lost. Maybe we're at the wrong end of it. We make our way to the railway tracks, or try to. Watch the big metal bridge held aloft by hope. I sit down on the sidewalk, my back against the wall, Sarah plumps down too. We've both got the meat sweats. We start to kiss again but it's too much effort. I think I might be actually falling in love, either that or it's a pulmonary embolism. Who are we to judge? Perhaps I can admit finally that... life is circular, it always takes you back too close to home? This is Chicago, one of this nation's big three cities, shouldn't I be losing myself in it, not thinking of a certain smile again?

"I think I might grow a beard."

"I think I might stop shaving my fanny."

In England this does not mean your ass.

I told you the English really are very filthy.

Was this a threat?

I decide to up the stakes.

"Maybe I'll grow a moustache."

"What? Like Hitler?"

Funny Sarah, funny. I was thinking more John Holmes, but, "…if that's what gets you off, girl."

She punches me and then I remember she's kinda Jewish and I can see an extra dimension to what I just said, but hey, didn't she bring up Hitler in the first place?

Then she says, "Where next, Mein Fuhrer?" and all my sympathy dissolves… and also I'm thinking, so now you want me to take the wheel?

Wait a minute. "You don't shave anyway."

"I trim."

Suddenly I see a denser thicket stretching out into my future, as if in my midlife I will find myself in the middle of a dark forest…

A long time ago I had thought that men and women were different, that this was the problem. Now, of course, I realize that the differences between individuals is far greater than the differences between the sexes, and, understanding that, it made me think that perhaps it didn't matter whom you became attached to. Or this could just still be the meat sweats talking.

Just one more spring roll, just one…

"You wanna fuck?"

I want to say I do, but it was me that posed the question not Sarah.

"Look at you, Mr. Romantic."

I try my best, maybe I'll even get good at that kind of gesture one day.

Suddenly out of nowhere, some magic forest kingdom, I think 'Maybe I'd like her not to shave?'- is that weird?

We kiss and I look at her top lip, does she wax there too?

Just a little? Wishing she didn't?

What the hell do I actually think?

I realize I can't tell the qualitative difference between oompah and punk rock anymore... between bald and hirsute, perhaps even cock and cunny?

I put the two together on a petri dish, disembodied, just for science, and my base simplification of my sexual indecision gets me where? Anywhere at all?

Then we get up, and would you believe it, I'm hiding a nearly newborn erection as we start wandering down the street, lost, aching for tradition, signposts, not knowing the way back to myself, should I follow the curve of my semi-tumescence... eventually settling on playing the old game of trading names for a club night we might start one day, cozying up to its familiar warmth, looking for a simple harbor.

The Shove Shack, Gay Jihad, Dr. Burpington's World of Gas, The Shove Shack Redemption, Whores Well That Bends Well, The Cabin In The Jimmy Woods, Chaka Khan's Stately Pleasure Dumb, Queer Hitler On Ice's Favorite Base Camp, Downstairs At Eric's, You'll Never Leave Alive, Deaf Wigga Storage, Marlon Brando's Sandwich, Marlon Brando's Other Sandwich, Marlon Brando's Sandwich Maker, Marlon Brando's Other Sandwich Maker, Marlon Brando's Gatorade, Cheetos, Scotch and Soda (Hold The Cheese) Or Whatever You Want To Call It Sandwich, Marlon Brando's Gatorade, Cheetos, Scotch and Soda (Hold the cheese) Or Whatever You Want To Call It Sandwich- Sandwich Maker, Marlon Brando's Other Sandwich Maker's Uncle Dave, Marlon Is That Your Sandwich?, Stop Huffing The Brie Marlon, Marlon Are You Sure?, Marlon Put Down The Sandwich We Can Talk This Thing Out... Over A Sandwich Maybe?, Don't Bogart The Mustard Marlon, Marlon Barnardo's Famous Kid-Bothering Dad, The Bod Particle, Breast Face 2000, One Eyed Jock's, Waco-A Go-Go, Eton Alive?, Porco Diablo, Black Jack's White-Out, The Good, The Bad, and The Seymour Hoffman, Fat Sam's Solihull Speakeasy, Saturday Night Beaver, Mos Def's Cantina, The Restaurant at the End of this Sentence- Nando's, Mr. F's Nightmare Sausage Fest, Club Troparcana, The Big Ball Room, The Left Big Ball Room, Studio 53.1415926535, PI's the Limit, No Jack-Offs Required, Harold And Claude (Van Damme's) Place, King Kong's Island, Wing Wong's Smile-Land, King Dong's Vile Hands, Cannabis Holocaust,

Ghostworld 2: Enid Does Dallas, Johansson's Septum, A Lap Dance From Steve Buscemi, We Warned You But You Wouldn't Listen, Bear Fruit, Let's All Hear It For Eugenics, G.G. Allin's Laundry Bill, The World According to Larp, Some Mothers Do Shave 'Em, I Learnt This From A Book, Turn It Down, and, of course, The Club. Then we start to discuss fresh info on a local Sausalito disc jockey; to be precise, what William and I called his 'counter-cultural credentials'- the large collection of piercings he had below the waist. It was whilst sorting through his perineum one weekend, filing bunched fold from fold, desire from rash discomfort, that Handsome Jake the dj had concluded that a butcher's shop window was the apogee of man's achievements. A unique insight, but Nobel Prize winning? Raw meat should hold no mystery for anyone, but I could appreciate how a pure aesthetic was fevering his passions. The lavatorial décor of grey marble and white tile, the cardboard breakfast of sawdust and fresh blood scent, the swaying row of cadaverous flesh hung on hooks.

Jake had resolved then, that, as his genitals were a poor paean to those salty cuts, a further course of spearing was the only logical option. He was already famous for being awash in intimate surgical steel, a local legend in that department, but perhaps, he had concluded, if 'I rattled as I walked, as my weight shifted in sleep, then, with a sound descended from the high-pitched clink as when hunks of decomposing tissue are lifted from adjacent S-bends of ravenous steel, well then, I could at least be partially satisfied in knowing that my own body gave echo of this mortal metaphor's beauty.'

I paraphrase of course.

As my brother put it, Jake's profound announcement was more like, "Shieeet, you know I think I'm gonna get my balls pierced again."

Still, the meaning beneath was clearly there for anyone who has lived amongst humanity as many years as I, and has learned to interpret the depth beneath the shallow discourse.

I had felt he was on to something too. I am not arguing that all butchers are Da Vinci. Although if one were to be branded with the smudged blue mark of herd ownership, I do not believe the skin would have reached its divine purpose until, when gripped by strong hairless fingers at nape, the master carver bisected the pre-ordained design through pursuit of the finest cut, the highest effect. We might as well make it artistic, for Death, a fellow of infinite pest, will come for us all, however much we live in denial.

Yeah definitely, meat sweats.

Myself, I have no aspirations to test the man with the scythe, no desire to run with the bulls, eat gator meat despite living in denial, or climb Mt Everest, or really to stand for Presidential office, certainly not rob banks or jump off of roofs. Tedium is a stranger to one who finds delight in the simplest of pleasures, and the greatest of art. Someone is always being born seemingly just to bring me gratification, the next Picasso slopping blue-headed and oblique-angled from his mother's womb, the world teeming with cultural Meccas. Paris is a fairground, everyone clowns, so what am I doing in Chicago?

No-one related to me has any ties to this place.

Not even a vintage one with a sweet screen print of the World's Fair.

Is that why?

Sarah's grandfather was a butler so he moved around as the work dictated.

She has a photograph of him in Berlin in 1931 wearing a Yarmulke. And one from 1937 of a tanned youth, in the same locale, performing naked calisthenics, which is also him. Hmm. Unfortunately she doesn't possess a signed one of Herr Hitler from the same period. They are worth a bomb on eBay. If you can still buy a bomb on eBay? My own grandfather didn't own a snapshot of the shouting moustache man either, not because of our shared antipathy towards celebrity, but because even he, who was astute but never a very political animal, could see that this was probably going to go 'tits up'. Cromwell entering Ireland, Andrew Jackson signing the Removal Act, the Balkan Wars... The same mistake again and again. That's because it's not a mistake I guess. Much like the opinion of a sexual predator, it's only a mistake for the victor if they are brought to justice. Two thousand years of expedient rape and murder.

I wouldn't mind but Mein Kampf doesn't even have any good pick-up lines.

Great uniforms, even better architecture but...

Suddenly I remember sitting on a low marble plinth at a bus station, same marble as the floor, no past to give away, no future, resting my hands in my lap. A monumental clock with fascist undertones and then a girl approaches, the solid tick, tick of high heels on the edge of black holes, weeping stars, that floor swallowing light, reflecting light. She's fierce blonde, in her early twenties, black rimmed glasses on a chain of tiny silver planets. Shaped like an hourglass, if father time was a dirty old man, uniformed like a librarian, if Hugh Hefner staffed the stacks. Am I hardboiled? Hardboiled like my brothers? Hardboiled like a dime-store detective? Like an egg?

I cross my legs, and, just to turn over a new life, remember me dreaming of hers, the echo of the crackle of a thousand dead silk moths, red seams are the devil's own highway, we shift gear, she walks on past, lipstick the color of Catholic regret, and I think I say something to Sarah, except is that really my voice? A rumbling cough, a horse dying, drowning in a ketamine kiss? I take another mini-donut, shake off the sugar, then wet my finger, pat some up, lick it. I can almost see William's as it tests the air, surfing it from a car window... time folding in again, with eggs and sugar and flour like a desert dust...

Blown in on who knows what new wave, an Emo kid, or what used to be called a death-rocker, which is what used to be called a goth, which is what used to be called a positive punk, which is what used to be called a Berlin-born New Romantic, which is what used to be called a faux satanic hippy, which is what used to be called a strung-out Rolling Stone drug groupie- all croak and jaggers, which is what used to be called a real satanic hippy, which is what used to be called a beatnik, which is what used to be called a Weimar cabaret hanger-on, which is what used to be called a decadent- the 1920's were roaring, the Charleston in felt slippers- I'm told, the wearer of which is what I believe used to be called a bohemian, a Romantic, a morbid fop, someone frightened of Visigoths, a witch, a soothsayer, shaman... back and back, walks past, and is that a swagger I see before me, full of the smug satisfaction of youth, of knowing you're a one hundred percent bona fide original... minor nobility of the Douche of Devilshire.

Asks me for directions in a low husk, super polite and I feel like a shit-heel now.

Boyd wanted to know if that was a boy or a girl 'cos he hadn't seen the face as he and William came careering over. Long bangs you see, and no waist, no tits, just like Thora Birch when she lost the weight. He was only interested 'cause her accent was 'foreign' sounding, and I tell him if he wants to know, why doesn't he go and follow his evolutionary imperative and find out. I paraphrase here, of course; I think it's more like, "Fuck off Boyd…"

I'm such a shit-heel. Especially as I know it was a boy.

Then Boyd comes back with *her* number.

Whaddya know?

Damn I must be getting old.

"Damn, you must be getting old…" Sarah is grinning, like she read my mind.

Thought police, weren't we talking about Nazi Germany?

I'm still sweating.

But that only gets us as far as the next stop on our itinerary.

I considered the National Hellenic Museum but something told me to beware Greeks bearing gift-shops. Boyd and William have already disappeared again. It's not like anyone told either of them to fuck off… Oh, yeah. Anyway, now Sarah and I are watching the demographics shift as we wander. Chinese turn into sullen-faced doughboys- Poles, then skinny terrorists- which Sarah tells me are Indians. This is plainly a lie as none of them try to sell me a dreamcatcher. Then I use the phrase 'oh, dot not feather', and yes, my arm really does hurt now.

"I wanted a sophisticated Californian."

"Does sophisticated have another definition in the OED?"

"Does racism not count if you're not really from the coast?"

"I don't know, isn't David Letterman from somewhere in the Midwest, and people think he's a liberal."

"Isn't he?"

"He thinks all the New York cabbies wear turbans and smell bad."

"In England we have a TV presenter called Richard Hammond who hasn't much time for Mexicans."

I know who Richard Hammond is.

And yes, I would.

"You guys don't have a lot of Latinos."

"You don't have many sub-continental Indians."

"So it's not racism, it's just plain bullying."

"Well, we do have the term 'racial minority'."

"We won't soon, except maybe for the Poles, though some of them are Catholics too so maybe they'll keep breeding."

"Maybe we should go back to the hotel later and stem the tide by making some nice blue-eyed, half-Jewish babies."

"Well, your Fuhrer is flattered, but I spent at least two dollars on these rubbers, and, goddamit, I will get my money's worth."

"What the..." Somehow we seemed to be walking in circles but we've still ended up outside this place. Two tiers of dull brick broken up by a white be-starred box stuck on one side and large garish writing, "Reggie's Record Breakers." It's a... well, what is it? A bar, diner-come-record shop-come-gig venue I guess.

The bar's just that right amount of dingy and we skirt the entrance, look in. We go in. Stand at the bar. Tattoos and bandanas but punk not biker. We order two Jack Daniels and cokes and drink them quick, then another two, just a very light afternoon buzz. Then we go round again... Sarah asks the bar-girl who's on tonight and she nods at a flyer on the counter.

"Never heard of them."

"They're good."

The girl doesn't know this is what Sarah does whenever she reads a flyer. It could have said Bruce Springsteen and the E Street Band and she'd still have said the same.

"Never heard of them."

I go for a piss and am surprised by how little the toilet smells of, well, piss.

When I come back the girl's telling Sarah that this is just the little stage, that there's another part of the building with a huge rock club, with a balcony-come-cage, and... I'm not really listening. I forgot the painkillers I was on and now I'm getting kind of fuzzy.

"...free pool on the roof deck..."

How big is this place?

Eventually we make it into the record shop part and it feels like the walls will fall in on us. Before the internet there were these things called record stores that sold t-shirts, incense, and Bob Marley tapestries- Reggie's still does. And pet parrots. Ok the parrot is not for sale. Lots and lots of vinyl and CDs. Mostly rock, punk etc., but it's pretty good on most genres except jazz. Sarah buys a cd copy of Red Star and for some obscure reason the first Sugar Babes single, vows to buy a player to augment the tape deck that William had gaffer-taped to the Aveo's glove-box. I try and find something that I can bear but will annoy the fuck out of Boyd... and fail. When we tumble onto the street it's lighter than we expected.

"You wanna go get another Jack Daniels?"

Then a guy walks past with a duck under one arm. Which is, to say the least, kinda spooky.

"You oughta go to Lake View."

We both stare.

"Just sayin'."

He carries on.

Red suitcase, a duck under one arm, shabby suit, dirty sneakers, about forty-five. We go back into the bar and the girl behind the counter gives us the number for Flash Cabs.

When we get there, Lake View's just a patch of grass, some skyscrapers.

The cab driver is Pakistani and probably thinks we stink of booze.

He tells us we have the look of chameleons in a terrible French accent and neither of us get the joke. Then he says he's going to take us to the Brown Elephant Resale Shop. Is this some kind of euphemism, or is he somehow being racist? For a moment we consider telling him to go fuck himself, but then stupor sets in and it turns out it's only two minutes away. He's taking us for a ride, not 'a ride'. Perhaps we were destined to get here?

Thrift stores are different when you're drunk.

We pull up next to another brick lump, this time next door to a Bank of America telling machine. There are pockmarks like bullet holes in a couple of the bricks. I muse again on this great nation as I squeeze the small of Sarah's back. In England 'open fire in every room' is an architectural description of what an old public house may boast in the way of heating, in America it's an invitation to pepper a seedy bar with lead. Then I realize they are just chips and Sarah's imagination has been working overtime. Valentine's Day is near but there'll be no massacres today.

A big white garage door proclaims, 'Donate. Shop. Support.' To the right an orange sign above the entrance says, 'The Brown Elephant'. In their window an anti-Thorazine poster that urges us to resist the 'American Gulag'. A picture of a doctor who looks like Freud injecting a woman who's been strapped down, 'Protest the American Psychiatric Association National Convention' It's a thrift store, so oddball is to be expected. They support Howard Brown- the Midwest's largest lesbian, gay, and bisexual health center. There are other posters inside, including one for the Chicago Department of Cultural Affairs exhibition, 'Cows on Parade'- they wanted $85 though...

The place is a big warehouse inside, large exposed steel beams, rainbow flags. The clothes live in a paint-peeled room that looks like the ballroom from a Jean Cocteau movie gone to hell in a handbasket, but they're a kind of boring selection- no real vintage finds. We rummage through well-ordered racks and...

In a strappy, high-heeled sandal.

In a leather Harley Boot with chains.

In a court shoe.

In an Ugg boot.

In a pair of training shoes.

In a Wellington.

In an Oxford brogue.

In a Manolo Blahnik.

In a Jimmy Choo.

In a thigh-high patent.

In a galosh.

In a sling-back.

In a slipper.

In a wedge heel.

In an open-toed mule.

Sarah delights me with her feet.

I love dress-up.

She's bored.

Then I find a boring, plain old tie which no-one has noticed has got a half- naked lady painted on the inside- how did the rag pickers miss this baby? I keep it on the down low and play $5 for a tie no-one would pay $1 for if they didn't know its secret. The rest of the stuff in here is better than the clothes. You know that this is halfway to being a proper thrift shop and not a waste of time by the layers of dust on the shelves and floor. So Sarah's browsing the adult bit of the vast book section when a skinny dude in an oversized coat puts his arms round her waist, but as that's me I guess that's ok and then she jumps and elbows him in the stomach and he goes down squeaking, "You want to get a coffee?"

She shoves an open page into my face by way of reply and being a good boy scout I read. It's an erotic account of love in a library.

I think of pencil skirts of a certain cut. Starched white blouses, immaculate. Junior employees with bullet braces, oh, and freckles. If they're older a bun. Librarians. A caricature of librarians. I believe that's the collective noun when you're jerking off between the stacks.

I'm sorry, I just couldn't help it.

My thoughts wander...

One minute you're forty, the next you're forty-two and wearing a smashing blouse and pushing a very small set of steps to... help... reach... the... top... shelf. Oh, God!

Here, let me help you get that off your trousers...

I should really look where I'm pointing.

Who does this work for?

A limited market, surely? File under D for deviancy.

We head for the door. "Yeah, coffee sounds good."

We come out. Opposite is the rather sinister 'Center on Halstead' building. Sarah's telling me it reminds her of what they did to the British Library. Not that the buildings, she says, are remotely similar, but it's still that cold shiver you only get when glass meets steel.

The old British Library was in the round, as she puts it, '...like an all-ceiling being without floors, an omni-knowledgeable deity accessible by handwritten prayer, carded request...' Now that they've updated their systems she hates the unfathomable transubstantiation of the electric into visible data and back, back, back into the seemingly immaterial realm. A binary trick of the light more marvelously opaque than a basement full of opiate dreamers could ever have speculated over a hundred years ago as they drifted into the crepuscular, became part vellum themselves...

Sarah asks a girl in jellies and a Le Tigre t-shirt and it turns out this modern monstrosity is a LGBT place that just happens to look like a CIA intelligence factory. We turn left and amble down Halstead a few feet till we get to the Whole Foods store. That isn't a whole foods store, it's the Whole Foods store, and you've got to get the branding right. It is as always a little dear, but not ridiculous and we... Why are we in here? I wanted coffee, a coffee shop. We walk back out into the sun. I ache.

We pass a beautiful old building on our left that's boarded up? Or are they the most inconvenient shutters that have to be unscrewed each evening; a nightclub? Then a Shell garage and I almost go in and see if they do microwave coffee but... we end up a little further down the street, jet-streaming behind heart-attack dodgers, through the blue water wake of the chlorine clouds of stale joggers, that swimming pool reek that hangs for days, right here to the Diva Thai and Sushi bar with a couple of iced coffees and mochi ice creams- a combination which gives us brain freeze beyond all understanding.

It's only when we leave the place that I finally notice that there are giant rainbow poles lining all the street, that and the suspicious number of women with 'can't make up their mind what they are' haircuts and overly groomed men, and I eventually figure out I'm not the 'only gay in the village', a catchphrase which I am reliably informed, by Sarah, is from the oeuvre of a buddy of the swimming cowboy.

Hey, maybe I am becoming straight, losing my radar. Sarah told me I didn't need to see the swimming cowboy's show 'Little Britain', I just needed to know that it's not only Americans that are epically crass.

I'm not so sure, can our hygiene-challenged cousins match this?

Cupid's Treasure, we're walking past a fat man in a window.

One of those mocha pink mannequins that aren't really mannequins at all, more the stuff of fairground nightmares. He's obese, barrel-bellied with man boobs, also angel wings, a red, white and blue leather target codpiece and… what? That isn't enough? The Treasure is a huge sex toy shop that caters for all tastes, as far as we can see peering through the window. Unlike my stupidly literal fever dreams we don't go in to buy a toy for my ass. I look around now, look at a couple of guys holding hands. If I was going to tell her…

Tell her what?

I used to be gay, up until a few days ago when I finally fell in love with a woman- whom for months now I've sworn I loved? Or that I'm bisexual and that there are a lot of men I find attractive and only one woman- which sounds suspiciously like I'm actually gay and that she's just overly mannish, or some sort of an honorary man, or I'm ashamed of who I am, or she looks like… someone I lost, and can't replace. Or that this loss is just a quirk, a psychological fault, a boyhood trauma? Like I haven't thought this through, over, under, around, into the very bowels of the twisting cardboard and popsicle-stick world of my rudimentary soul? Or that, maybe I'm not confused anymore and that you can find many men attractive and only love one woman or at least a small number of women who have the right smile?

She kisses me on the nose and simultaneously I feel like I don't need to tell her anything but that also I morally should, or at least should have already. What is love, Captain? Can it be so changeable? One minute a fire and then it became sexless, cut off at the waist, or is it a biological imperative or a dead-end, or… It's all been done before, including this, and probably right in the middle of the road, so what's the fuss? A la recherché du temptress perdu?

Her phone starts vibrating, a text from William.

'This Bud's for Homer."

It's a shared joke.

My brother always sends a message to let her know the text that's coming next is for me to read not her.

As a security system it has its faults, but this time she abides by the rules.

"You gonna let me see?"

She always asks the same question, and gets the same reply.

"No, it's a secret."

There's a pause, too long.

We're already crossing the street, she hands me the Android and I wander into a car lot, crouch down in the shade of a red-brick building.

She puts her hand on mine and her eyes are sort of dewy, distant. Like marbles in a can of paint.

"A secret..."

Like she wants to confide in me, and for a second I think she's going to tell me she's gay... because hey, absurdity is what punctuates all of life's tedious parade.

Instead?

Absurdity *is* what punctuates all of life's tedious parade.

"I'm pregnant, I didn't get rid of it, I'm... I'm really sure I'm pregnant..."

The first thing I think?

Honestly?

Again, even if I was gay, my balls sure as fuck aren't.

"You gonna read that now?"

Is this a test?

Am I supposed to look at the phone or throw it at a wall, or what exactly?

"You... you're..."

I can't quite say it, she interrupts anyhow.

"I want to keep it."

14. Our Little Miracle

So holidays are for new experiences, isn't that what they say? Certainly I've never wept in a car lot just down the road from a sex shop.

Well, only with Joy and her boyfriend, and hey, we all experiment in college.

Is this joy?

Fear?

Panic?

Misery?

All four?

I'm holding her and she's crying too. After a while even this has got to stop, hasn't it?

It's like when you get too much earwax and you think it's time for the dropper. You lie on your side and plop the oil in and seal the hole with cotton-wool and everything becomes real close like your own footsteps crunching in the snow, your own breathing coming back at you on a long hike. Then you turn over and the oil comes out and... you're still deaf, the pressure feels like it's going to bust your eardrum, and you realize you're in for the long haul. A week of tinnitus, shouting at people to get them to repeat themselves and fiddling with your lobe trying to dislodge the boulders of gunk deep in your ear canal. It is HELL. How long does it take before children leave home?

I sit down, we sit down, a little dirt won't hurt us now, we don't say anything, our backs against warm brick. She's not even waiting for me to speak, because that would just make her like everyone else? Too much of a girl? She can't be more female than right now, can she? I still love her.

Eventually when we've stopped shaking, but somehow before we start talking, I open the text.

'Dear Sir, please find enclosed the Viagra as promised.'

It's the same way he always starts.

'Hey, I hope you're paying attention because this is it, you'll get no more from me.'

I can see she's reading over my shoulder, so I do what I always do and turn my shoulder against her, and she does what she always does and stares off into the distance. I carry on reading.

'Is she staring off into the distance? Good.'

He always puts that too. I laugh, she never knows why and one of the reasons I love her is she's never asked, never needed to know.

'By the time you read this, you won't be able to stop me.'

Stop what?

The world's longest text message?

The longest he's ever sent me.

'I just couldn't go on with... Doesn't matter now, maybe Boyd'll get a kick out of how I left the building? Dad always said it was a sin and I just wish he was alive. One more thing to piss him off. But then I wouldn't want him to know either, because I don't want them thinking I failed... so just call it an accident. You'll see, let them think it. You better delete this afterwards. You will, good soldier, you still got that BB gun pellet in your ass? Not anymore. Tell Boyd he can keep the hat...'

To anyone else it wouldn't make much sense, but I could see the tunnel, where it was going, the brick wall at the end, no light, no matches.

'Don't tell all the truth to Boyd, either, if he's so smart, he'll figure it out... yup, I'm still a comedian. I've taken the car back already, by the by.

P.S. this has nothing to do with you being a homo, you self-centered prick.

What?

It's a shock that I knew?

Boyd's a fucktard and Sarah's just too fucking super-smart, but this baby bear's just right. I never told them so don't get your mankini in a bunch. If I keep talking about your love of man meat then this little epitaph will be more about you than me, which seems right, on reflection, maybe..?

So let's get to the end.

You know I never asked you...

Why don't homosexuals like African grey parrots?'

In my head I can hear his voice take a pause, hold for the punch-line. 'Because they prefer a cockatoo. Take care you fuckin fag, ok?'

And that's it.

Well, except that one last line.

The one I can't repeat.

And now I'm crying?

Again I'm crying?

Or I want to cry but instead I'm numb, lifting Sarah up, straightening my legs.

"I think…"

I stop, change direction, then delete the text.

I hate practical jokes, what's practical about them? They serve no purpose. Like even a corpse feeds the worms. This has got to be one, right?

You can't get taxis to drive faster.

Cajoling doesn't work.

You can't get elevators to rise faster.

Pressing the button, over and over, doesn't work.

You can't get hotel doors to open faster, when there is…

Someone's removed the casters off this chair.

It won't ever fly.

It just jams the door to our hotel room, and I'm pushing and pushing, squeezing into an end, full stop.

William is slumped behind the door.

There was no fanfare for this.

I was silent all the way here, pretty much, and William is slumped behind the door.

And Sarah probably thinks I don't want to keep the baby and William is slumped behind the door.

But don't worry he's taken the car back to the rental place already.

So that's ok.

A form of heavy tunnel vision, the edge of the room in shadow, in glaucous gloom- or the center stage is too compelling to pay attention to the drab setting.

Is this an actual regrettable condition of the years passing, the slow fade from widescreen to silent-era circle and then the television's disappearing dot, exposing by decreasing degrees this decrepit treat of dim yellow bulbs, half-drawn curtains, the last performance, the last show for these failing eyes tonight, and what do we have for our delight, ladies and gentlemen?

Not even a decent score, there's a cd player, but no cd, and I'm wondering what the last song he heard was before he... before this.

I've forgotten to obey my own mantra for living life.

There is no distance between us.

There's a sport sock in his mouth.

And a belt tied round the door-knob.

And a magazine full of skinny Victoria's Secret girls that I'm going to have to hide because not even Boyd is that stupid.

And William is slumped behind the door.

His trousers around his ankles, still erect.

Does this happen?

Happen a lot I mean?

Who would hide the embarrassment of suicide with this?

I mean William would, but he's nuts, but what about others?

Was nuts.

Is no longer nuts.

I remember kicking him in the nuts, and now...

He's slumped behind the door.

Look there's his nuts.

Is it good for a pregnant woman to scream, or cry or tear at her hair?

Does it depend on what trimester you're in?

I want to read that message again.

But I've already deleted it and she's got the phone, and...

Want to read it again.

That one last line.

'Sarah told me and I think the baby might be mine, but that's got nothing to do with it either. I just can't go on...'

So that's ok then, and if it's a boy we'll call it William and if it's a girl we'll call it Alice?

When he finally turns up I thought Boyd would take it worse.

Well done Boyd, you're a man now.

Once you can't feel anything you'll know the transformation is complete.

Just ashes.

Can we say anything now?

Do anything?

I went to Chicago and all I came back with was this lousy toe-tag.

I'd never been to a morgue before.

So holidays are for new experiences, isn't that what they say? Holidays don't last forever. The bubble bursts.

In Chicago airport Boyd farts and nobody laughs.

In LAX there's a girl holding a Chihuahua, it's blue-fawn.

Is she German?

Boyd doesn't try to pick her up.

I want a dog, but with a baby coming?

You want the kid to grow up with a pet though, don't you?

To let the kid see it arrive, to see them learn together, to see the kid out-smart the dog if the kid's not Boyd, to see the kid's heart break when…

Boyd said he's thinking of going up north.

It's that vague.

He wants to be an explorer or maybe a writer… and writers need the cold?

I'd leant him a copy of the novel 'The Slynx' which he thinks is pure science fiction when anyone with half a brain would read it as heavy allegory.

Also I think he believes he can change Sarah Palin.

Make her his woman, the Alaskan exotique, inculcate her with Stockholm syndrome, run guerrilla raids against the oil companies, just like Don Kyoto, write her name in yellow in the snow. I thought it was William who liked sturdy girls in glasses?

Momma bear.

The labor is only eight hours.

Only Sarah is allowed to refer to this as 'only'.

We do call him William.

He has his mother's teeth, his auntie's too and his uncle's love of stunts.

One time I found him tight-rope walking along the thin edge of the cot.

Well I would have if I wasn't out cruising for guys.

Am I that much of an ass?

Actually I just went out wandering the streets.

I wasn't looking for men.

They just found me?

"It's like taking a work of art and turning it into a Picasso."

Say what, now?

"It's a life-size sculpture of a dragon."

Every conversation sounds like the babbling of idiots round here.

The babble of our little idiot is growing profound, even if I don't know if it is 'our' little idiot. Can you get a DNA test that distinguishes between brothers? That's how much I follow science. Was Boyd the dumbest after all?

This is Santa Monica Boulevard.

So...

Everyone is from somewhere else and yet still they all seem inbred.

Who moves to L.A. to raise a kid?

This is a gay-bar.

These are the people.

Open your mouth, swallow the steeple.

William would have marched me straight home.

Made me a good dad?

It wasn't like that.

Nothing mattered anyways.

I just talked and talked, sealed my status as a pariah.

Who goes to this kind of place to talk about his kid?

Maybe I should try picking up men at Sarah's post-natal class.

'Dilf' has not really entered the English language.

I need to avoid sex altogether.

It should be easy.

Sarah's hardly ever in the mood... maybe that'll change, maybe I'll want it to one day? She's currently taking pity on me for all the wrong reasons, misplaced assumptions and... is this going to end in self-pity?

Hell no. The sun is shining, we kissed, hugged, yesterday afternoon we even went a little further for the first time in... and now look the sun's shining, stop bitching, get on the freeway, drive.

She's taking him to the park today, and I'm absent, but it's ok, just the mood we're both in for once, it's all gonna be alright, and did I say the sun is shining? Which is hardly news for California but still... if he grows up to be super-smart he's mine and if he loves that cheerleader's costume and getting ploughed by the entire football team- he's surely mine. Can you really be homophobic against yourself?

None of this matters.

My girlfriend is British and is kinda cool and sometime soon I bet I'll get laid again one way or another and hey, our baby boy is healthy and the sun is shining and I'm not with them, so let's just enjoy life, have fun, isn't that what my shrink would say if Sarah let me have one?

I go to leave the house.

I open the door, just a crack, unshaven- I laugh, it's all so funny?

Fun, fun, funny...

I pull over next to a diner.

Think about going in, but I noticed lately that I'm getting a little pot-belly just like Ren Hoek.

You've got to nip that in the bud.

I walk past and onto the beach.

Sarah always used to say that when she saw more than two girls in bikinis walk past she always wanted to yell, "Cut!"

Does she notice now she's resident?

There's almost no-one on the beach, just a guy off in the distance with a dog.

We need to get a dog.

I watch the waves, waiting for a sign or at least a troupe of Fellini's dwarves.

Suddenly they will get bigger, bigger.

The waves I mean.

Not even a clifftop would protect you.

I remember Sarah and I when we first met, we ended up stoned, running from the chalk edge of a cliff at midnight. The waves bigger than Godzilla in our tiny pulsing brains. They will swamp us...

"Aaaargh!"

Breathless, there is no escape.

Today they're just little crests, white fluff on an azure backing.

I wish I smoked tobacco.

Instead I count pi in my head and pray that'll send me to sleep.

Eventually it does.

I wake up with sand in one ear and a low thrum like the telegraph moan from David Lynch lost in Istanbul, "Hello, can you hear me, agent?"

I'm off the case, off the leash, downstream, paddle-less, rudder-less, hopeless.

I'd like to say the sun's gone down but this is L.A. so we're going to have to wait for a little miracle. I hum 'California Uber Alles' and go digging for landmines in the sand. Is this the bit where I take off my clothes and just walk into the surf?

I'm crying again and I wish I had a dog or a dad or anything except maybe my brother. William would have been able to help me get through the grief of losing a sibling, but Boyd? Was all we had now what I remembered? That time Bill dragged me and Boyd out to the nightclub his Irish pal Samuel's father owned in the middle of freakin' nowhere ostensibly on a mission of near-national importance. They'd bonded over what William called 'indoor Gaelic sports' and it wasn't until we'd gone over two hundred miles that he revealed the nature of this late night- early morning run, and that this atypical interest, the very friendship itself, the one he'd cultivated with Sam over six weeks- a teenage lifetime, was just so he could sing, some time after midnight, to his bleary-eyed brothers, '...I left my darts... in Sam's dad's disco...'

That is the kind of guy my brother is... was.

Two years gone by and you'd think the wound wouldn't be so raw for a heartless prick like me, what will it be like after ten? Who will I be?

There's a girl in a wetsuit out on the waves now, cutting back and forth, but she doesn't have the grace of a true athlete. No Cheetos, no Gatorade, no office chair and missing teeth.

You'd think I wouldn't miss Boyd as well, but I'm getting that weak.

I've got a bladder infection, an anal fissure, sporadic tinnitus and a subscription to a pay-to-view internet service I hope Sarah never finds the electronic receipts for. If I was gone tomorrow no-one would option a mini-series about me, and after all isn't that what life is all about now?

I think about Knievel, dead at 69.

I think about some long dead morning, the closet in my dad's house.

Faded polaroids, like seventies film stock.

I keep thinking I can hear Evel Knievel on the television in the den, but that can't be right, the chronology all wrong, still the recollection keeps coming back as apple-fresh as American Pie and as bleak as a starry night can be.

I always believed Knievel was a bullet to the general consensus that nostalgia was an old man's game, that it wasn't what it used to be, never was. I can remember his fingers- slicker than Django's, faster than the splenetic spray of a Gatling gun whipped from a wooden kimono, fiddling above the abyss, bathed in the Sony Trinitron Van Gogh glow of lost youth, 'ear today and gone tomorrow'- the line that never quite made the cut of Don McLean's clunky paean to the insanity of genius- 'Vincent', the black shadow refrain as our great showman maps out the course of his trajectory with a wave, then that last tacit pause before the shattered fret of a shambling twitch of tumbling notes, the muffed intent, the descent into oneself, a man become silence as the rocket plummets, the parachute opens early and the lazy breeze belches out the one prayer it can bestow... then there's that final whistle, the afterthought, the memory rattling in your head, the comfort a warm wind only finds for itself when gamboling through the hole in a drummer-boy's chest.

Even with all the bravado?

As he danced his hand out over Snake Canyon's void I knew then that the Evel one wouldn't get across, but somehow knowing that made me worship him more. It made me understand that in the years to come I'd still be dreaming of the day Knievel made it...

Well, nearly...

The truth?

I knew he wouldn't get across because it was a re-run.

Hindsight is like that, like your first kiss, it only makes sense in...

Well, hindsight.

Was there ever a time when we were all young enough to believe that Bond might not always win?

Were we always this flightless, bereft of imagination?

Or is that just me?

Is that me?

The last couple of grainy polaroids.

Searching for those couple of Halloween shots of Boyd dressed as Princess Leia. The freedom of heterosexuality. Did I really think I could blackmail him as a child?

I remember looking through a shoe-box but I can't find the right ones, William impatient grabs two of them from my fingers, "These are not the Boyds you're looking for."

I always thought Alec Guinness looked like an ice-cream salesman.

I need something to eat.

I don't really, but it's always worked before.

A way to not think, just shovel it in.

The menu is simple.

Tables under palm fronds- plastic of course, a BBQ pit and a picture of Lisa-Marie Presley on the wall.

Did she sing 'Black Velvet'?

The older I get, the more it all drifts...

Did William fade back into stardust before the millennium or how many years afterwards?

I can remember the date, just not the year.

All these things getting squashed, mashed, ground and scattered to the warm wind...

Certainly it seems a shame how quickly we forgot that Matt 'The Condor' Hoffman used to jump over the moon on a regular basis.

Well, more regularly than a cow ever did.

I order a 16 oz steak, it comes with home fries, creamed corn, and a salad- just for my doctor to patronize later at his own discretion.

I'm as smart as he is, he's just a mechanic... and I'm just a car?

Not sure where I'm going with this.

I play with the latter portion of the meal 'till it's squashed, mashed and ground... and I want to scatter it to the warm wind, but, honestly, you do need something to soak up the remaining grease.

"Yeah, I'll be home in an hour, missed you, bye..."

When did we start communicating like normal people?

What happened to the magic?

The cheating?

The epic lies.

Gone...

At what point are you no longer gay?

And if you no longer fuck your wife either, then, what are you?

I'm not talking about a preference.

Embracing asexuality is a choice or an imperative, this is...

LGBTQA... D for dead?

I do love to exaggerate, it must be my effervescent personality.

It's such a passport to adventure...

I remember going to see a band when I was nineteen, higher than I have ever wanted to be, in retrospect. Rich kids, a collection of scuzzy neo-new wavers fighting for space on a stage primarily occupied by shop dummies. The lead singer was dressed as a cartoonish Adolf Hitler with gumboots on. Did we all think seventies English comedy was that hip, that Freddie Star was a proto-punk rather than the last gasp of their vaudeville? As the first song struck up, the Fuhrer started to simulate sex with one of the mannequins and then these crappy little television monitors flickered to life and a constant 30-second loop of a huge black cock going in and out of a white ass began, as a bleach blonde moppet put their hand on my knee and asked if I was with anyone? Outside we got into separate open-topped cheap-o sports cars, held hands across the tarmac as we were raced through a red light... at the moppet's parent's place I walked up a flight of open plan stairs into an expensive modern apartment which would have smelled of fresh carpet but something insidious was permeating everything. The moppet's parents had been away half the summer, and when I found the steel pail of vomit that was congealing in the wardrobe, the little blond minx informed me that they were loath to dispose of it because it brought back happy memories of last weekend...

None of that matters exactly.

You know, I can see their face, just about.

Peeking out from underneath that bleached explosion of hair.

The white, white, white of their gorgeous teeth.

I just can't remember whether I should be pretending that I can't remember whether they were a girl or a boy anymore...

I can hear the Ween song 'Sarah' playing in my head, then I think of Boyd and 'Waving My Dick In The Wind' pops up, if you know their oeuvre then 'Mr. Richard Smoker' seems just as appropriate to me right now, though infinitely more offensive.

A warm blanket of homophobic self-loathing envelops my soul.

Will mine be the last generation that cozies up inside that womb?

If I screamed it from the rooftop of a Seven Eleven would anyone care anymore? Again, at what point are you no longer gay? When you come out as bisexual? Or when you can't remember the last time you sucked cock? Does it matter when you last fucked a woman? Is there an expiry date on all this? Do you have to hand in your badge and give back your pistol before the timer runs out? The sand in the hourglass is turning to mud...

Outside it's started raining, which is frankly ridiculous.

I think of a traditional California New Years' when children fall to bed, listless, their eyes gummed with fake snow, still dreaming of last week's tomorrow, of presents yet unwrapped, the vig yet to be creamed off from a year-long lifetime of their better self's noble deeds, the teeth once brushed far into the night, rooms left approaching tidy, prayers and hopes traded for the promise of a sweeter world to come, and now all that good behavior left to atrophy, grown weak, over-tired in the aftermath of one too many slices of enchantment, washed away into disappointed tears and tantrums.

Were we beyond that?

We had made our own fun and blamed no-one for it, long ago.

Grown, our parents were now all on a permanent vacation, dead or, god forbid, somewhere near Milwaukee- which seemed far further by Greyhound than the spectral option.

I should be at home with her and the bundle of joy, but I'm still driving.

Is this even L.A. anymore?

I could just keep going, straight on till Norman.

William always did say that Master Bates was a deliberately comic name for a Freudian serial killer. I know Hitchcock was that crass but wouldn't it be better if even he didn't know? A subconscious riff on the subconscious.

I turn the car around.

I won't be staying in a motel tonight.

The road to West Hollywood is short.

Still, the sooner we can move to Santa Barbara the better for all of us.

Did I really just think that?

Till then... I'm at L'Scorpion which is between Jameson's and Supper Club and I'm in the middle of a dark chocolate booth drinking Tequila- just the one, two, three... talking to a Mexican dude about the bartender, who I think is called Sean.

The place looks like something from Dusk Till Dawn, lots of Spanish ironwork and dark reds, but the music is mainly hip-hop.

Is that Laura Prepon?

"Yeah, I'll have another..."

What am I going to do, go home?

Well, it is starting to get crowded.

"...Hey, no... forget it..."

I skip the next drink.

Wish I hadn't parked my car so far away.

I'm not exactly drunk, just lazy.

Which frankly is un-American.

Need a coffee?

Want to look like a friend of Edward Hopper?

Ed's has gone so I end up at Starbucks.

Me, myself and I.

Is this how it works now?

You spend the first third of your life frightened of ghosts, the last third frightened you'll never see one, what do you do in the middle? Act all smug in the full knowledge that you aren't scared anymore, avoiding the thought that one day you really will be? Materialism is a cold comfort. Death is... This really is going to be a night to remember.

Ill met by moonlight.

The greatest story ever told... that's enough David McCallum film titles, a trick of mine to sober up, dial down the panic. I usually can't put the effort in after King Solomon's Treasure- to be honest neither could he.

Would I look good in a turtle-neck?

A cashmere walking cape?

As good as he did?

I start the car, drive into gridlock, 9 AM.

This will take some explaining.

Feels like I'm on my last go round...

There's a douche come on the radio telling me more and more about some useless information, adverts Iggy Pop did for a car insurance firm in the UK. The DJ's playing them to prove what point exactly? It gets worse, he finally cues up a song, "... if I leave here tomorrow..." its parting gift is more than I can bear so I turn it off, choose not to continue testing my faith in Iggy either, shut up the argument in my head, take the sacrament and cue up the 'Ballad of Hollis Brown' on the iPod and refuse to believe he's sold out or ever will, whatever that means nowadays. Then realize I can't hear a damn thing in the car with all the hiss on that track and go for 'Funhouse' instead.

Start to sing, bang the steering wheel like an ape.

Have we been separated far too long?

Is this fun yet?

Am I having fun?

Is this fun... now?

We get to the end of the track and I turn off again, or I turn it off, turn off the highway... I sit watching the cars go by at a distance, the keys in my lap, the tuneless shrill of the AC falling away under the throb of the traffic.

It's not like you need a manual to have fun, is it?

If you did it'd all be Greek to me.

Have you ever sucked cock?

Not for fun of course.

Who would do that?

That'd be crazy.

Like corn chips dipped in root beer...

The real truth?

The truth of who you've always been in love with, the truth at this moment and, let's face it, only this moment, or at least probably not the next...

I never fucked my sister.

Never even wanted to.

Is even that a mask?

The teeth aren't even convincing.

You think maybe that's my own rictus behind it?

A grimace, a set grin against the resistance of the wind, freefall. We want to hear its note, the rush of air against the wheels, but it's only the song still echoing inside the skull, a single stuck chord feigning stillness, and then we know we cannot stop.